Persecution Of The

Saints

TOM BAZOW

Published in 2014 by Tom Bazow LLC

Ordering Information: Amazon Author Page

amazon.com/author/tombazow

ISBN: 978-0977772544

Cover design by Maria Crockett - Five 29 Design

314.808.8236

five29design@gmail.com

Printed in the United States of America

Acknowledgements:

It is amazing how the Lord can prompt you to take one point from a certain message and turn it into a book idea. Several years ago I was privileged to hear a sermon by Evangelist Perry Stone at Life Christian Church (now Life Church-Fenton) on the mark of the beast. That one point led to Persecution of the Saints and I thank God I listened.

I cannot go without thanking my beloved bride, Warrine. Your faith in me and your never ceasing encouragement helped make this project happen. You are, my best friend.

I'm also grateful to Pat Bradley and Amy Goodberlet for taking the time to read my original manuscript and offering outstanding feedback.

As always, Hannah and Molly my cherished daughters, being around you two inspires me to be the best, always.

Lastly, my awesome graphic designer Maria Crockett. I gave you a concept and you gave me an outstanding cover.

And there was war in heaven. Michael and his angels fought against the dragon, and the dragon and his angels fought back. But he was not strong enough, and they lost their place in heaven. The great dragon was hurled down-that ancient serpent called the devil, or Satan, who leads the whole world astray. He was hurled to the earth, and his angels with him. **Rev. 12:7-9**

ONE

High above "fly over country":

"Doctor, from one professional to another," retired Air Force Colonel Carlin Hather spoke in a hushed tone. "If you don't have a gun yet, get one. And make sure the darn thing's unregistered."

Doctor Benjamin Palmer sighed deeply. The sparkle from his hazel eyes diminished but for a second. Immersed in thought, he wondered what need an internist would have for a gun. He strained to straighten his six foot two frame within the cramped confines of coach. Reaching up to adjust the air, the initial blast parted his wavy blonde hair. Doctor Palmer hated flying.

Waiting patiently for a response, Colonel Hather stole a beady glance to his right. In his peripheral vision the Colonel caught the movement of another man seated across the aisle. Slowly he turned. He stared directly at the person in question.

Pastor Jacob Conley was trapped. The intense glare from the military-looking man caused him to be on edge. Sure he had been listening in on their conversation. Jacob knew he was wrong. He realized he needed to come clean, fess up, if you will.

Meeting Colonel Hather's gaze, Jacob proceeded to confess, albeit reluctantly. After all, how would it sound for a pastor to be caught eavesdropping on someone's private conversation?

1

Leaning in to the Colonel, he mustered his most sincere look. "Sir, I'm really sorry for listening in on your conversation." Gesturing with his right hand, Jacob continued. "I swear to the God I serve, I didn't mean to, I just...

"You say you serve God?" Colonel Hather interrupted. "Are you a pastor?" Hather's right brow rose.

Jacob's face reddened. Running a hand through his sandy brown locks, he could only manage to smile. His beam evinced a sense of warmth, a sense of trust. The good Lord blessed Jacob Conley with two physical attributes that stood out from all the others: smiling brown eyes and a sincere grin.

"You really got me in a pickle," Jacob said. "Yes, I am a pastor. I know I shouldn't been eavesdropping. Forgive me." Jacob offered his hand toward Colonel Hather.

The Colonel firmly grasped Jacob's hand.

Leaning to his left, Jacob shook Doctor Palmer's hand as well. "Pastor Jacob Conley. It's a pleasure, gentlemen."

"So, how much did you hear, Pastor Conley?" Doctor Palmer asked, across the aisle.

"Well, I must admit when I heard the word gun," Jacob spoke in an even more hushed tone. "My ears definitely perked up."

Being suspicious by nature, Colonel Hather glanced about the plane. Darkness cloaked the aircraft as it raced away from the setting sun. Aside from the melodic hum of the engines, silence surrounded them. Not a single soul was stirring; no flight attendants were in sight. Most of the seats were empty, which allowed the Colonel to feel a bit more at ease.

Glancing first to his left, then slowly to his right, Colonel Hather remained cautious. "So, Pastor. Where is your church located?"

Jacob wondered how he should proceed. Should he simply answer the question and bow out graciously? Or should he answer and continue to enlist the Colonel's trust? God purposes circumstances and people in our lives for a reason. It was at that moment Jacob strongly felt he needed to know more.

"I pastor a bible believing church in the heart of America, Colonel." Returning the Colonel's stare, Jacob added. "First Christian Church, St. Louis, Missouri. In Missouri, we not only believe in the right to carry arms, we believe it's our duty to defend it."

The Colonel nodded in agreement. He felt more relaxed. "I wasn't joking, gentlemen. Like Pastor Conley indicated, the right to protect yourself is a serious issue. Who knows how long the second amendment will actually be around?"

All three men remained silent. Jacob responded first. "So why now, what makes you say that?"

"You probably wouldn't ask that Pastor Conley, if you had heard what I originally told the Colonel."

"Feel up to repeating it, Doctor?"

Taking a moment to look around, Doctor Palmer continued. "I should think, pastor, this bit of information comes right up your alley...I believe it is in Revelation that speaks about the mark of the beast?"

Tilting his head slightly, Jacob answered. "Yes, it does."

"I've recently been made aware of an undertaking within the government. They've developed, well; I should say acquired a process that will require all patients of any hospital to be affixed with a tattoo on their skin."

"A tattoo?" Jacob mouthed.

"Well, a tattoo, for the lack of a better word. Actually the process applies an invisible code to the skin that when scanned with the proper instrument will provide the entire patients profile." Pausing for effect, Doctor Palmer continued. "Basically, the procedure will be required of all patients in order to receive treatment at any medical facility."

"And if they refuse?" asked Jacob.

"That's simple." Colonel Hather interrupted. "No mark, no treatment."

"But surely a patient has a right to refuse this, this tattoo," said Jacob.

"Since the government virtually runs all health care they can do what they want."

"And it's all in the name of progress, or so they say," added Colonel Hather.

Dumbfounded, Jacob reflected on what he had heard. The mark of the beast was the first thought that came to mind. "Surely not, Lord." He quietly prayed.

"Pastor Conley?" Doctor Palmer tried to get Jacob's attention. "You seem lost in thought."

"Or perhaps prayer?" asked the Colonel.

"I'm sorry," Jacob apologized. Turning his attention toward Doctor Palmer, Jacob continued. "When you mentioned the book of Revelation I was pleasantly surprised. You obviously know scripture."

"Well, Pastor, being a man of science doesn't necessarily mean one can't be a man of faith, now does it?" Dr. Palmer grinned at Jacob.

Offering his hand once again, Jacob leaned in toward Doctor Palmer. "Good to have you aboard, Doctor." Jacob gestured to Colonel Hather, his smiling eyes ablaze. "And you, Colonel Hather? Do you have a faith?"

Hather paused and eyed Jacob. "First twenty years I served this country on my own. Last twenty; I've come to realize I needed a better source. To be honest, don't know how any soldier can get through without Christ."

Staring ahead, all three sat silently.

"Now, about that gun." Colonel Hather glanced first to his left and then to his right.

TWO

Washington DC / the Oval Office

Sitting pensively at his desk, President Stuart Pollard gazed blankly at a document. Signing this new Bill would be the proverbial nail in the coffin against those in opposition to his plans. All of the clandestine meetings that occurred during his campaign, all the ground work laid out during the first year of his term, led up to this point.

President Pollard gazed across the room. He felt a sense of empowerment from the history encompassing the Oval Office. The desk he sat behind was a story in itself. The Resolute desk came as a gift from Queen Victoria of England to then President Rutherford Hayes in 1880. Constructed from the timbers of the British Arctic Exploration ship Resolute, the desk had been used by many past Presidents. Now it was President Pollard's turn to sit behind this storied piece. Sliding his fingers across its weathered features, the President looked up.

Upon one wall hung a portrait of Pollard's Presidential idol, Woodrow Wilson. The portrait stared back as if giving knowing approval. President Pollard drew strength from the progressives of the past, such as Wilson. He had nothing but contempt for those who did not share his same beliefs.

There was so much to be accomplished for such a young leader, albeit a man showing early signs of aging. With silvered temples, a head of slick black hair, and an average size frame, the President appeared far older than his 38 years. Yet it was a smile that charmed the masses that vaulted Stuart Pollard into the office of President.

His had been a meteoric rise from promising second term congressman to the office of Presidency. No place could be prouder than the great state of Nevada. It was the home of Sin City, legalized prostitution, and the now President of the United States.

Stuart Pollard's victory came relatively easy. The conservatives seemed almost unprepared or even unwilling to put up much of a fight. Inevitably his inherent charm and the power of those who backed him put him in this position. Now it was time for payback. For those who stood against him, this was only the beginning. For the ones who directed his campaign, the power was truly theirs. The President knew the "Association" called the shots, and he answered to them.

He anxiously tapped a pen against his massive desk. Pollard realized with one quick swipe another piece of the plan could be put into action. But not until his special guest arrived.

"Mr. President," Jenny Davis knocked and immediately poked her head into the office. "Mr. Farman is here."

Rising from his chair, Pollard smiled. "Thank you, Jenny, please send him in."

Striding around the desk, President Pollard stopped in the middle of the room. He eagerly awaited his close friend and mentor, Ra Farman. The two men greeted each other, but not in the traditional westernized way. Two fake kisses to each other's cheeks along with beaming smiles set the stage for their meeting.

Ra Farman towered over the President. At six foot three his height most assuredly came from his Muslim father. Yet his dark hair and olive skin tone was a blend of both Middle Eastern and western heritages. Born 52 years ago in a small suburb of Chicago, Ra Farman expressed very Americanized views learned from his Caucasian mother. But it was his strong hatred toward Christianity that greatly influenced the President.

Each man sat in close proximity to one another. President Pollard was seated in his favorite chair while Ra sat at the end of an adjoining sofa.

"Did you see the news this morning, especially their reaction?" asked the President.

Stroking his dark goatee, Ra paused in serious thought. "The Christian Coalition is certainly up in arms, are they not?"

"And the association, are they pleased?" asked Pollard.

"Our associates are content, but let us not talk about them."

Ra grinned with satisfaction at how he manipulated the President. To President Pollard everything revolved around the fictious group that funded him. In essence the association was just a word. But to Ra it represented something entirely different. The association was the great deceptor. The association was the ancient enemy. It was in fact the most evil presence on earth. Ra reported to "it", and the President reported to him.

8

"Let's discuss C.E.A.T," Ra said.

The President smiled. He spoke with confidence. "My plan is to sign the document immediately, then send it over to the Hill." Pollard gestured with a wave of his hand. "The media has been notified regarding our press conference this afternoon. To unveil the new law, if you will."

"Excellent," Farman immediately stood. "Don't let me keep you from your executive duties."

"Oh, but you must witness this signing."

President Pollard approached the resolute desk. He stared at its beauty. With the Presidential seal etched on the front of it, he realized the significance the desk portrayed. The course of the world, let alone this nation, would be changed while seated behind it. And it was his agenda to alter history, not follow it.

The President sat and reached for a pen. "One more step toward removing free speech." Signing the document, President Pollard glanced up at his mentor. "How long before we can anticipate the next step?"

"Should be a matter of months," Ra smiled at his protégée. "Just be prepared for an uproar from the conservative talking heads by tonight."

"I'm not worried about them," President Pollard stood in response. "It's the Christians who will eventually be most vocal."

Heading toward the exit, Ra turned back. "Then let them," he replied smugly.

THREE

St. Louis, MO / First Christian Church

"Unbelievable!" Hollered Getta Carter. She pushed away from her computer screen. Reaching for the television remote, with her well-manicured hand, she tuned into one of the 24 hour news channels. Getta's youthful smile turned to a frown. "Pastor, you have to see this."

Pointing to the television screen, Pastor Jacob Conley's feisty secretary was steaming.

"What are you all up in arms about, Get?" Abbreviating Getta's name always drew her attention. "You've got to quit watching the news."

"Pastor, I think you better have a seat for this one." Getta gestured toward the screen. Pointing the remote she clicked back to live TV.

"With the utmost consideration, my administration has decided to enact a new piece of legislation that I have just signed into law this morning." President Stuart Pollard stood behind the Presidential podium.

"Effective at midnight tonight, the Compulsory Equal Air Time act, or CEAT for short, will take effect whereby the FCC will regulate all radio stations AND television stations to assure they are in compliance with allowing opposing viewpoints to be broadcast on their respective stations."

Dumbfounded, Getta stole a quick glance at her boss.

"In addition," the President continued. "Those stations not allowing opposing views to be aired for the same amount of broadcast time will be in violation, whereby the FCC can and will impose not only a potentially substantial fine, but also have the right to revoke the station's license."

Jumping to her feet, Getta hit pause and shouted at the television. "He can't do that!" Who does he think he is?"

Jacob shook his head and simply replied. "He just did. Turn it off, Get. We need to go to prayer."

"Go to prayer, more like go to war." Getta took a moment, realizing what she had said. "I'm sorry, Pastor Jacob...but this is totally ridiculous." It didn't take long before Getta's small office was crammed with other staff members, vehemently expressing their shock.

Jacob quickly retreated to his own sparsely decorated office. At one end an entire wall of glass showered sunlight across the room. At the opposite were two antique bookcases filled with every version of the Bible known to mankind. In front of them sat an old rickety wooden desk; providing space for a laptop, two family photos, and an ornate clay reading lamp.

To the right of Jacob's desk was a single tan leather couch. The sofa and two matching wing back chairs were the only signs of taste within the confines of his office. His beloved bride, Linda, insisted on it.

Jacob's favorite picture of all time hung on the wall across from the couch. Modestly framed in dark oak, it depicted a picture of the Savior propping up a fallen man. He couldn't even remember who had given him this treasure. In times of turmoil Jacob envisioned himself being held by the Lord.

Bowing his head in silence, Jacob's mind drifted to that picture. He thought of Jesus reaching out, and calling to him. When in truth, it was we who should cry out to Christ. He meditated for several moments before lifting his head to the sound of knocking.

After clearing his thoughts, Jacob said. "Come in."

He motioned to Will Foxx, his associate pastor, to come in then Jacob responded to a buzz from Getta.

"Pastor, Dr. Benjamin Palmer is on line one for you, and needless to say you have four other calls waiting. I'll go ahead and take messages."

"Thanks Get." Jacob motioned towards his associate. "Mind if I take this call?"

"No, not at all," answered Will. "I'm kinda curious to hear what you have to say to Dr. Palmer about this press conference."

Jacob thought about how God first orchestrated his meeting Dr. Palmer and Colonel Harter. Time went by so quickly. It was as if he just stepped off that plane. Now, a couple months later and a few follow up meetings, Jacob was beginning to understand why.

Jacob reached for his phone. "Ben, I was thinking of you. I guess you beat me to the punch." Glancing at Will, he added. "By the way, mind if I put you on speaker? I have Pastor Will in my office."

"That's fine, Jacob," Doctor Benjamin Palmer replied. "Pastor Will, how are you?"

Leaning forward, Will stretched his wiry frame. "Dr. Palmer, the question is, how are we going to counter this absurd new law?"

"Ah, you both have no doubt heard about the President's speech to the media."

"Unfortunately yes, Ben. It appears he's taking a stab at eliminating freedom of speech."

"That's not what worries me, Jacob. Something tells me he's gonna take this momentum and run with it."

Glancing at Will, Jacob replied. "How so?"

A bit of silence elapsed before Ben continued. "The last time we met in your office the Colonel mentioned he felt that something big was on the horizon. You remember?"

"Like it was yesterday. Only, at the time he wasn't sure what."

"Well now we know," Ben said. But, that's only the beginning."

Jacob remained silent. Lost in thought, he wondered what could be next.

"An unknown source within Pollard's administration recently contacted a media person whose friends with Colonel Hather."

"Can you mention the media person?" asked Jacob.

"Not sure who it is, but she spoke with the Colonel recently."

"Go on."

"Anyway, this source claims to be a Christian and is upset about hearing what the administration wants to do."

"This doesn't sound good," Will interrupted.

"Why does something tell me this has to do with the church?" asked Jacob.

"It does, Jacob."

Jacob sighed at the prospect of what might be coming next.

"Pastors," Doctor Palmer continued. "The word is churches will soon be classified as for profit. Consequently, 501 (c) (3) status would be taken away."

"What!" Will exclaimed.

Motioning his exuberant associate pastor to calm down, Jacob spoke up.

"So in essence, our tax exempt status will be gone and we'll all be scrutinized by the IRS."

"That's right. Of course any little discrepancy noted by them will basically shut the doors of hundreds if not thousands of churches."

"Unbelievable," Will muttered.

"How can the government accomplish this, Ben?"

"That's the part I'm not sure of, Jacob. I guess the how is by simply introducing legislation to that affect." Dr. Palmer sighed. "Churches would close because they wouldn't be able to afford the taxes."

"I would imagine contributions would no longer be a write off for our tithing members as well." Jacob paused before he asked. "How reliable is this source?"

"We, or Colonel Hather and his media friend, really don't know. Needless to say, it's probably best if we don't mention this to others. At least at this point."

"I'm not sure I agree," said Will. "Wouldn't it be better to get this out in the open and let the ire of the people rise? At the very least it could head off this motion before they move forward."

14

"Possibly," Ben answered.

Looking at Will and offering his opinion, Jacob replied. "But in the same token this unknown source could be very helpful to us in the future. That is, if she's not exposed."

"I agree," added Ben. "We probably need to see how this plays out and react to it then."

"I hope it not's too late, that's all I'm saying." Will said.

"Agreed." Focusing on Will, Jacob spoke directly to his assistant pastor. "Could you excuse us for a moment, Will?"

Rising from his chair, Will's eyes met Jacob's. "Gentlemen, thank you for allowing me to be part of this conversation. I don't take lightly what I just heard."

Jacob nodded in response.

"He's certainly a passionate young man, wouldn't you say?" asked Ben.

"I've known Will for quite a few years, Ben. He's nothing if not loyal."

Dr. Palmer remained silent. He sensed Jacob was in prayer.

"Ben, we need to meet soon. I have a stirring within my spirit like never before."

"Absolutely, I'll touch base with the Colonel and get back to you. Take care, Pastor."

"God bless, my brother." Jacob hung up and slumped back in his chair.

Glancing up at the ceiling, he softly whispered. "What is it you want me to do, Father? What should I do?"

FOUR

Dillon, MT

The pristine wilderness of the Montana region has always been a haven for outdoor enthusiasts. Regardless of the season there is always some activity one can enjoy. For those clamoring for warmth, and plenty of sunshine, they got their wish; because winter suddenly took a vacation. Frigid weather and mounds of snow were replaced by sunny days with temperatures hovering in the mid-forties.

None were happier than the residents of Dillon, Montana. Many took to the trails and hill country in droves. Local hiker Art Rawlins was certainly no exception. Setting out on foot, reaching the Dillon Reservoir was his immediate goal. Art's long gangly legs made short work of the beaten path to the lake.

Flanking each side of the trail stood evergreens gently swaying from the slight breeze. The close proximity of each tree combined with the meandering pathway reminded Art of a maze rather than a passageway to his destination. Barely breaking a sweat, he adjusted the rag beneath his floppy brown strands of hair. Within a matter of minutes he was within sight of his objective.

Approaching the outer edge of the forest Art glanced up and stopped dead in his tracks. Wisps of chilled breaths shot forward in rapid succession, only not from exertion, but more from shock.

Propelling him forward Art's hiking boots seemed to have a mind of their own. Reaching the edge of the lake, Art cried out. "My God, what's happened?"

Little did Art Rawlins know, it was indeed, God.

Typing furiously at her keyboard, Sherry Rawlins was on a roll. With a deadline in one hour, Sherry knew it would be close. Her editor, Mark Granger, was not the most patient man, but at least he let her work from home. The Wednesday edition of the Dillon Gazette was set to go to press. There was no stopping her now.

Tranquility was all Sherry asked for, and thus it was a big reason she worked from home. Momentarily pausing, she was suddenly startled by the ring of her cell. Sherry debated whether to check out the caller. She merely glanced in its direction, then continued. After four more rings the call went to voicemail.

Collecting her thoughts, Sherry felt agitated by the interruption. Her fingers were poised above the key board, when once again she was interrupted. This time it was the land line phone.

"This better be important." Sherry reached for the phone, recognizing Art's caller I.D. "Honey, I'm right in the middle of my story."

"You're not gonna believe it!" The voice screamed into her ear. "The lake. Ya gotta see the lake."

Turning towards the window Sherry's mind brought about images of Dillon Reservoir. "What is it? What's wrong?"

"Sherry, I'm standing here at the lake, and it's, its red!"

"Red, what do you mean red?"

Kneeling at the edge of the shoreline, Art's shaking hand reached out. "I'm telling you Sherry, the water is all red. As far as the eye can see."

"How can that be?" Now standing, Sherry peered through the glass pane. "You sure it's not the sun?"

Dipping his forefinger into the liquid, Art quickly withdrew it in disgust. "This isn't water; I mean it doesn't feel like water."

"What? You touched it? My gosh Art, if the water's not right, why'd you touch it?"

Rubbing his thumb along his forefinger, Art could tell the substance was thick, not watery. "It's all right, but I'm telling ya it's not lake water. It's heavier. It almost looks like blood"

"Listen, don't go anywhere," Sherry turned back toward her desk. "I'm hanging up the house phone and I'll call you right back on my cell."

"Why, are you coming out here?"

"You bet I am." Sherry reached for her cell. "This story takes precedence over the drivel I'm writing now."

Slamming the cordless into its base, Sherry Rawlins sprinted for the door. By the time she reached her car she had her editor on the line. "Hold the press, Mark. There's something fishy at Dillon Reservoir and I don't mean the kind that swim."

FIVE

St. Louis, MO

Romans was always one of Jacob's favorite books of the Bible. It so clearly pointed the way. Written by the apostle Paul, Romans presents the facts of the gospel. The good news such as; salvation by grace, freedom from sin, and why it's important to live in complete submission to Christ. Was there ever a man who saw more clearly so soon after losing his own sight than Paul?

Continuing to read but not knowing quite what he was looking for Jacob scanned his King James Version. Forgiveness of sin kept weighing heavily on his mind. This was the message that would be so vital to his sermon on Sunday. Stopping at 3:22 Jacob read, *the righteousness from God comes through faith in Jesus Christ to all who believe.*

With reading glasses propped at the end of his nose, Jacob lifted his head toward the ceiling. His eyes focused above the rims, and he softly prayed. "Show me Lord, exactly what you desire me to see."

A moment later, Jacob finished reading 3:23-25, and then abruptly stopped. Words from the page became blurry. Letters soon faded away. Blinking rapidly, he panicked at the sudden loss of his vision. Instinctively his hands reached toward his face, fingers probing both eyes. Darkness barren blackness. Like the apostle Paul, Jacob was blind.

Reaching out for the edge of his desk, Jacob tried to rise from his chair. His legs gave out. He fell back into his seat. Thoughts coursed through his mind. He was losing control of his body. Why was this happening? What should he do?

Jacob's rapid breaths diminished in intensity. He felt himself calming down. Only, it was not by his own effort. He felt the presence of the Lord. Over and over in his mind he kept thinking, control, I need to give up control to God. Finally he completely shut out all other thoughts.

Jacob Conley ultimately submitted to the presence he had so fervently cried out to. The Holy Spirit was in total control, and he feared not. A warmth Jacob had never felt before permeated throughout his body. Quickly a new thought appeared in his mind. It was the blood, the blood, the blood. Over and over the word blood danced throughout his thoughts.

"Why this word? What is it I need to do, Lord?" Jacob cried out in darkness. "What is it about the blood?" Then a different vision appeared before Jacob. In his mind he saw a mass of people swimming under water. Each time one tried to surface they were prevented from breaking through.

Again, the words; the blood, the blood danced all around. He continued to see people struggling in the water. "What does this mean, Lord? What is it you want me to know?" Jacob strained against the chair.

Still paralyzed from all movement, yet comforted from any fear, he whispered heavenward. "What next, Lord? Show me and I will follow." The images in his mind faded and were soon replaced by a brightness.

Jacob opened his eyes. His sight was restored. Quietly he sat focusing on the window. Shaking his head as if it were all a dream, Jacob blinked rapidly. But it wasn't a dream; it was much more than that.

For the first time in his ministry, Jacob Conley was blessed with a vision. He had no idea what it meant. But he knew someone who might.

SIX

San Diego, CA

Having dozed off for a moment, Mollie Mae Jeffers reached for her glasses. "Jeffey, are you all right?" She called out, after being startled by his voice. "Land's sake where are those glasses?"

Once again she could hear his voice trailing off in the distance. She knew it was coming from his room. Where else would Jeffey be? He was always in his room.

Finally out of part frustration and embarrassment, Mollie Mae peered at the end of her nose. Her cross-eyed vision produced one pair of errant eye glasses and a slight level of disgust at growing old. Golden year's aside, being seventy definitely had its trials and tribulations.

One of Mollie Mae's biggest trials and greatest joys stemmed from taking care of her precocious and challenging grandson. Only Jeffey wasn't your ordinary child. Trapped in a teenager's body was the mind of a seven year old autistic child. Not just any mentally challenged individual, but one with a uniquely gifted ability. Jeffey Jeffers could talk to God!

"I'm coming Jeffey, I'm coming," Mollie Mae cried out.

Approaching his room, she could hear him giggling and talking out loud. Mollie Mae always knocked first before entering Jeffey's room. She seldom waited for an invitation to enter.

22

Sitting on one side of his bed, Jeffey was bent over. His head tilted away from her. She could see he was staring at his toy chest. Jeffey rhythmically rocked back and forth as if he was listening to some melody. Who knows, maybe in his mind he was hearing music.

"Jeffey, what are you looking at?"

With his head still tilted away from the door, Jeffey simply answered. "God. It's God. He's hiding."

"He's hiding, Jeffey? Where is God hiding?"

Straightening up and turning his head ever so slightly, Jeffey replied. "In the toy box, M & M."

"Oh," Mollie Mae giggled. She always loved hearing him call her M & M. No one else ever did, just Jeffey. Then again, there was no one else. Only Mollie Mae and her sixteen year old autistic grandson. And she would have it no other way.

Mollie Mae had sole custody of him ever since her only child, and Jeffey's mother, died in a tragic car accident. It was sixteen years past. In his world he knew no one else and the love he would occasionally shower upon Mollie Mae made life all worthwhile.

Their life was very simple, living in the inner city of San Diego. Not far from Balboa Park, Mollie Mae lived in the same four room house for the past forty years. She survived on a modest pension from her deceased husband and the warmth from their church friends. Jeffey existed on the love from M & M and God.

The two of them were always a sight, and a welcome one at that, whenever they arrived at Holy Baptist Church. Jeffey's six foot two frame towered over the diminutive Mollie Mae. But none stood taller in the eyes of her tight knit congregation than she.

Stepping towards the bed, Mollie Mae's kind brown eyes beckoned a smile from Jeffey. As she sat next to his slender body, he immediately ran his hand across her close cropped scalp. He loved to feel her stubbly mane. Jeffey called it Jesus fuzz, because Mollie Mae's hair was pure white. It contrasted immensely with her brown skin.

"What were you and God talking about?" She asked.

"Lot's a things," Jeffey continued rocking, while looking away.

"Anything I should know about?"

"Just one." Jeffey stared at the toy box once again.

Mollie Mae tried her best to get him to look at her, but he seemed fixated on the toy box. She stood. She knew the only way to make eye contact required standing between him and the box. Only Jeffey did something she never expected.

Grabbing her hand he pulled Mollie Mae back to where she was sitting. "Sit down, M & M. Sit down." Jeffey spoke somewhat agitated.

Allowing him to continue holding her hand, she glanced into his eyes. "What is it, Jeffey, what is it?"

"Pastor's in trouble." He quickly looked back at the toy box.

"Trouble," she asked. "Pastor Vernon? From church?"

Rocking back and forth at an excitable pace, Jeffey refused to look at Mollie Mae.

"Jeffey, you need to answer me," she pleaded.

Squeezing his hand, Mollie Mae asked again. "Jeffey, is it Pastor Vernon?"

"Don't know," he answered, his head still tilted away.

Frowning, she remained silent for a moment. She knew she couldn't force an answer from him if he wasn't ready. Calmly, Mollie Mae let go of his hand and walked away. Reaching for Jeffey's door handle, she heard him speak one more time.

"Not Pastor Vernon, M & M. God told me it's not him."

Through all the years that Jeffey spoke about having conversations with God, Mollie Mae never doubted him. She wasn't about to now. Yet for some reason, she felt shivers crawl down her spine. For the first time in her life she felt fear for Jeffey. Not for who he was, but for what he may come to know.

SEVEN

Dillon, MT

Sherry Rawlins fidgeted in a chair inside her editor's claustrophobic office. With his door shut and the blinds partially open, the only light source emanated from the fluorescent ceiling. Tugging at the turtleneck clinging to her throat, Sherry stared at his phone.

"For the umpteenth time, will you relax already?" Mark Granger sighed.

"I can't, Mark. We're sitting on the biggest story to come out of this town and the big guys are taking their time getting here." Sherry shot daggers back at Mark. "How can you sit so calmly, just waiting?"

"We're small potatoes, Sherry. You know that." Drumming his fingers on his desk, Mark added. "When the boys from Butte get here, they're gonna take over this story and you know it."

"Well, I wanna be the first one interviewed," Sherry interrupted. "I broke this story, Mark." Sherry peered through the blinds. "By golly, I want credit."

"And you'll get it, as soon as they arrive. Is Art still up at the lake?"

"Yeah, at least he better be." Sherry whipped out her cell hitting speed dial in the process. She stared at her boss as she waited for the call to go through.

"Still there?" she asked as Art answered his cell.

"How long do you want me to stay, Sher? For crying out loud it's gonna be dark soon."

"The news boys from Butte said they would be here any minute now. I need you to let me know if anything changes."

"Believe me, nothing's changed except a few more people gawking at the water."

Sherry looked down at a jar sitting on Mark's desk. The sample of water was still bright red. At least she had some evidence. "All right, all right," said Sherry. "Come on home, Art, that lake's not going anywhere."

Ending the call, Sherry held the jar in her hand. Stealing a glance at her editor she commented. "Right here, Mark. This stuff's a Pulitzer." She smiled, setting the jar back on his desk. "Yep, this paper's about to hit the big time."

"Unlike the jar you're holding," Mark answered. "I'll believe that when I see it."

"KXLF TV just pulled in." Mark's assistant announced, poking her head through the door.

Grabbing the jar again, Sherry beamed at Mark. "It's show time."

EIGHT

St. Louis, MO

Adjusting his Bluetooth, Pastor Jacob sat patiently at a red light. He wasn't sure if he'd get through to the one person he trusted to help sort out all that happened. But, if anyone could, it was him.

The light turned green. Jacob merged onto the highway when his call hit voice mail. "I'm sorry I'm not available," the male voice responded. "Please leave a message and I'll get back as soon as possible."

Frowning, Jacob formulated what he wanted to say. It was always amazing to him that it was not only the message you left but the tone that was so important. "Hey, Jim, this is Jacob Conley." Jacob paused to decide exactly what he wanted to say. "Listen, can you give me a call, I had a really strange thing happen to me; well, it wasn't strange at all, Jim. It was incredible, glorious." Jacob paused again, knowing his emotions were taking over. "What happened to me is right up your alley, Jim. Please give me a call as soon as you can."

Living close to the church was definitely a blessing in Jacob's view. The only other person he desperately wanted to share his experience with, he hoped was at home. Jacob pulled into the garage. He was pleased to see her car parked in the other bay.

Jacob ran swiftly into the house. He called out to his beloved wife. "Linda, Linda, where are you?"

28

Sitting in the den, Linda Conley had finished playing a piece on their baby grand. An accomplished pianist, she adored her recent anniversary gift compliments of Jacob. With slender fingers that were meant to play, they easily matched her long legs. Linda stood just under six feet. Long, flowing, sandy brown hair complemented her hazel eyes as they sparkled upon hearing her name.

"In here, Jake. What is it?" Linda peered around the corner in his direction.

Jacob's eyes lit as he approached his wife of thirty years. "You gotta sit down, hon." Jacob guided Linda to a nearby sofa.

Sitting next to each other, their knees touched at an angle. Jacob held her hand in his.

With penetrating eyes, Linda asked. "What happened?"

"Everything's fine," Jacob reassured her. "In my office today, while I was silently praying, I had a vision."

Linda tilted her head slightly. It was her way of letting Jacob know she was intrigued.

"It was amazing, Lin. The Lord took complete control of my entire body." Pausing for effect, Jacob stared into her eyes. "And my mind."

"Are you saying you couldn't move?"

"I couldn't move and I couldn't see."

"What? Where you blinded by some light?"

For some reason Jacob closed his eyes as he continued. "No, I was totally blind. I couldn't see a thing."

Taking a deep breath, Linda asked. "Then what happened?"

"This is the part I don't understand." Leaning slightly in, Jacob first glanced up at the ceiling, then back down. "I kept seeing the word 'blood' flowing through the darkness." Shaking his head, Jacob continued. "No, actually it was two words."

"What two words?"

"The blood." Jacob put an emphasis on the word the.

Squirming somewhat on the sofa, Linda responded. "Okay, so it's completely dark, then the words, 'the blood' swim around over and over again?"

"Exactly, but that's not all."

This is getting good, Linda thought to herself.

Intensely Jacob added. "The bizarre part was when I saw a mass of people under water. Each time one tried to surface he couldn't."

"Was there something holding them back?"

Shrugging his shoulders, Jacob answered. "I think it was the blood. The blood in the water."

Linda paused, to let it sink in. "Or maybe the water wasn't water at all. Maybe, it was blood they were swimming in."

"I don't know, Hon. To be honest I don't know what the Lord is trying to tell me."

"How long did this go on?"

Running his hand back and forth through his hair, Jacob thought before answering. "I wanna say everything happened in a matter of moments. I really don't know."

"Obviously everything returned back to normal. Have you had any reoccurrences?"

"No, not yet at least. I kinda flew out of my office and jumped into my car. Probably freaked Getta out." Jacob chuckled slightly.

Linda placed her hand over Jacobs. "So what next?"

"I tried calling Jim Calhoun on my way home. Ended up leaving a message."

Linda nodded in agreement. She knew how much Jacob valued his friend's wisdom. Jim was not only a fellow pastor, but also highly respected throughout the world. Linda paused for a moment before asking a question. "What about calling your dad, Jake?" She tried to gauge Jacob's response. "Maybe he can shed some light on this."

Rising from the sofa, Jacob stared out a nearby window. "I'm just not sure how he'd receive it." Frowning, Jacob added, "to be honest, I don't want to bother him with it."

"Well," Linda replied. "Let's wait and see what Jim has to say."

NINE

The Oval Office

With his "unofficial" advisor, Ra Farman, sitting to his right, President Pollard glanced at a staff member. Sitting across from them was Anne Givens, the President's press secretary. Anne was a fireball of excitement who spoke a mile a minute. Her curly red tresses only added to her animated nature.

"Mr. President, we need to address this anomaly that has occurred out in Montana." Gesturing wildly with her hands, Anne continued. "This story has the potential of scaring the American people."

Holding his hand up in a stop position, Ra turned to whisper in the President's ear. This only agitated Anne even further. She was certainly supportive of the President but, she didn't quite get the connection between President Pollard and his friend.

"This is what we need to do, Anne," the President spoke. "We need to carefully craft a statement for the public. One that reassures them nothing is wrong."

"But Mr. President," Anne interrupted.

This time it was Stuart Pollard's turn to hold up his hand. "Believe me, Annie."

Anne Givens sank back in her seat knowing he was about to patronize her. The President was always sarcastic when he referred to her as Annie.

"The people will be better served if you tone down the rhetoric," President Pollard paused for effect. "The less we make of it, the sooner it will go away. Understood?"

Rising to her feet, the President's press secretary answered the only way she could. In a defeated tone she replied. "Yes, Mr. President, I'll wait for the release."

"That's good, Annie. You go ahead and schedule with the press for about 3:00 this afternoon."

Anne turned about and headed for the door.

"Oh, and Anne." Turning, she faced her caller. "Remember, control your tone."

"Yes sir," she frowned, addressing Ra.

Still smiling, Ra glanced at the President waiting for his question.

"How does the association want to proceed with this press release?" Stuart asked.

"To make it as insignificant as possible. We don't want some small town mishap stealing the thunder from our agenda."

"I understand." Rubbing his chin while in thought, the President asked. "But what do you make of this strange happening out in Montana? My experts tell me that it is actually blood in that lake."

"If we ignore it, it will go away." Ra's eyes darted from one end of the room to the other. He acted as if there was something only he could see. "But I think if we give it attention, it could potentially grow."

"Grow into what?" The President peered over his left shoulder.

Placing his hand on Stuart's right shoulder, Ra seized his friend's attention. "Distractions are not an option, Mr. President. In a few days' time, the anomaly will go away and the media will become disinterested."

"And if this doesn't happen?"

Standing to his feet, Ra Farman glared down at the President. "Then the association will take matters into our own hands. You do understand, correct?"

Nodding in agreement, the President replied. "Understood."

TEN

Outside the White House

Pulling over to the side of the road, Ra Farman peered out his window at the White House in the distance. Smiling, he brought his cell up to his ear waiting for a response.

"Yes," a voice spoke.

"Are you and the others ready to proceed?" Ra asked.

"Just tell us what you want done and how soon."

"Good," Ra glared out his window at a passing police vehicle. "Summon whatever you think you need. Go immediately to the site. No delays, go immediately. Do you understand?" Ra concentrated on the person he was speaking to.

"I do. We'll take care of it by the end of the day."

Slamming his fist against the dash, Ra became enraged. His eyes turned to a smoldering red. "You will have it done immediately!"

Outside, a woman pushing a baby carriage stopped in her tracks. Peering inside Ra's car she searched for the source of the commotion.

Sensing her presence, Ra calmly acknowledged her with a simple nod. As she went on her way, he continued his conversation. "Make sure the lake is transformed back to its natural state by this afternoon. No later than 3:00 my time. Understood?"

"Yes sir." Ra's line went dead.

Through his windshield Ra stared at the woman with the carriage. His fury once again started to rise. Summoning the darkness from within, he unleashed his powers toward the child. Within seconds the woman stopped. Bent over, she tried to tend to her screaming infant. Wails of grief penetrated Ra's vehicle, even from a great distance.

Grinning with satisfaction Ra quickly sped away; leaving a panicked mother, and a tormented baby to deal with unknown forces.

ELEVEN

First Christian Church

With notes in hand, Jacob tried focusing on his sermon for Sunday morning. His mind kept shifting from his paper to the vision from yesterday. Concentrating did not seem to be an option.

Finally, giving into frustration, Jacob sat in his chair. Perhaps if he flipped open to Romans once again, inspiration would take over. No sooner did he reach Romans 3 Jacob's cell rang. Glancing at the ID showed unavailable. He answered on the third ring.

"This is Jacob."

"Pastor Jacob, my friend. Jim Calhoun here."

Jacob felt relieved. A sense of peace fell over him. "Jim, I'm glad you called."

"Not a problem, Jacob. Though there seemed to be urgency in your message."

Sensing the concern in his friend's voice, Jacob immediately replied. "No, no, I didn't mean for it to sound that way...actually I had an incredible experience, Jim."

"How so?"

Collecting his thoughts, Jacob took a moment before talking about the previous day. He mentioned losing control of his body, the words that kept appearing in his mind. He finished by stating that this was clearly a vision from the Lord, but he wasn't sure why. Jacob paused, waiting for Jim Calhoun's response. There was nothing but silence.

In a muffled tone, Jacob heard his friend softly praying. He was praying for the revelation Jacob received and he was praying for how his friend should proceed.

Jacob's head bowed in reverence and his eyes remained closed. He could feel tiny streams of tears slowly cascading down his cheeks. Silently he prayed in conjunction with Jim. Both men called upon the Lord's Holiness. Feeling the presence of the Holy Spirit Jacob felt awestruck.

"I need to come see you," Jim suddenly remarked.

Wiping the tears from his face, Jacob simply answered. "I know, I know."

"I can't make it until next weekend, Jacob. What do you have scheduled for the following Sunday?"

Running his hand through his hair, Jacob thought for a second. "I'm in the midst of a new series." Realizing what the question really meant, Jacob continued. "But, I'd like nothing better than to have you speak, if you're willing."

Chuckling, Jim replied. "That would be perfect, my friend. I'll call you with my flight arrangements...and Jacob?"

"I'm here."

"I sense this is just the beginning. You realize that, don't you?"

For the second time in the last ten minutes Jacob could feel his eyes welling up. "I do, Jim. I believe this vision is a piece of a puzzle, with many more parts to come."

"I agree. Blessings, brother, I'll speak to you soon."

Jacob clicked off his phone. He sat back staring at the ceiling. Prayers of utterance ushered from his lips. With eyes closed, grinning as large as he could, Jacob Conley laughed like a little child. Like a babe adoring his mother. Like a man in awe of his Father. And he just knew his Father was smiling back, too.

TWELVE

Dillon, MT

Dillon Reservoir was still popping with excitement. After all, a true phenomenon had occurred and news like this drew attention. The news media was camped out as close as the local authorities would allow. Sight seers and gawkers were kept back to a manageable distance.

No one was allowed to take a sample of the tainted water. The odor from the pooling blood wafted through the atmosphere, yet amazingly nothing dead floated upon the surface. The sight of the shimmering substance seemed to satisfy the curious, for the time being.

The media continued to report the lake as being transformed from water to blood, though no one had attempted to submerge and see how far the red liquid penetrated. Divers were scheduled to officially take a look later in the afternoon. Scientific analysis still needed to be conducted before the authorities would permit this next step.

Meanwhile the people who gathered nearby were content to speculate what happened to the lake and what it probably meant. Theories seemed to range from all the fish dying at once and somehow bleeding out, to environmental whackos polluting the lake to make a statement. Bottom line, no one knew how or why. No one knew what to expect next.

One man had a different mission, though. Clothed entirely in black with sunglasses to shield his eyes, Gaether Lahash stood off to the side of the gathering crowd. Almost everything about him was average. He was of average height, build, brown eyes, and brown hair. He even appeared to be in his mid-thirties. All these characteristics helped him to do one thing; blend in. But the one thing that made him different from anyone else was what was inside. Gaether was comprised of pure evil.

Blending in with the shadows of the tree line he gazed at the body of water. He had one assignment and one assignment only. Change the current condition of the reservoir.

Gaether knew who was responsible for the blood in the water. Because of this knowledge he also knew there was not a power on earth that could change it back to the way it was. There was however a way to eliminate the actual substance within the reservoir.

Walking away from the crowd and proceeding downhill, Gaether made his own path through the forest. Arriving at a point he determined to be sufficiently below the shores of Dillon Reservoir, he stopped.

Gaether was well hidden in darkness from the surrounding woods. He dropped to his knees and summoned the power to do his bidding. Immediately he fell backwards. A tremendous jolt emanated from deep below the lake bed that only he felt.

Powers unseen to man and unimaginable scurried about. At home in a realm that no human could ever witness, they burrowed straight down to the depths of hell. The creatures possessed deformed scale like limbs, with razor sharp six inch claws. With gnashing teeth and a stench that permeated the air, the beings had only one goal. They were ordered to eliminate all evidence of the lake. Within moments everything was gone.

Off in the distance Gaether heard the astonished cries of the people along the lake shores. Grinning, he righted himself and walked away from the calamity of the scene high above. When he reached the roadside, Gaether pulled out his cell.

Pressing one button he was instantly connected to the person who ordered this mission.

"Is it done?"

"Yes," Gaether answered. Pausing, he added. "Will there be anything else?"

Grabbing his remote, Ra turned the television to the first news channel he could find. Transfixed by the scrolling headline at the bottom of the screen exclaiming "breaking news", Ra replied. "Not right now, but I may need you, yet soon enough."

Turning the volume up, Ra listened to the frantic voice of a newscaster reporting live from Dillon, Montana.

"In an incredible turn of events something truly stunning just happened at this once serene, majestic lake in Dillon, Montana. At approximately 12:53 local time what authorities are calling a possible earthquake may have occurred deep beneath the Dillon Reservoir. The result of this has led to the complete draining, if you will, of this lake through some kind of fissure at the bottom of the reservoir. Authorities can only speculate that the substance, and we call it that because it certainly didn't appear to be water, disappeared through some kind of sinkhole in the bottom of the lake. Experts think this fault line may have even contributed to the strange red substance in the first place. Now we can only…

Sitting back in his arm chair, Ra smirked at the now silent screen. Taking in the frenzy of the news media gathered around the empty lake he spoke softly to himself. "Not an earthquake dear lady, but the work of my minions." Ra, briefly glanced away, then back at the television. "Yes, this is only the beginning."

THIRTEEN

St. Louis, MO

Jacob wrapped up his day by putting the final touches on his sermon. It was important to at least have the key points memorized by the end of a work week. Having accomplished this he decided to call Ben Palmer and touch base with his dear friend.

He figured it would be hit and miss reaching Ben. Who knows if he was on call? Jacob took a chance and dialed his cell number. He was in luck. Ben answered on the fourth ring.

"Jake, how are you?"

"Hi Ben, wasn't sure I'd get you. Hope I'm not disturbing you."

"Naw, finishing up some paper work. Even though I've reduced my practice hours significantly, the red tape menace seems like it's quadrupled."

Jacob leaned back smiling at his friends comment. "Now that you're working for the government does that surprise you?"

"Hey, everything takes longer with universal health care. That's why I'm slowly getting out."

"Well, at the rate you're going the second coming will have come and past, Doc."

Ben laughed and quickly added, "Don't get me started. The good Lord couldn't come soon enough far as I'm concerned."

"Amen brother. Amen."

"So to what do I owe this call?"

44

Jacob paused before answering, knowing that their conversation was about to take on a more serious tone. "Listen, Ben, some interesting things have recently happened. What are the chances of you getting away next weekend to visit?"

"Should I ask what happened now, or do you want to fill me in when I arrive?"

Jacob wondered how he was blessed with such a good friend. "Sure you'll be able to get away? I realize its short notice."

"To be honest, Amy and I have been pining to get out of here for quite some time. I know she'd love to see you and Linda, as would I."

"Perfect." Jacob glanced at his calendar before continuing. "Just so you know you won't be the only guest."

"Well now you've got me intrigued. Care to fill me in?"

Jacob smiled knowing he couldn't be surrounded by any better people. "All I can say is you're about to meet one of the world's most anointed men of God."

"Really. Jake, that's enough right there to get me to visit."

"Good," Jacob answered.

"But I have one pressing question."

"Just one?" asked Jacob.

Ben paused before asking. "What do you need me for?"

Swallowing hard, Jacob answered. "I need and trust your instincts, Ben. Jim and I feel something significant is about to happen. I want you onboard when it does."

There was a silence after Jacob's last statement. He knew his friend was lost in thought.

"Jim wouldn't happen to be the Jim Calhoun you've spoken of before?" Ben asked.

"Yes, he is."

"Then if it's that important we'll be there," Ben replied. "We'll shoot for Friday morning and make it a long weekend…sound good?"

"Perfect." Jacob hung up and gathered his notes together. It was hard not thinking about next weekend. He still had the present one to contend with and everything it was about to bring.

FOURTEEN

The White House

The vibration from his shirt pocket momentarily distracted President Pollard. He glanced away from a man sitting to his right. Holding up a single finger, the President instantly silenced Gary Addison, his Department of Commerce advisor.

Without even offering an apology for the interruption, President Pollard reached in and pulled out his cell phone. Looking at the phone, the President started to read the text. The message was both simple and direct. Call me ASAP.

"Why don't we wrap this meeting up, gentlemen," President Pollard addressed all three staff members.

Within a matter of five minutes President Pollard sat alone at his desk readying himself to place a call. He hesitated. He knew Ra needed something. The question was what? Ra didn't actually contact the President that often. In fact, during the first two years of his term the vast majority of their contact was infrequent at best.

Lately, though, the President sensed a growing agitation in his associate. Something was definitely pressing at him. None-the-less, Ra Farman was not the kind of man one kept waiting. The President realized one significant fact. When you sell your soul you're no longer in charge. Ultimately, he answered to Ra.

Placing the call, the President waited for Ra to answer.

"President Pollard, good of you to call me back. I trust I wasn't interrupting anything."

The President was a little taken back by the greeting. Ra was known for getting right to the point. "Everything all right, Ra?"

"Absolutely, my friend."

Relaxing a bit more, the President responded. "So exactly what might be pressing my mentor and friend this Monday morning?"

Keeping his tone cordial, Ra answered. "Can we meet this week, perhaps tomorrow?"

"Of course, I'll need to check with Jenny and see what my schedule is set for.

"Cancel what you must, Stuart." Ra interrupted in a more direct tone. "It is imperative that we meet. I think thirty minutes should suffice."

Muting his cell, Stuart rose to his feet. He glanced at the intercom button and pressed it.

"Yes, Mr. President."

"Jenny, I need about an hour set aside for tomorrow morning. Reschedule or cancel what you have to. Understand?"

"Uh, yes sir, Mr. President. Is there a particular time you need?"

"One moment, Jenny." The President reached for his cell. As he prepared to un-mute the phone he was startled by Ra's voice.

"9:00 AM will do fine." Ra hung up without waiting for confirmation.

Quickly glancing at his cell phone, The President hesitated. How did he know? He wondered.

Returning to the intercom, The President responded. "I need 9:00 AM open, Jenny."

Just enough silence lapsed that prompted the President to reply. "Is that doable, or do we have a problem?"

Sensing the agitation in his voice, Jenny answered. "I'll move some things around; it should be no problem, Mr. President."

"Very good."

"Mr. President," Jenny asked hesitantly. "Whom should I schedule for the 9:00 AM slot?"

"I'll be meeting with Mr. Ra Farman, Jenny. Thank you." The President was about to walk away from his desk when Jenny added one more thing.

"And Mr. President, just to remind you, Senator Tucker is waiting to see you."

"Right." Glancing at his watch, the President realized it was now 10:23. His meeting with the Senator had been scheduled at 10:00. Taking a big breath, he replied. "Please send her in."

Still trying to wrap his mind around his conversation with Ra, the President felt like a child who had his toy taken away. He didn't like it, but there was nothing he could do.

Mentally preparing for his meeting with the Senator, the President mustered a plastic smile. He realized he was doing that a lot these days. The odd thing was he didn't mind at all.

FIFTEEN

The White House / Next morning

Stepping lively through the main corridor leading to the Oval Office, Ra Farman uncharacteristically greeted everyone with a smile. Why not? He was looking forward to his meeting with President Pollard this morning. But he was most anxious to tell him about the next part of their plan.

Punctuality for a meeting was important to Ra. Arriving early was his known trademark. No one disliked this part of Ra Farman more than the President's assistant, Jenny. In fact there was very little she liked about the man. But her job wasn't to pass judgment, if she wanted to keep her position. Much like many others in this administration, she had to pretend.

Jenny glanced at her watch. It read 8:52 AM. She debated whether she should engage in small talk with Mr. Farman. He did seem in a particularly good mood. In the past, he never gave her the time of day.

"Jenny, how are you this morning?" Ra asked.

Straining to smile, Jenny responded as genuine as possible. "Just fine, Mr. Farman, and you?"

"Couldn't be better. Is the President in?"

That was short lived, she thought to herself. "I'll check and see if he's available." Jenny picked up the phone and pressed the intercom button. Smiling at Ra, Jenny spoke into the phone. "Mr. President, Mr. Farman is here. Are you ready for him, sir?"

Jenny waited for the President's response. "Very good, Mr. President, I'll show him in."

Not waiting for her, Ra proceeded toward the door, before Jenny cut him off and reached for the handle. Turning slightly toward Ra, she said. "Protocol, Mr. Farman. Allow me to announce your arrival."

Stepping back, and gesturing toward the door, Ra simply answered. "By all means, young lady."

Jenny knocked twice then opened the door to the President's office. Before she had a chance to say anything, Ra moved swiftly past her.

"Thank you, Jenny," the President said. She closed the door behind her.

Sitting back behind her desk, Jenny exhaled a great breath. Let it go, just let it go, she thought.

President Pollard motioned to his friend to take a seat. Ra wasted no time sitting in what he considered the power seat. He chose a single wingback chair that ultimately led to the President sitting to his left on a couch.

The President knew Ra well enough to know that pleasantries or beverages were never of interest. Diving right in, he asked. "So my friend, of what importance do you have for us today?"

Turning his head slightly to the left, Ra answered. "The association would like you to move ahead with a new initiative."

51

Hearing the word association prompted the President to sit forward. "What initiative? I wasn't aware they had anything new on the drawing board."

Ra smiled at the President's response. "And how could you, Stuart? This is an idea that, how shall we say, just came to mind."

Shifting in his seat the President leaned in closer toward his guest. "So, apparently they're no longer interested in 'not for profit' at this time?"

"On the contrary, my friend." Ra made sure he emphasized the words, my friend. "They still want you to act on that measure. Soon I might add. Only we wish to have you enact something new at the same time."

The President sat back and hesitated before speaking. "Exactly what is this new initiative, Ra?"

Ra's eyes gleamed with satisfaction as he responded. "We would like to have a special rule put in place that would heavily regulate all Christian Colleges and Universities. But we would like this be under the radar, so to speak."

"I'm afraid I'm not following."

Nodding, Ra replied. "Let me explain. Basically this rule would regulate Christian universities and colleges by requiring them to conform to what the state deems morally acceptable."

"Go on," the President urged.

"I see a sparkle in your eye, Stuart. That's good."

The President smiled in return.

"We would restrict freedom of religion by wording a document that prohibits intolerance or discrimination in regards to religious belief."

Resting his chin against his hand, the President asked. "Why would this restriction be necessary?"

Ra paused briefly, making sure he had the President's full attention. "Because it would protect the safety, health and morality of our citizens."

"Of course." The President grinned.

"Now you see," Ra responded.

The fact that the President understood this concept was exactly what Ra had expected. Through the power of suggestion and constant manipulation, Stuart Pollard continued to feed into his plan. What was not expected was the ease in which the President fell. Their relationship had been a work in progress that started many years back. Stuart Pollard had aspirations of the presidency and Ra Farman needed a candidate. Because Stuart was a well-known charismatic politician, he fit the bill. Ra could provide the backing and Stuart could be the front man. But the characteristics that attributed to this match made in hell were that Stuart Pollard was of the world, and he was willing to be used.

Leaning forward, the President asked. "But, how we define what is moral is the key. Is it not?"

"Absolutely. Thus, the significance of the fine each institution would incur would ultimately drive them out of business."

"And out of our way, I might add." The President now looked more relaxed than ever.

Pleased with how things were proceeding, Ra paused before reeling his protégée in. "How do you suggest we implement this rule without stirring up too much dissension?"

Reaching for a note pad, the President jotted down a few items. Looking up at his guest, he replied. "That's simple, we bury it among the not-for-profit law that is about to be changed."

Nodding in agreement, Ra asked. "I assume you're confident in the votes for this bill to be passed?"

"My sources tell me the opposition is already conceding," the President smirked. "Why, they have distanced themselves so far from the Christian coalition that taking this tax exempt status away is a non-issue."

"Splendid." Ra stood to his feet. "How soon do you expect the vote?"

Rising as well, the President responded. "At the very latest, end of summer. But I suspect even sooner."

Reaching out his hand, Ra pulled the President in close. "This is very good news, my friend. Very good news." Releasing the President from his vise like grip, Ra Farman retreated for the door. Turning around before exiting the office, he added. "I'll be in touch soon, Mr. President." He then winked, and walked away.

SIXTEEN

St. Louis, MO

The weekend came in what seemed like a whirlwind to Jacob. Nothing out of the ordinary occurred but he was busy none the less. It always took more time to prepare for a guest speaker at the church than to prepare for one's own sermon. For this guest Jacob wanted everything absolutely perfect.

Jim Calhoun was not only a dear friend but a much respected minister to the congregation at First Christian. A sort of "buzz" filled the air when the saints knew he was coming to preach. Word generally spread throughout the Christian community whenever Jim came to town.

Preparing for an estimated overflow of attendees on Sunday morning kept the First Christian staff hopping. Jacob was no exception. Not only did he have to prepare at the church but he needed to help Linda prepare at their home as well.

At least he had a good excuse to leave early for the day. After all, Dr. Palmer and his wife, Amy, were due to arrive at the airport around 11:00 AM. Then Jim Calhoun and his wife, Lisa, would arrive later in the afternoon.

The good news was Jacob had arranged for Pastor Will to pick Jim up at the airport. He would then bring them to Jacob and Linda's home. The bad news was he needed to hustle if he was going to make it to the airport in time for Dr. Palmer's flight. Last minute details always got the best of him.

SEVENTEEN

San Diego, CA

Mollie Mae always felt anxious waiting for the school bus to bring Jeffey home. It wasn't because she didn't trust the driver. She never knew what kind of day Jeffey might have had. Today was a good day though. He bounded up the walkway smiling and carrying on.

"What's got you so chipper, Jeffey?" Mollie Mae opened the door as he bolted past her.

"Gotta watch nature channel," Jeffey plopped down in front of the television.

"Well wait, Jeffey. I want you to tell me about your day."

Approaching the already seated Jeffey, Mollie Mae stood between him and the television.

Scooting back and forth Jeffey tried his best to see around her, even though there was nothing on. "Nature channel, M & M," Jeffey pleaded.

"Now, Jeffey," Mollie Mae countered. "You know the rules. No television till you do your homework."

Continuing his see sawing efforts, Jeffey's mind was set on one thing. "Gotta watch nature channel...right now."

Mollie Mae reached for the television remote, but Jeffey beat her to it. Extending his right arm past her, he clicked the remote and the television sprang to life.

"Now give me that remote!" Mollie Mae demanded. She took a step toward him.

"Stop, M & M. Stop."

Placing her hands on her hips, Mollie Mae glared at Jeffey. "What has gotten into you?"

Tears started to stream down Jeffey's face. He pleadingly looked up at her.

"Child, what's wrong?" Mollie Mae took a seat next to her troubled grandson.

Placing her hand on his now rocking body, Mollie Mae asked again. "Jeffey, what's wrong?"

Turning his head from the TV, he peered through imploring eyes. "God told me to, M & M. He told me to."

Taking a big breath, Mollie Mae reached out her hand. "Then let me put it on for you, child."

Without hesitating, Jeffey handed her the remote. The incessant rocking continued, as he stared at the TV.

EIGHTEEN

St. Louis, MO

The Conley house couldn't have been more boisterous. Having finished a wonderful meal prepared by Linda Conley, the three couples retreated into the den to relax and get to know each other further.

Much to Jacob's pleasure Jim Calhoun and Ben Palmer seemed to hit it off quickly. Jim had always been a trusted friend. Like a brother in more ways than one. At sixty two years of age, Jim possessed the wisdom of past prophets. He had a full head of gray, and sparkling blue eyes that seemed to twinkle when he spoke of the Lord. People naturally gravitated to him. Even his stature exuded an aura of confidence.

Now that both men were present Jacob felt a sense of peace engulf him. It was as if the Holy Spirit was sitting among them, just like an old friend.

Sitting forward on a sectional right next to his soul-mate, Amy, Ben seized the moment and gathered everyone's attention. "You know what?" He announced. "I for one am honored to be in your company." Gesturing with his right hand, Ben continued. I'm really looking forward to the rest of this weekend. Something tells me it's going to be eventful."

"I agree, but I also think it's simply the Holy Spirit guiding you." Jacob said. "As a matter of fact, I can sense His presence right now."

59

Seated on the same sectional to the right of the Palmer's, Jacob felt Linda gently pat his hand. "Without a doubt, Jake." Linda added.

Across from the two couples sitting in a loveseat were Jim and his wife Lisa. She was the matron of the group, yet youthful in spirit.

"I say we go with the flow of the spirit," interrupted Jim. Scanning everyone's eyes with the intensity of someone truly convicted, Jim Calhoun closed his eyes. Calling upon The Lord he prayed for clarity, righteousness, and blessing.

Upon finishing his prayer and without skipping a beat, Jim turned to Jacob. "Now my friend, tell us about your vision."

Feeling as if the eyes of the world were upon him, Jacob hesitated trying to collect his thoughts. Leaning forward, Jacob first glanced down, then turned to his right to face Jim Calhoun.

"Before you start, Jake, let me get comfortable." Amy Palmer scooted to the floor directly in front of Ben. Looking around after she settled in, Amy giggled as all eyes fell upon her. "What? Can I help it if I know he'll rub my shoulders?"

"What about me?" Lisa elbowed Jim. "We've been married over forty years and I'm still waiting for that back rub."

"Sorry, Lisa, but this doctor doesn't make couch calls," Ben replied.

"Well," Jacob shook his head while laughing. "If you guys are done with the lame jokes, I'll begin."

"Please," Ben said. "Don't mind us."

Still focusing on Jim, Jacob spoke next. "Through all my years in ministry I have always been able to hear from God. But I've never been able to see things that I felt were clearly sent from God." Jacob paused, before he continued. "So, about a week ago I was reading Romans…

"Which passage?" Jim interrupted.

"3:23-25, I believe." Jacob scanned the eyes of the others before moving on. "I was planning to use scripture from Romans for my sermon last Sunday." Jacob hesitated. "All of a sudden the page became blurry and I started to lose my sight."

"You couldn't see, or had you closed your eyes?" Amy asked.

"No, no, I couldn't see. I had lost my vision."

"So what happened next?" Ben asked.

Jacob could feel Linda's hand squeezing his. "I remember trying to stand. I was disoriented. I kept thinking I'm losing control. Then, in the darkness I started to see the word control. It was though God was telling me to relinquish all control." Squirming somewhat in his seat, Jacob paused. "Actually, He was telling me that. I didn't get it at first."

Looking up from her seat on the floor, Amy added. "I can imagine."

"So, Jacob," Jim asked, already knowing the answer. "Why do you think He wanted you to give up control?"

"In order for me to truly understand, God needed to be in charge."

"Wow," Ben murmured.

"Wow indeed," Linda added, squeezing Jacob's hand once more.

Seizing control of the conversation, Jim held his index finger up. "Jacob, you were praying for the Lord to speak to you." He now held up two fingers. "He forces you to lose the sense of sight." Now three fingers were held up high. "Then in darkness you see the word control and nothing else, which forces you to focus on Him."

"Exactly," Jacob replied.

Leaning forward, Ben asked. "So what next?"

"This is where it became beautiful, then a little strange." Holding Linda's hand even tighter, he continued. "I was at total peace. There was an overwhelming sense of His presence about me."

"Glorious," Lisa commented.

"Yes," focusing on Lisa, Jacob replied. "Yes, it was." Moving his shoulders about, emphasizing his discomfort, Jacob paused. "Then it became somewhat eerie."

"How so, Jake?" Ben asked.

Closing his eyes, Jacob reflected. "The next thing I saw was the word blood."

"Blood?" Lisa asked, leaning into Jim.

"Well, not only the word, but then I saw a group of people struggling in what appeared to be blood."

"Jacob," Jim spoke up. "Did you recognize any of the people in your vision?"

"Yeah, was there anyone you knew?" Ben asked.

Shaking his head no, Jacob didn't say a word. After the momentary silence, he then added. "The people, they were struggling to get to the surface. Trying to get out of the substance, or blood. But they couldn't."

"Did anything else happen, Jake?" Jim asked.

"Well, at this point the words 'the blood' were circling around the people over and over, and then the vision disappeared. I, I was back to normal."

Pervasive silence filled the room for quite some time. All appeared to be reflective in thought, until the prophet among them spoke.

"My brother, Jacob, could you stand for a moment?"

Rising from his seat, Jim Calhoun approached his now standing friend. With all eyes focused on the two men in the center of the room, Jim placed his right hand on Jacob's left shoulder.

His eyes closed and silent in prayer, Jim felt the presence of God speak through him. "Son, I have commissioned you to take on a tremendous task, says the Lord. For years your heart has cried out for something to be done to help your pleading brothers and sisters across this land. God wants you to know, He has listened to their pleading…and He has listened to your call to service."

With a burning intensity Jim stared into Jacob's melting eyes. "You need not call any longer. For it is time to act. I will use you to lead the charge. I will use you to cry out to the masses. I will use you to start the revival."

Sensing that his friend was weakening, Ben instinctively jumped up and placed both hands behind Jacob's back.

With tears cascading down his face, Jacob's knees buckled slightly as Jim continued.

"This is the calling I place on you, says God. There will be a combination of signs you must heed. Not just visions that I will bless you with, but others to give you words."

Peering through moistened eyes, Jacob felt a jolt course through his body. Jim placed both of his hands on Jacob's shoulders. Twisting his face as if stricken with pain, Jim hesitated before continuing.

"Lastly, take heed to what I say next. The enemy is close and will be on the attack. You will face great challenges and so shall your accomplices. The conflict will be intense. You must not grow weary from the battle."

With his eyes aglow and a grin that exuded warmth, Jim squeezed both of Jacob's shoulders. "Now take courage and remember this, it is I with you, do not be afraid."

Falling back into Ben's arms, Jacob drifted off into another vision. Entering into the spirit world, a great battle ensued. The forces of darkness clashed with those of light while the rest of the world was oblivious.

In this realm reality unfolded. For countless ages the factions of good versus evil have waged on, long before mankind ever existed. But that which Jacob was allowed to see did involve man. Though darkness may rule the earth, man still has a choice.

Being of faith Jacob knew this but it didn't prepare him for what he was about to see. In the distance, beings so hideous gnawed at the souls of the unsaved. Grieving angels of indescribable beauty could do no more than stand by. The immediate surroundings were neither Heaven nor Hell. In fact, every scene that unfolded was all too familiar to Jacob.

In homes, offices, prisons and even schools, the torment inflicted was very real. Demons entered and left bodies freely uninhibited. Clinging to many, were creatures not willing to let go. Others sat upon shoulders whispering commands into unsuspecting ears. Violence perpetrated from person to person was directed by powers within.

All the images of darkness that Jacob observed led to one disturbing fact. No human could see what was occurring, and very few seemed to care. But why? Why was this happening and why did God's angels stand back?

Jacob's gut writhed in heaviness and his face twisted in grief. He cried out again and again. "Why? Why, Lord?"

Falling to his knees, weighted down from despair, Jacob sobbed. He watched men and women in agony stemming from the suffering inflicted. So many, there were so many. Gently, he felt a touch of a hand caress his heaving shoulders. Peering up at the glowing presence before him, Jacob could mouth no words.

"This is not your burden to carry," said the spirit before him. "These are the souls that have refused grace from the Savior."

"How can I not hurt for them? Don't they still deserve a chance?" Jacob pleaded for an answer.

"Some you may still save, many you will not. But you, Jacob, have been called for a different purpose."

Rising to his feet, Jacob followed behind the angel. They walked past those who had sold their souls. "Where are we going?" Jacob cried out.

"To your destiny. To those who will follow."

A scene unlike the other materialized before Jacob's eyes. Before him stood men, women and children. Shoulder to shoulder, arms lifted in praise. As far as the eye could see was a vast army of worshippers. Praises were sung. Shouts cried out. People simply worshipped.

But not all were in sync throughout the throngs. The further back that people gathered, the more they looked confused. It was as if those newly arrived somehow didn't get it. Even though they knew something huge was happening, they weren't sure what to think.

Then Jacob saw something truly astonishing. The sea of humanity parted in two as if a hand swept across the people. A pathway was opened creating a single aisle from the back to the front. What seemed like an invisible barrier held everyone back on each side.

The next moment, a sound thundered over the shouts of the people. Immediately the maimed and the injured entered the aisle. Forward they struggled. Some in wheelchairs, others on crutches. All were determined to get to the front. Remarkably the line kept moving because of one reason. Healing was instantaneous.

Those standing up front healed all who came forward. Those who were cured then moved throughout the crowd. The power of faith and the movement of the Holy Spirit flowed like a river. It restored everyone it touched.

"This is remarkable," Jacob cried out in awe. "Who are these people?"

"Do you not understand?" The spirit's glow intensified as more and more people rejoiced.

Warmth engulfed Jacob. He took in the glory before him. "I think I do," he turned to face the angel. "These are the saints and they're bringing forth revival."

"Now you truly see," the angel replied. "To bring forth revival, healing must occur. But in order for true healing, one must first know Christ."

"Why am I here?" Scanning the vastness of individuals Jacob softly murmured. "What exactly does He wish me to do?"

"Lead!"

Feeling humbled, yet overwhelmed at the same time, Jacob remained silent. He stared directly at the angel. "What do they call you?"

"I am called Briathos, the warrior."

Jacob nodded in acknowledgment. He turned once more to take in the sea of humanity reaching out to Christ. For what seemed like hours he remained still allowing himself to absorb the energy.

Tears streamed down Jacob's face. He was not unlike them. He knew he had the ability to do more, but for some reason he hadn't. Standing high above the masses, Jacob finally understood his assignment.

Facing Briathos, he paused. Then Jacob spoke with a new conviction and purpose. "If I'm to lead the saints, then let the battle begin. It's time for our persecution to end!"

Opening his eyes abruptly, Jacob immediately realized the revelation had ended. Gathered around him were those he dearly loved. Smiling like never before, he leaped to his feet. In a childlike manner he asked. "So what are you all looking at?"

Throwing her arms around him, Linda embraced her husband. "I don't know what you went through, but I can sense you're a changed man."

Stepping back, Jacob's eyes seemed to be on fire. They glowed with burning intensity. First he stared at the Calhoun's, then the Palmers, and finally back to Linda. "I've never felt more energized than I do right now. But I beg you to indulge me for what I need to do."

Cocking his head slightly, Ben immediately asked. "What is it Jacob?"

Jacob's eyes found Jim before responding. Jim instantly knew.

"Stay here and pray, brother. Now more than ever you need to be alone with the Lord." Jim motioned for the others to follow him as he turned to leave the den.

Grasping Linda's hand Jacob drew her near. "I just need some time. I need to be with Him."

Leaning into Jacob, she placed a peck on his cheek. Linda turned to join the others. She had no doubt the conversation at breakfast was going to be very lively.

NINETEEN

Sunday morning / First Christian Church

Sitting at a conference table in a back room of the sanctuary, Jacob, Ben and Jim finished praying together. As predicted there was an overflow of people attending the 10:00 AM service. Many were anticipating the sermon of Jim Calhoun. They were in for a special treat. The Holy Spirit had plans for both Jim and Jacob.

"You sure you don't want to join us on stage, Ben?" Jacob asked.

With eyebrows raised, Ben replied. "You gotta be kidding me. The last thing these people want to hear is the opinion of some doctor they've never heard of."

"Don't sell yourself short," Jim said. "You may not think it, but you have a lot to offer."

"Thank you, but I'm fine just listening."

"How about you Jacob?   Are you ready to make the announcement?" Jim asked.

Glancing at one friend, then the other, Jacob replied. "I have never felt more ready to fulfill my calling." Closing his eyes, he glanced upward, silent for a few seconds. "Shall we?" he motioned toward the door.

Persecution of the Saints

The sanctuary was quite literally rocking. Over two thousand people sang along with the praise and worship band. The pulse of the music rang out. It shot throughout Jacob's body. No longer could he just stand in worship. He had to jump.

At that very moment, the lights dimmed and the next tune took on a decidedly slower melody. The worship team played the Revelation song. It was an obvious favorite among those in attendance. Ben turned to look at the people behind him. Not accustomed to a church as charismatic as First Christian, he was awestruck. As far as the eye could witness appeared a sea of hands uplifted. Genuine heartfelt joy. Everyone sang in harmony for the love of Christ. They had all drawn close to the King.

Turning toward Amy, speaking as loud as he dared, Ben stated. "This is incredible. The people are truly shouting out to God."

Smiling, Amy simply replied. "I know, isn't it wonderful?"

As the song started winding down, Jacob walked up on the stage. Reaching for a microphone he stood motionless. Silently he prayed. Jacob waited on a word from the Lord. Taking his cue from his beloved pastor, the worship leader discreetly nodded to the other musicians. The melody continued but at a much more subdued level. Jacob addressed the anxious audience.

"Oh my, oh my," Jacob spoke into the mic. "Thank you Holy Spirit for being here, right now, in this sanctuary."

Hand claps and cheers rose up from the congregation, urging Jacob on.

"Yes, yes, give Him praise." Jacob remained silent. He listened to the people shout out to the Lord. As the praises started to die down, Jacob spoke again. "Worship Him, just worship Him. Show Him how much you love Him."

Throughout the sanctuary individuals prayed to the Lord. Some prayed silently, some vocally. But all prayed earnestly. Seizing the moment, Jacob cried out. He called for The Lord's continued presence, guidance, inspiration, revelation, and so much more.

***

Outside the church was an entirely different scene. Stragglers continued to filter into the sanctuary. But invisible to the naked eye, an intense spiritual battle was taking place.

Shielding the building with a formidable presence Briathos and his angelic comrades held back an army of darkness. Led by the demon, Lahash, minions of evil charged forward. They hoped to gain an entrance. Swooping in and out and clashing against the light, they relentlessly searched for an opening.

Swords of light were drawn, to combat the slashing claws of evil. A new regiment of demons advanced forward. They were the size of a hyena but had the ferocity of a badger. The demons attacked with abandon. Sheer numbers suggested victory was imminent. Salivating profusely, Lahash's confidence grew. He was pleased with the reinforcements.

Despite being outnumbered, Briathos' legion held fast. All efforts to protect the sanctuary were successful. Frustrated by their thwarted attempts, scores of evil turned their attention elsewhere.

A new attack came upon unsuspecting humans, still arriving for service. Some were successful in swaying hesitant church goers. They gnawed at their souls. They placed doubt in their minds. The vast majority of worshipers made it through the doors. But minor victories caused celebration among the darkness. They knew that each soul won equaled an eternity of torment to feed upon.

Hunkered down out of harm's way, Lahash kept in contact with the one who called for this siege. Each report was always news of success. For in a fallen world there is constantly someone to tempt, and to sway. Someone to convince that the rules of this world are not the same as in Heaven.

Off to the side of the building a door opened. Exiting at a brisk pace a young woman made a beeline for her car. She shook her head as if in disagreement. Briathos sensed there was trouble. Swooping down for the kill, Lahash grinned with excitement.

"Wait, Julie, wait!" A man called out. Jogging after her, he hustled to catch up.

With minimal spirits protecting her, Lahash ordered a legion of demons to attack. Instantly, Julie felt a jolt within her being. She turned to meet the young man. Feeling her hands ball up into fists, she now stood poised for a confrontation.

Briathos stopped short of the two humans standing face to face. Realizing he could do nothing unless he was called upon for help, he waited.

The enemy went to work on the spirit within Julie. Filling her mind with images and thoughts of rage, he knew he was close. He battled to capture another soul.

"What!" She screamed. "What do you want from me, Michael?"

"Don't listen to him," the demon whispered. "You know you don't want to be here."

"I don't understand, Julie. Why'd you take off?" Michael tried to grab hold of her hand. She yanked it away.

"This is your scene, not mine," Julie spat the words out.

Briathos continued to hover. He waited for an opportunity to converge. But there was none. The demon within her grew in size each time she lashed out at the young man.

"What's wrong with you? I don't get it. What happened, Julie?" Michael tried to take a step closer, but she retreated toward her car.

"I knew this was a mistake," Julie glared at Michael. "You know what, I'm outta here." Turning to grab the door handle, she was stopped by Michael.

Sweeping her around so they were again facing, Michael replied. "Don't do this, Julie." Looking around as if he felt a presence, Michael returned his focus to her. "There's, there's something wrong. Don't you feel it?"

"Everything's fine," the demon whispered. "You don't need him, or his god."

"You know what," Julie brushed his hand aside. "The only thing wrong is you and this stupid church."

"Is there a problem here?" A man approached. He was dressed in all black.

Feeling his own anger rise, Michael lashed out. "This is private, pal. Do you mind?"

Standing to the side of the young couple, the man answered. "Yeah I do. I'm part of security. You look like you're hassling this lady."

Instantly Briathos stood guard in front of Michael. He was not seen, but his presence definitely felt.

Backing off slightly, Michael glanced at the security guard. He then looked back at Julie. Somehow he knew there was nothing else he could do. "Fine," he replied. "You go and head out. I'll call you later." Michael turned and walked away.

Stepping into her car, Julie looked back as she drove off. The guard was gone.

Briathos covered Michael as he continued to walk back to the church. He waited for an attack, but there was none. Gloating high above them Lahash grinned. Then he disappeared, savoring the victory he helped accomplish.

TWENTY

Inside First Christian Church

Standing up on stage, Jim Calhoun stood next to Jacob. He waited for the audience to quiet. Turning to whisper into Jacob's ear, Jim said, "Wait. Stay here with me after you address the congregation."

Peering out over the hungry audience, Jacob wasted no time introducing his guest. "Everyone please give a warm First Christian welcome to our dear friend, Jim Calhoun."

Seizing the moment Jim addressed the crowd. "Dear Brothers and sisters, I'm humbled by such a warm reception. It is so wonderful being here. I want you to know that today marks the start of something great."

The audience once again clapped in approval. Jim hesitated. "Let me tell you something. Your excitement is for the Lord and not something I or your pastor have to say."

Glancing at Jacob, he reconfirmed he wanted Jacob to stay. "I have asked Pastor Jacob to remain up here with me. You'll see why in a moment."

Motioning to two stools just to the right, Jim paused. He waited for Jacob to take a seat. "Two nights ago I was privileged to witness something incredible." Smiling at Jacob, Jim returned his focus to the audience.

75

"Your pastor received a revelation so remarkable and at the same time so important that I feel it must be told."

Not expecting this to happen, Jacob stepped down from his seat and approached Jim. Placing his left arm around Jim's shoulder, Jacob pulled his friend close to him. "You know, I gotta admit I wasn't sure when I should talk about this," Jacob spoke. "But when a prophet tells you to speak, I believe you should."

Joining the audience in a subdued laugh, Jim took a step to the side and added. "After the other night we'll be soon calling this man a prophet. For the main purpose of prophecy is to communicate God's message to the people."

When the noise in the sanctuary died down, Jim once again motioned to the two chairs. Once he and Jacob were both seated, he continued. "There has been a great outpouring of cries to God over the past years, but none so much as today." Pausing, Jim continued. "I know, because I have been one of those who have pleaded for the Lord to intervene. We as Christians are being persecuted like never before in modern times. I don't need to tell you that law after law has been put in place to not only discriminate, but eliminate the Christian way of life here in this country."

Now standing, Jim approached those in the audience closest to him. "Just like the Hebrews back in Egypt. God called upon a little known man, a man named Moses. He called upon him to lead his people out of persecution. I feel the same is being done today."

Pacing back and forth, Jim emphasized what he had to say next. His voice was loud and clear. "Now, I doubt we're ever going to see Moses again. No, I don't believe it is God's intent to lead the saints of today out of the nation that was founded on Christian values. But it is the intention of our most high God to hear the cries from the brothers and sisters." With an even greater emphasis, Jim added. "To stop the discrimination and the ELIMINATION of what we stand for!"

With the crowd worked up in a frenzy, Jim waited for the sanctuary to quiet. In a subdued voice he started to speak again. "No, my brothers and sisters, we don't need another Moses. Noooo, we just need someone to stand up and lead."

His voice inflecting a louder tone, Jim stood directly in the center of the stage. "We need scores to start a revival. We need many to gather the troops." Jim motioned with his right hand gesturing to all in front of him. "Yes, we need someone to stand up to the corrupt elitist in charge and say, enough is enough."

With his voice getting louder yet, Jim added. "Christians founded this country. Christians made this country. And Christians will, once again, lead this country. Because God has heard our cries. And let me tell you, He will not let us down. We serve a God who is faithful. We serve a God who is righteous. We serve a God who is all-powerful. And we serve a God who sacrificed His only begotten son, so we could be forgiven. We must give all the honor and glory back to the One. The One, who helped build the greatest nation on earth."

Having no choice but to remain quiet because the noise within the church was at a fever pitch, Jim stared into the audience. He knew he had the crowd's undivided attention. He knew they waited on his next word. Jim prayed silently for what the Lord wanted him to say next.

Slowly the crowd started to quiet. Every once and awhile someone shouted a word of encouragement. Still, Jim remained silent. With eyes closed, and his head tilted slightly heavenward, the audience respectfully waited for Jim to continue.

In a voice not much louder than a whisper, Jim spoke again. "Brothers and sisters, now is the time for us to act." Speaking a little bit louder, he continued. "Now is the time to take back this nation. Now is the time to say enough is enough."

Turning toward Jacob still seated in his stool, Jim pointed directly at him. In a voice just short of someone shouting, he asked, "will you follow the man I feel God has appointed?" "Will you allow this man, the man whom the good Lord has destined to speak for us, to lead?"

Jim stood next to Jacob. He then called out. "Pastor Jacob Conley may very well be our Moses." Jacob's eyebrows instantly shot up feeling uncomfortable being compared to the greatness of Moses.

Sensing his uneasiness, Jim patted Jacob on the shoulder and added. "Now I know Jacob Conley is far too humble to allow me to say his name in the same breath as Moses. But, we are in need of a leader today…in this country, right now. Who are we to question what God is planning?"

"I have seen what God has in store for Brother Jacob. I have heard from this man what God wants him to do. Let me tell you, it is no small thing."

Again, addressing the audience in a more subtle tone, Jim continued. "All I ask is that we listen to what God has to say to Pastor Jacob." Getting a little louder once again, he added. "All I ask is that we follow Jacob's plan for us. We allow this man to lead. Now I think it's time I turn this over to my dear friend and allow him to tell you the revelation he experienced. Brothers and sisters, I give you Pastor Jacob Conley."

Stepping aside, Jim Calhoun clapped like never before. But all for naught, because his claps were drowned out by the standing ovation Jacob received. The crowd cheered over and over. He sheepishly tried to calm them down.

Finally after several minutes Jacob was able to gain control of the audience. In a bit of laughter he spoke. "My golly, shouldn't you save that for after what I have to say?"

Taking a seat next to Jim, Jacob simply smiled at the crowd. With his image projected on the twin screens at both ends of the stage, the crowd was able to see the sincerity in his face.

"Quite frankly, I don't know how to follow up on what I just heard." Jacob shook his friend's hand and sought approval from Linda and Ben sitting in the front row.

As Linda nodded to her beloved husband, Ben simply gestured for him to continue.

"What I'm about to tell you will seem both astounding and possibly alarming at the same time." Jacob waited for the full attention of his audience before he continued. When he was finished telling his story from his first vision of the blood to his revelation of being told to lead, Jacob had taken almost thirty minutes.

By the end of his sermon the audience sat riveted to their seats. Jacob became so energized he paced like a caged animal. Sensing that there was nothing left to add, he abruptly stopped and stared at the ceiling.

With arms raised heavenward, Jacob tilted his head back and smiled. His smile seemed to fill the screens and prompted those in attendance to do the same. Within a matter of moments came his laughter. It was a genuine God loving laughter that only the Holy Spirit could bring.

Soon it became so infectious that individual chuckles broke out as well. A Holy laughter broke out within the sanctuary. It became so contagious that very few souls were not affected.

Opening his eyes, Jacob took it all in. Throughout the congregation was a church full of the spirit. It was a mass of people ready to serve God. And he realized one other thing of great importance. This was the beginning of a Christian army. Jacob needed to prepare himself to lead.

TWENTY ONE

Late April / Northern Nevada

Deep beneath the earth's surface something peculiar was happening. Methodically and slowly, the blood that once filled the Dillon Reservoir flowed in a southerly direction. The substance pooled with underground streams heading for a sole destination.

No human had any idea what was happening, nay no creature as well. Soon enough it would affect all inhabitants living below by forcing them to surface. And for those living above the soil, they were about to be invaded.

But this was not the work of darkness, nor did the evil ones have any idea this was happening. This was the work of a higher power, with a message meant for one group in particular: stop persecuting my people.

TWENTY TWO

Elco Motors / St. Louis, MO

"Sir, sir, are you all right?" The car salesman pounded on the SUV's window. "Mister, I said are you all right?" He backed away from the vehicle and looked around for anyone within shouting distance.

After a few moments another car salesman approached. Waving his arms, the first man shouted. "Over here, Skip. Check this guy out."

Skip approached his associate and the car. Nothing seemed unusual to him. The SUV appeared to be in great condition.

"What's up Tony?" Skip stood off to the side of his associate. "What are you yelling about?"

Pointing to the driver's side window, Tony replied. "That guy. The one behind the wheel. He's been sitting like that for about five minutes."

Skip peered through the window and saw what Tony was talking about. Tapping on the glass, Skip asked. "Hey mister, you all right in there?" Getting no reaction from inside the vehicle, Skip frowned at his friend.

"You think he's drunk, or on drugs or something?" Tony asked.

"You say he's been like that?" Skip reached out toward the door.

"Already tried it. It's locked." Tony stood with his hands on his hips. "Heck, I'd let him sleep it off if I thought I'd get a sale outta him."

"Aw, leave him alone. We'll check back in a few minutes." Skip turned to walk away.

"Might as well," Tony conceded. But before leaving, he slipped his card between the window and the door frame.

A few minutes passed before the car's occupant woke to a startling surprise. Gasping for breath, he blinked rapidly, trying to get his bearings. Surveying his surroundings, the man appeared lost.

Turning his head to the left he saw something stuck between the top of the window and the frame. He hit the automatic window button and the object fell onto his lap. It was a business card.

Picking the card up, he read the bold faced print.

Tony Tucker

Used Car Sales

Elco Motors

Then it hit him, like a wave smacking into a pier. Jacob Conley didn't come here by choice. God sent him. He remembered driving down the road and feeling light-headed. He quickly pulled over. Jacob parked his car, not realizing his destination. Then, everything immediately went blank.

"My God," Jacob whispered. "Why am I here?" Glancing at his watch, he realized over twenty minutes were unaccounted for. But why? Why did he end up at a car dealership?

Feeling somewhat embarrassed and a little confused, Jacob started his vehicle and pulled out onto the road. Looking into the rearview mirror, he caught the dealers sign. It stood out like a sore thumb.

"Elco Motors! What in the world is that supposed to mean?" Jacob sighed. "Linda's not gonna believe this one."

TWENTY THREE

Platte City, MO

Hannah Tanner rocked back and forth, arms wrapped around her petite legs. The third step from the bottom of the stairs offered little room to accommodate her gently swaying body. She dared not move from it. Everything in her four year old mind urged her to react. But how?

Sensing that it was another one of mommy's talking to God moments, she opted to stay put. Hannah stared at her mother writhing at the base of the stairs. The golden wooden floor that seemed to envelop her beloved mother frightened her. In her mind it was a mighty sea that Mommy could not escape. The frantic strokes, the crying out; Hannah's mommy was drowning.

Even though this wasn't the first time that mommy fell down and chanted out loud, it scared her none the less. Pushing long brown strands of hair out of her face Hannah finally summoned up the courage to respond. "Mommy, are you okay?" Her rocking stopped momentarily waiting for a hopeful reply. There was none. She only heard strange words emanating from her mommies voice.

Hesitantly, Hannah approached her mother. Her movements lessened from a moment ago. Gently her little fingers reached out edging so closely to the figure. Finally, she laid still. "Mommy, please answer me. You okay?"

Sensing a physical presence, then the touch of a finger, Gail Tanner immediately opened her eyes. She peered up at her daughter's pleading eyes. She swiftly surveyed her surroundings. Without hesitating, Gail snatched Hannah into her arms.

It was now Gail's turn to gently rock back and forth. Holding onto Hannah she softly whispered into her ear. "It's okay, baby girl. It's okay."

Hannah pulled back just enough to look into her mother's striking green eyes. They were eyes that always brought her comfort. They conveyed absolute love.

"It happened again, didn't it Mommy?"

Gail's auburn strands, now moistened with tears, clung to her high cheek bones. Gently, with a touch only a child could produce Hannah moved the strands first from the left side of Gail's face, then the right.

"That better, Mommy?" Her angelic voice whispered softly.

Fighting back the gusher of tears that was sure to follow, Gail embraced her child and prayed out loud. This time in a way that Hannah understood. "Dear Lord, thank you for this precious child I now hold in my arms. Please help her somehow understand what is happening to me. Let her know everything is all right and give her peace. Thank you, Father."

Looking into her daughter's eyes, Gail invited her to end the prayer together. "Amen," Gail stated.

"Amen," little Hannah added.

"Mommies okay, Sweetheart. Are you okay?" Gail asked.

Taking a step back, then peering over Gail's shoulder, Hannah replied. "Can I watch TV now?"

Giggling, Gail pretended to reach out and grab Hannah, but she was too quick. She ran off to another room. Calling out to her daughter, Gail stated. "Honey, Mommy is going to use the phone now, all right?"

"Okay," Hannah replied. She smiled at the program on the television.

Gail dialed the phone as quickly as her fingers allowed. Nervously, she stared out the dining room window at nothing in particular.

After the fourth ring, he finally answered. "Hey hon, what's up?" Chris Tanner asked.

"Chris, it happened again."

Hesitating, Chris asked. "What, the visions? Did you have another vision?"

Choking back tears, Gail tried her best to keep her composure. "Yes, and Hannah witnessed it. I did my best to comfort her. I think she's okay."

"How about you? Are you all right?"

Pulling a chair away from the table, Gail took a seat and continued to look off in the distance. "I'm fine. But I really need to talk about what happened." Gail sat silently, collecting her thoughts. "Chris, God is telling me to intercede for someone. But this seems bigger than any of the previous times."

"Why do you say that?"

"It just does. I, I don't know why."

"Well, do you at least know who it is?"

Gail tried remembering the image from a few moments ago. "No, but his face is now becoming much clearer."

"Well, that's good, isn't it?"

Extending her right arm, Gail stared at her trembling hand. "Chris, I'm worried."

"Why, what's wrong?"

"I can see his face, I know him from somewhere."

"What, Gail? What else are you seeing?"

"There's this darkness, Chris. He's being surrounded by something, strange. But I sense he doesn't know it, at least not yet."

"Okay, try to calm yourself; I'm pulling into our subdivision right now."

Jumping up from the chair, Gail placed her hand over her mouth and drew a great breath. New images flashed before her. She then saw Chris pulling into their drive, but she wasn't able to move.

"What is happening, Lord?" She continually asked.

Hearing her voice, Chris rushed to Gail's side. She continued to stare ahead until she heard Chris say, "I'm here, Gail. I'm here."

Throwing her arms around her husband, Gail spoke softly into his ear. "I know his face, I know his face. But I don't understand why he's there."

Tilting his head to one side, Chris asked. "Who? Who did you see?"

Gail hesitated before answering. "We need to call Pastor Phillip. He'll know how to contact him."

Chris guided her toward a chair. He sat nearby. "Gail, why do you think Phillip would know this guy?"

With a saddened expression, Gail said, "the man spoke at our church, Chris. I think it was last fall."

"Last fall? I remember we had two guests at the church."
Pausing, trying to jog his memory, Chris added. "And one of them
was a female."

"That's right. I can almost see his name; it's at the tip of my
tongue."

Placing his right hand on Gail's left knee, Chris peered into her
eyes. "It'll come to us. So, what was the other thing you saw?"

Shaking her head, Gail replied. "It was really disturbing. He
was sitting at a slot machine. All I could hear was the noise. You
know, the noise those machines make? Over and over again."

"Okay," Chris continued focusing on her eyes.

Shuddering, as if a cold draft entered the room, Gail continued.
"Then the room became black. It was just him and the one slot
machine. Everything else disappeared."

"What happened next?"

Gail's eyes widened. "He pulled the arm down on the machine
and loud music went off. He hit the jackpot. But instead of coins
coming out, blood gushed out. It drenched him, and everything
else."

"Blood, are you sure, Gail?"

"It was a red liquid, Chris. I know it was blood."

Standing to his feet, Chris then asked. "Was that it? Did
anything else happen?"

Shaking her head, no, Gail remained silent.

"Well, one thing is for certain," Chris said.

Looking up, Gail asked. "What's that?"

"We definitely need to call Pastor Phillip. Somehow this man
needs to hear about your vision."

"His name is Jacob Conley." Gail blurted out.

Stunned, Chris sat back down. He stared at his wife. "How do you suddenly know his name?"

Tears streamed down Gail's cheeks. She sheepishly glanced at the floor.

Placing his hand gently under her chin, Chris urged Gail to meet his eyes. "Honey, what is it? What's wrong?"

"Why is God showing me this?" Trying to catch her breath, Gail continued. "Out of nowhere his name came out of my mouth." Gazing into her husband's eyes, Gail added. "This is serious, Chris. I really think this man might be in trouble."

Chris stood and stared out the window. "It's either that, or this might be some piece of a puzzle he needs to know."

TWENTY FOUR

Washington, DC

Wrapping up a briefing with his press secretary, Anne, President Pollard glanced down at his muted cell. Recognizing the caller, the President allowed the call to go into voice mail.

Turning his attention back to Anne, the President asked. "Will there be anything else, Anne?"

Taking her cue, Anne rose from her seat. "No, Mr. President. That should be it."

"Thank you, Anne." Stuart Pollard pulled his phone back out of his pocket. Listening to the message left for him, he quickly deleted it. He then hit speed dial.

"This is Ra," the voice on the other end replied.

Reclining back in his chair, Stuart said, "I got your message. It sounded urgent."

In a very direct tone, Ra responded. "We may have an issue."

Straightening up, Stuart asked. "Do you need to come by?"

"That won't be necessary." Ra paused. "My sources tell me there may be an individual who is primed to stir up trouble. Trouble, against our cause."

"Oh, are the associates worried?"

"Do not be concerned about the associates, Stuart." Ra's voice inflicted arrogance. "This man and his connections are our main focus. At least for now."

Standing to his feet, Stuart looked out the nearest window. "So, who is this person and what's he trying to do?"

"As for who he is, let's just say he's part of the coalition. But what he's capable of doing is a major concern."

The President ran his right hand through his hair. It was a habit he resorted to when he felt stressed. "If there is someone out there who can jeopardize our mission, Ra, I need to know who it is."

Ratcheting down his tone, Ra replied. "In good time I will fill you in. For now, we need you to ramp up our efforts."

"Which efforts, Ra?"

"Calm down, Stuart. I need you to focus."

Stuart nervously glanced about the room.

"See what you can do about moving up the nonprofit initiative. The one slated for a vote this summer." Speaking in a louder tone, Ra added. "Put some pressure on those colleagues of yours. You know the drill."

"I have no problem twisting some arms, Ra. But it would help if I knew why. You know, in case others ask."

"Is it not our objective to squash the religious right?"

"Of course it is," the President answered. "It always has been."

Pausing before speaking, Ra responded very calmly. "Then WE would like it done sooner than later. Are we on the same page, Stuart?"

Taking a seat at his desk, the President quickly realized something. He was being called out on the huge debt he owed for getting elected. He also knew it was time to cash in some personal favors as well. "I'll get to work on it."

Ending the call, the President let out a tremendous breath. He stared blankly out the window. There was a lot of work yet to be done.

TWENTY FIVE

St. Louis, MO / First Christian Church

Sitting at his desk, Jacob flipped through his Bible hoping to get a sign. Perhaps a clue pertaining to what had happened at the car dealership. He and Linda had spoken at length about the experience. But he was no closer to understanding what it meant.

Wisely they had written in his journal everything significant from that day. There were four points that stood out. He was in a parking lot. The lot was part of a car dealership. The name of the establishment was Elco. The name on the business card was Tony Tucker.

The obvious parts to him were the names of the dealer and salesman. It wasn't as if he could do a search through the Bible for those three names: Tony, Tucker, Elco. What Jacob had hoped was by re-reading Romans he might somehow be led to associate a passage with the names. After all, it was Romans he was reading when he had his first vision.

Finishing chapter three of Romans, Jacob took pause. Something about lines 29-30 stood out. There was no correlation between the message of these verses and the names from the dealership. Jacob saw something else.

Paul wrote: Is God the God of Jews only? Is he not the God of Gentiles as well? Yes, of Gentiles too, since there is only one God, who will justify the circumcised by faith and the uncircumcised through that same faith.

The word "faith" kept standing out to Jacob. For in this modern age, we too must live by faith much like the Hebrews needed to. That was over two thousand years ago. But God grew impatient with the Jews for continually displaying a lack of faith. Is God growing impatient with today's Christians for the very same reason? And is God commanding those of faith to make a stand?

Rising to his feet Jacob stared at the ceiling with arms upraised. "I'm so sorry, Lord. I'm so sorry. We haven't been standing up for ourselves. Have we?" Jacob wondered why there are so few of the faithful left. What it would take to once again be the majority. There was clearly one answer. "Now I see why it's time we take a stand," Jacob spoke. "Why it's time we say enough is enough."

Slumping back into his chair, Jacob solemnly added. "I just pray your patience isn't nearing an end."

Jacob's intercom brought him back to life. It was Getta. "Pastor, you have a call from Pastor Phillip Hurley in Kansas City."

"Oh, thank you, Getta." Jacob picked up his phone.

"Pastor Phillip, how are you?"

"Hello, Jacob, I'm great. Do you have a moment?"

Jacob sensed urgency in his friend's voice. "Absolutely."

Using a tone a little more at ease, Phillip asked. "I trust all is well at the opposite end of the state."

"Couldn't be better, Phillip. How about you?"

"The church keeps growing, praise God. But ever since your visit, I'm having a hard time following up after your message." Phillip chuckled slightly. "You really made an impact on my congregation, Jacob."

"Glad to hear it, but of course I take no credit."

"Amen," Phillip added. "Listen, the reason I'm calling is I may have a word for you."

Shifting in his seat, Jacob glanced down at his opened Bible. "Really, please go on."

"We have a dear sister, here at the Rock, who has a gift of intercession."

"What's her name?" Jacob interrupted.

"Gail Tanner. Gail's been a member for quite a few years. I've never known her to not hear His voice."

"Wonderful," Jacob replied.

"She called me yesterday and told me about a strange vision she had involving some man."

Jacob continued to listen intently.

"She couldn't place his image at first but she knew she had seen him before. Anyway, in her vision this man was sitting at a slot machine. He was in a casino."

"A slot machine?" asked Jacob.

"Wait, it gets better," Phillip added. After a few moments while the man was playing the machine, everything around him turned black. Then the most bizarre thing happened."

Sensing that the man in the vision was probably him, Jacob started to squirm in his chair.

Pausing for a brief moment, Phillip continued. "After he pulled the handle one more time he hit the jackpot. All the bells and whistles went off, but coins didn't come out of the machine."

"I'm afraid to ask what happened next," Jacob replied.

"Jacob, obviously you realize the man she saw was you."

"Just tell me what came out of that machine, Phillip."

"It was blood!"

Not a word was spoken for almost twenty seconds. Phillip realized he had struck a chord. In almost a whisper he asked. "This means something to you, doesn't it?"

"Unfortunately yes. Now I have an even bigger puzzle to solve."

"How can I help?" Jacob's friend asked.

For the next ten minutes Jacob told Phillip about everything he had experienced. He started with his first revelation, including his encounter with Briathos. Jacob ended with what happened at the car dealership.

After Jacob spoke of three key words from his last vision, Phillip interrupted him.

"Oh good Lord, Jacob."

"What, what is it?"

"Gail's vision had nothing to do with a casino. It had nothing to do with blood."

Staring straight ahead, Jacob asked. "Then what?"

"You probably didn't see the news this morning, did you?"

"No, I came straight to my office," Jacob replied. "What happened?"

"Elko, Nevada...it's all over the news."

TWENTY SIX

Elko, NV

Statuesque Jackie Billups was completely stunned by what she saw. Never in her ten plus years of reporting did she encounter anything like this. Stepping cautiously, she tried her best to avoid squashing any of them. Then again, wherever she moved they tried to scatter.

Finally, finding a good vantage spot, Jackie's emerald eyes stared at her camera man. Addressing a live feed, she exclaimed. "It is utter pandemonium here in the little town of Elko, Nevada. I think you'll appreciate that I didn't use the word "zoo". For as far as the eye can see," gesturing to her right, Jackie guided the camera away from her and then back. "There are literally thousands and thousands of frogs. Quite frankly, everywhere."

Again stepping cautiously as the camera followed, Jackie did her best to side step the creatures. She settled on one spot. "The obvious questions are where did they come from? Why are they here?" The camera now zoomed into a close-up of Jackie. "Adding even more intrigue to this bizarre story is that our very own President, Stuart Pollard, is from Elko. In fact, his parents still live here."

Fielding a question from the anchor desk back in Las Vegas, Jackie paused to listen. "Go ahead, Ted," Jackie said.

"Jackie, what are the local authorities telling you in regards to their theory? Why have these frogs shown up?"

"Yeah, Ted, what they're saying is that with the Green Frog's hibernation cycle ending, it is not unusual for them to surface at this time of the year. But it's their numbers that are shocking. The Green Frog population in this part of Nevada has been down over past years."

"So this city has never had that many frogs to begin with?"

"Exactly, Jackie replied. "They have no idea why there are so many and why they seemed to be confined to this community."

"Now, Elko borders the Humboldt River. Is that correct?"

"It does, Ted." Pointing off in the direction of the river, Jackie continued. "Authorities are speculating that the frogs came up from the river. Again, why there are so many, no one seems to know."

"Jackie, are President Pollard's parents in any kind of jeopardy from this frog invasion?"

"The secret service has not allowed anyone access to the Pollard's home. Thus far the White House has not issued any statements. So, we really don't know."

"But as far as you can tell, Jackie, their home has been invaded by Green Frogs as well?"

"Absolutely, Ted. As a matter of fact, the Pollard's home sits above the river. It was probably one of the first to be invaded."

"Well, the town of Elko, Nevada has certainly encountered something of Biblical proportions. Wouldn't you say, Jackie?"

"Indeed it has, Ted." Smiling as comfortably as she could, Jackie finished her closing statement. The camera continued to pan over the vast number of frogs. "We'll continue to gather more information as the day wears on. For now, this is Jackie Billips reporting."

TWENTY SEVEN

St. Louis, MO

Leaning against Getta's desk, Jacob watched in awe at the spectacle taking place in Elko. Joined by Getta and Pastor Will, the three of them were riveted by the news coming across the screen.

"This is amazing," Getta said.

Obviously intrigued by the expression on Jacob's face, Will asked. "What do you make of this, Jacob? You ever heard of something like this before?"

Pausing before replying, Jacob continued to be focused on the TV. "Just one other time, Will. And it occurred over two thousand years ago between Moses and Pharaoh."

Not expecting such a divine answer, both Getta and Will turned to look at Jacob.

Jokingly, Getta asked. "So, pastor, you telling us that this might be the start of the ten plagues?"

"The frogs came second, the first plague was blood." Will said.

Suddenly realizing what Will had said, Jacob stared off in the distance.

"Now wouldn't that be something?" asked Getta. Ever since she was a little girl, Getta had been fascinated by the Book of Exodus. She marveled at the miracles God created and the people He used. But the most intriguing part of Exodus was the ten plagues. Could this somehow be happening again?

101

Also realizing the significance of his statement, Will rose and approached Jacob. "Pastor, both of these events have recently occurred. Haven't they?"

Without replying, Jacob simply nodded yes.

Jumping out of her seat, Getta joined her two pastors. "Pastor Jacob, are you serious?"

Glancing first at Getta and then Will, Jacob replied. "A little over a month ago, a small town in Montana was in an up roar over their reservoir having what appeared to be blood in it."

"I vaguely remember that," Will interrupted.

"It happened so quickly that the news media barely reported on it," Jacob continued. "Some have said that the Pollard administration put a hush on it, news-wise."

"Now I remember," Getta replied.

"For some reason they didn't want the public getting wind of it. That's what I've been told." Glancing up at the ceiling, and smiling, Jacob added. "But my sources have confirmed it did happen. So yes, if you want to be truthful, two plagues have occurred."

"Why do I get the feeling there's something else you're not telling us?" asked Getta.

Patting her on the shoulder, Jacob turned toward his office. "As soon as I know more, you'll know more." In a serious tone, Jacob added. "But I do know one thing. The revival is going to start here. And it's going to start soon."

Taking a step into his office, Jacob stopped and poked his head back out. "Do me a favor, Getta. Hold any calls that might come through. I've certainly got some important ones to make myself."

TWENTY EIGHT

Washington DC

"I don't care what it takes," the President shouted into the phone. "Figure it out now! You got it?"

Slamming the phone back into its receptacle, President Pollard turned his attention to two people standing nearby. "If I hear one more person say the press wants to know," he glared with anger.

The President's intercom interrupted his thought. "Mr. President, your father is on line three for you."

"I can't take his call right now," he answered. "Jenny, take a message and tell him I'll be in meetings most of the day."

"Mr. President," press secretary, Anne Givens interrupted. "What exactly would you like me to tell the press?"

Sensing that the President was about to explode, Martin Ayers, the President's chief of staff jumped in. "Tell them we'll have a statement later today. Give no specific time." Diverting his eyes back to the President, Martin waited for an acknowledgment.

"Tell them that, Anne." President Pollard rose from his seat, and glanced at his watch. "I'd like a full cabinet meeting in one hour from now. Understood?"

"Yes sir, Mr. President," Anne replied. "I'll get right on it."

Upon her leaving his office, President Pollard turned his attention to Martin Ayers. "I want you to head up this meeting, Martin."

Feeling a little blindsided, Martin asked. "Will you not be in attendance, Mr. President?"

"I can't guarantee it, but you'll have all the information you'll need to discuss and draft a statement." Returning to his seat, the President glanced up. "Now, if you'll excuse me."

As his chief of staff exited the office President Pollard's anger seethed inside. He knew the only person he really needed to discuss this issue with was Ra.

Having spoken with both his parents several times today, the President was fed up with the issue in Elko. How do you tell your own parents that even the President is powerless to fix something like this? How will he explain it to the media?

This was beyond explanation and beyond his capabilities. It frustrated him to no end. Picking up his cell, the President hit redial once again. After a few rings, the call went immediately into voicemail.

Smashing his fist on the desk, Stuart Pollard felt his blood pressure rise. Unseen forces about him danced in delight. The more he raged inside, the more they fed off his frustration. Gnawing and biting at his soul, tiny demons encouraged the fury within.

Darkness engulfed him. His world spun out of control. The most powerful man in the world was so close to being under total control of the most dominant evil known to mankind. And he didn't even realize it.

Losing all ability to maintain self-control, the President's mind was flooded with thoughts of manipulation. Thoughts of how he could truly take control of this country. How he could change it to his liking. But more important, change it to their liking.

Here he sat, with more power than he could imagine. He just needed to embrace it. Learn how to use it. Then a thought occurred to him. All this time, he wanted so much to be part of the association. But in truth, the association was now part of him.

As if on cue, the ring of the President's cell brought him back to the real world. Placing the phone to his ear, he heard a voice more clearly than ever before.

"I got your message. But more importantly, I see you got mine."

"I did, Ra." Stuart replied. "Now, how do we take care of this inconvenience out in Nevada?"

"Well, this will not be quite as simple as the last time."

"Especially since it's all over the news," Stuart replied.

"But I know of a way. A way, we can turn to our advantage."

"How so?"

Changing the demeanor of his tone, Ra answered. "Stuart, you do realize that for every initiative we put forth against the demise of the Christian faith, He is trying to warn us to stop?"

"I do now, Ra. It didn't make sense before. Why...these so called plagues were happening." Pacing about the room, Stuart continued. "But if God thinks He can thwart our efforts."

"Make no mistakes, my friend." Ra interrupted. "This is only the beginning. You will be sorely tested, even with your newfound powers."

"Then how do we, as you said, turn it to our advantage?"

"First things first," Ra answered. "I have sent to your personal email account an entire press release that will need to be read this afternoon. This will appease both the press and the American public. Then, we will need to meet very soon to discuss our next step against the opposition."

"And in the meantime, you'll take care of the nuisance in Nevada?"

"As we speak, my friend," Ra added confidently. "As we speak."

TWENTY NINE

Elko, NV

Staring out his window Reverend Francis Curry was awestruck by the sight before him. Thousands of green frogs ran amuck throughout the city. But none crossed onto the church property. Thankful that his home was also adjacent to the small church, Reverend Curry had no reason to leave the church premises. Then again, leaving would be a difficult task.

Christ Redeemer First Assembly was without a doubt one of the oldest buildings in the city of Elko. The two-story all brick exterior looked more like a storefront rather than a place of worship. The only distinguishing symbol was a tiny white cross affixed to the roof.

As far as members go, Christ Redeemer was the smallest in the community. Reverend Curry always said it's not the amount of worshippers. It's the amount of your worship that counts. With sixty seven members who met three to four times a week, Christ Redeemer certainly had that covered.

As he continued to gaze at the spectacle before him, Reverend Curry decided to step outside the church building. A mixture of anxiety and intrigue filled his senses. Literally thousands of frogs were nearby. They were separated only by the sidewalk he stood upon.

Taking a step into the street, as if he was wearing some kind of frog repellent, the amphibians moved away from him. Stepping back onto the sidewalk the green creatures reverted back to hopping along the street. They kept a safe distance from the church property. Grinning like a little boy in a toy store, Reverend Curry did next what any kid would do.

Dancing back and forth between sidewalk and road, Reverend Curry cried out in laughter. Praising Jesus, he danced a jig in front of the church. Not caring who might see, Reverend Curry continued his dance for what seemed like an hour. Finally, he fell to his knees from exhaustion.

He kneeled on the side of the road. The only sounds Reverend Curry could hear were the frogs hopping and chirping. Reaching out to grab one, he was startled by the ringing of his cell.

Glancing at the caller ID, he didn't recognize the number. Reverend Curry stepped back on the sidewalk and stopped at the doorway. Taking one more look at the miracle before him, he answered his phone.

"Hello, this is Francis Curry."

"Reverend Curry, you don't know me. But my grandson just had a vision from the Lord."

"Who is this?" he asked.

"Oh, my, my, where's my manners. I'm Mollie Mae Jeffers."

Intrigued, he asked. "Well, Ms. Jeffers, how can I help you?"

"Oh it isn't us who needs help, pastor. According to my Jeffey, you're the one who needs it."

Shutting the sanctuary door he sat in the nearest pew. "What's this all about, Ms. Jeffers?"

"I didn't mean to startle you, but my grandson Jeffey, well, he has this kind of gift. He can talk to God. By golly He answers Jeffey back."

Feeling slightly alarmed, the Reverend asked her. "How did you get my number?"

"Through Jeffey. I already told you. He speaks to God."

"I see."

"Pastor, I don't make it a habit calling folks to scare them. Especially ones we don't know. But Jeffey sure was insistent on me calling you."

"Don't worry, Ms. Jeffers," Reverend Curry chuckled. "After what I just witnessed, being frightened is the furthest thing from my mind."

"Well that's good that you don't scare easy. Cause there's some powerful things going on at your church right now."

"How do you know I'm at my church?" Reverend Curry could hear her talking to someone in the background.

"Tell him what, Jeffey?" Mollie Mae's voice trailed off.

"Ma'am, ma'am are you still there?" asked the reverend.

"I'm sorry pastor, kinda hard to carry on two conversations at the same time."

"Perhaps it would help if I spoke directly to Jeffey."

Pausing before answering, Mollie Mae then replied. "Well, there's one problem, pastor. My Jeffey's autistic and he doesn't often talk to people he doesn't know."

"Okay, I understand. But what exactly is he trying to tell me?"

For a brief moment there was nothing but silence, as if the phone had been put on mute. Reverend Curry was beginning to feel both agitated and perplexed. There was something about her voice that told him to stay on the line.

"I can do it, I can do it," the voice on the other end said repeatedly.

"Jeffey? Is that you speaking?" asked, Reverend Curry.

"It's Jeffey," was all he said.

"Son," Reverend Curry replied. "What is it you wanted to tell me?"

Again, there was silence on the other end of the line. Then without warning Jeffey screamed. "Get out! Get out! Get out!" Jeffey paused. "Pastor's in trouble, get out now!"

A sudden chill coursed through Reverend Curry. It was unlike anything he had ever felt before. Sensing that he was indeed in danger, Reverend Curry hurried to the front door. Opening it, he stood in shock. Hundreds upon hundreds of the green frogs no longer moved throughout the street. Every one of them faced the church. They were completely still, not uttering a sound.

"Not that way, pastor," Reverend Curry could barely hear Jeffey shout. The phone dangled at his side.

"The back, the back," Jeffey cried. "Go out the back!"

Instinctively, Reverend Curry brought the phone up to his ear. He backed away from the door. "Jeffey?" He asked.

There was nothing but silence. He continued backing up along the aisle of his church.

"Jeffey, Mollie Mae, are you there?"

In what sounded like a whisper, Reverend Curry heard a voice speak through the phone. "It's clear out back, pastor. Gotta get out now."

Turning about face, Reverend Curry bolted for the stage. Stopping in his tracks, he reached for his Bible sitting on a podium. Taking one last look at the front of the church, he gazed in amazement.

Filling the sanctuary in a tremendous swarm, the frogs converged in total pandemonium. The noise inside was deafening. The green frogs continued to fill the sanctuary piling upon each other. Within minutes the church was filled as high as the pews.

Holding his Bible out in front, Reverend Curry cried out. "Lord God, please help me!"

No longer did the frogs advance toward him. They simply massed on top of one another. The sight was sickening. They squirmed. They fell. The frogs continued to stack, croaking with abandon.

Standing with his back against the wall, the reverend saw that the creatures were advancing once again. With no place to go but forward, the frogs were literally stacked to the ceiling.

Gazing at the mass before him, Reverend Curry froze in fear. Three enormous frogs leapt onto the stage. They sat mere feet in front of him. Their eyes glowed red. The beasts gradually opened their massive mouths.

Shock overtook fear as the reverend witnessed three demons emerge from the frogs. Grotesquely misshapen, one demon stood while the other two squatted. A black leathery skin encased the two that crouched. Tiny claws protruded from their chests. The sole demon standing was covered in matted grayish fur. The three then screeched in unison beckoning their powers.

The deafening roar of the frogs was unbearable. Reverend Curry slid against the wall. He desperately tried his best to get to the back door. He inched along. Clutching his Bible firmly against his chest, Reverend Curry prayed out loud.

Summoning his courage, he turned his back to the revolting spirits. He lunged for the door. Crossing the threshold from darkness to freedom, Reverend Curry embraced the beckoning twilight.

He raced across the lawn, stumbling abruptly thirty feet from the building. Instantly a tremendous whoosh blasted over him as he lay prone on the ground. Heat coursed across the back of his head. In his peripheral vision an orange glow radiated.

But nothing compared to the sound of the explosion that followed. Rolling onto his back, Reverend Curry witnessed a spectacular sight. His beloved church now in flames, burning like an inferno. The structure was leveled within a matter of minutes.

Bending at the waist, he realized he amazingly had the phone in his hand. Gingerly, he brought it up to his singed ear. Breathing heavily, Reverend Curry spoke. "Jeffey, Jeffey, you still there?"

"Pastor made it." He heard Jeffey's voice.

Francis Curry collapsed to the ground, dropping the phone, in the process.

THIRTY

Washington, DC

"In an incredible twist of events the small city of Elko, Nevada, hometown of President Stuart Pollard no less, has gone from nothing short of a frog infestation to not a single croak left to be heard."

The President sat transfixed before the screen, smiling broadly at the news report. What a way to start a new day, he thought. One day prior he was facing a crisis and now this was all over the news.

Even with his newfound confidence, the President had his doubts that the problem would be taken care of this swiftly. Turning his attention back to the newscast, the President was anxious to hear the comments about the explosion that rectified the frog invasion.

Strangely enough the burning down of a small church was downplayed in light of the sudden disappearance of the green invaders. The President realized no one had any idea how the frogs had met their demise. Except, for those in the know like him.

As for the outlandish story being perpetuated by the pastor of the destroyed church, well, who would believe such a thing? That was the beauty of having the media in one's pocket. The party in power was the one who controlled everything. Fortunately, the President ruled the party.

Clicking off the image on the screen, the President strutted to his desk. His swagger had new meaning. His confidence had greatly increased. Summoning Jenny, the President sprang into action.

"Yes, Mr. President?"

"Jenny, get me Senate Majority Leader, Dugan. I'd like to speak to him ASAP."

"Yes sir, I'll put a call in immediately."

Grinning at the draft of a new Bill, the President scribbled a few notes in the margins. He then paused. Rereading the entire page, he stopped about midway and crossed out an entire sentence. "What was I thinking?" he said out loud.

Glancing at the notes in the margin, then back at the deleted line, he held his pen poised above the draft. Starting at the beginning of the paragraph mid-way down the page, the President read out loud.

"According to "AID", the Assembly of Islamic Defense. Speaking out against Islam will be considered a hate crime." Adding his notes to the new sentence, he continued. "Consequently, evangelizing by others will also be considered a hate crime."

Pausing, the President set his pen down and grinned. "Much better." Reaching for his cell, he connected instantly to his intended party.

"I made a slight change to the draft you sent over," the President spoke.

"I knew you would, my friend." Ra answered. "One other thing."

"Yes?"

"Make sure the senate knows punishment will be severe and swift."

"Absolutely, I plan to meet with the majority leader today. Although, it may take some heavy arm twisting to get him on board this time."

Offering no immediate reply, Ra finally responded. "I don't particularly care if the Senator is up for reelection or not. Do what it takes, Stuart."

"Understood. I'll get him on board."

"Oh, and Stuart," Ra added. "Any issues with the media concerning the occurrence in Nevada?"

Chuckling, the President replied. "It's as if there was never a problem at all."

"Oh," Ra snickered. "What problem would that be?"

THIRTY ONE

St. Louis, MO

Jacob listened in on a three way conference call. He doodled on his desk calendar. It was a habit he had ever since he was a boy. It somehow helped him think. Stopping in mid stroke, Jacob quickly looked up from the calendar. Breaking into the conversation between his two friends, Dr. Ben Palmer and Jim Calhoun, Jacob spoke.

"Wait a minute. I think we're all missing the point."

"How's that, Jake?" Ben asked.

"Okay, so far two miracles have happened, correct?"

"If you'd call a lake filled with blood," Jim jumped in. "Then a town over run by frogs nothing short of miracles, then yes."

"That qualifies in my book," Ben added.

"So we agree that God is trying to get our attention?" Jacob asked.

"Without a doubt," Jim confirmed.

"Then my point is, we're not the only ones He is trying to reach."

A slight chuckle could be heard. "He's certainly got the rest of the nation's attention too, wouldn't you say?" Ben asked.

"Not to the degree it should, Ben." Jacob said.

"You talking about the lack of media coverage?"

"Or the lack of interest by the Pollard administration," Jim added.

"Exactly. I'm willing to bet, though I'm not a betting man that every time the President announces something new, God seems to answer with a modern day plague. He wants to get their attention."

"So are you referring to Moses and Pharaoh?" asked Jim.

"Indeed I am. Think about it. Centuries ago God allowed Moses to perform miracles against Egypt. He did it in order to let the Israelites have their freedom, right?"

"True," Ben replied. "But God used Moses as his deliverer. He acted as a go between, God and Pharaoh."

"And of course, God's point was to free the Israelites from bondage," Jim said.

"Yes, yes, it was," Jacob replied excitedly. "And now He is trying to get the President's attention. Just like He did with Pharaoh."

"To do what?" Ben asked.

A slight pause of silence occurred before Jim answered. "To back off."

"Back off, as in stop with all the changes?"

"Partly, Ben," Jacob replied. "But we have to ask ourselves what one thing is there in common between today and over two thousand years ago?"

Without hesitating, Jim answered, "persecution."

"Wow," Ben chimed. "I never thought about it that way."

"It makes sense. Just as the Hebrews were God's chosen people back then, Christians are God's people today." Jacob said.

"Even if the rest of the world may not believe that's true, we as Christians know better," Jim added.

"Sadly to say, not all get it. This is a wakeup call. Not only for those doing the persecuting…

"But to those who are persecuted for their beliefs, Jacob." Jim interrupted.

"In other words, God is saying enough is enough," Ben replied.

"Exactly. The big question is, will either side listen?"

"We are, Jacob. We're listening," Jim responded.

Without even realizing it, Jacob had drawn a crude looking cross on the pad below. Stenciled across the horizontal portion of his cross was the word "lead" in bold letters. Staring intensely at his rendering, Jacob spoke in an authoritative voice.

"Gentlemen, God has given us a unique glimpse at what He has in store. Through Biblical scripture we know what to expect next. We just need to figure out where the next plague will occur."

"Then what?" asked Ben.

"We convey to President Pollard why we feel God is doing this?"

"Plus, in the meantime we must rally all Christians to make a stand," Jim added.

"I gotta admit," Ben said. "I'm more hopeful than I've ever been. It's time we take back our country. One way or another."

"But make no mistake, brothers. We're up against an evil this nation has never seen before," Jacob replied. "If you've never experienced supernatural warfare before, you're about to get a taste of it."

"Okay, now you two have got me spooked," Ben said.

"I can't lie to you, my friend. It's going to get serious. Based on the glimpse I had when my spirit left my body, the evil one will not take this lightly."

"Nor shall we," Jim added.

"What, exactly, can I do?" Ben asked.

"First off, we need as many people praying for a revival as possible. Secondly, we need prominent Christians to speak out to whoever will listen."

"We also need as many friendly media types as possible," Jim said. "We've got to get the word out."

"Guys, I agree with all this. I also think we need an extremely strong candidate to rise up and face the President in the next election."

"Ben, you definitely have a point. All of this is for naught if we don't have someone willing to change the current policies," Jim replied.

"Absolutely," Jacob agreed. "Grassroots or not, without a candidate to believe in the people won't stand firm."

"Let me handle that side of the issue," Ben said confidently. "You two will have your hands full starting the revival."

"Speaking of which, Jim. I'm gonna start putting out calls to my list of church leaders and I suggest you do the same."

"Way ahead of you. I might add I want no argument from either of you on what I must say next."

"What's that, Jim?" asked Ben.

"I plan to make it loud and clear to all, and believe me I can make my point known, that we have a person destined to lead us."

"I couldn't agree more, Jim." Ben interrupted.

"That person is you, Jacob." Jim finished his statement. "We have all seen how God has brought you to this point. We have to have someone to turn to."

"Amen, Jim, amen."

Jacob remained silent for a moment, reflective in prayer. Opening his eyes he stared once again at the cross drawn on the calendar. This time something else stood out besides his artwork.

Just to the left of his drawing was a date circled in red. At no time did Jacob remember circling this number. For that matter he didn't even think he owned a red pen.

Even though today's date was the 25th, he had circled the number 19 on the calendar. Jacob prayed for continued guidance, for clarity about this date. Nothing significant happened. As in all things he resigned himself to the fact that it was in God's timing. Perhaps something would be revealed at a later time.

"Jacob, you still there?" asked Ben.

Hearing his friend's voice revived Jacob from meditating.

Intuitively, Jim asked. "What did you see, Jake?"

A smile appeared on Jacob's face. "I can always count on you knowing something is up, can't I?" Chuckling lightly, Jacob continued. "Your compliments had me quite humbled, brothers. But then I became lost in prayer and when I opened my eyes..."

"What'd you see, Jake?" Ben interrupted.

"I'm not sure, but something tells me the 19th of next month, or perhaps of the months to follow will be significant."

"The 19th, huh?" Ben asked.

"Why that date, Jacob?"

"I don't consciously remember doing it, but it was circled on my desk calendar in red."

"You know, I don't know if I'll ever get comfortable with your visions, Jake." Ben murmured. "But I have learned one thing."

"And what is that?"

"When God speaks to you, something big's gonna happen. Now, we just have to figure out what."

THIRTY TWO

San Diego, CA

Bolting upright, Mollie Mae woke to the sound of agonizing moans coming from Jeffey's bedroom. She glanced at the clock on her night stand and it read 2:44 AM. Mollie Mae sat, feet dangling over the edge of her bed, listening. There was nothing.

Surely it was not a dream she had. The moans were so clear, yet she heard nothing more. Driven by instinct, Mollie Mae rose to her feet. She slipped her robe on and shuffled off in the direction of Jeffey's room.

Not wanting to startle him, she resisted turning on the hall light. Instead, she felt her way along the wall. In her peripheral vision she sensed some type of movement. Startled, she froze in place and waited. Moments passed. Mollie Mae prayed silently for the Holy Spirit's guidance.

Finally, reaching the edge of Jeffey's door, she gently nudged it open. Complete silence engulfed her. Mollie Mae listened for a noise, any noise to come from his bed. Nothing but silence.

From the corner of her eye she caught sight of a figure. It scurried hastily away. Enough was enough. Mollie Mae reached for the light switch and screamed out, "Sweet Jesus, make it go away."

She flipped the switch. The room became engulfed in brightness. A brilliance occurred she had never detected before. Could it be because her eyes were still transitioning from darkness to light? Could it be something more?

With a new found confidence and the help of the guiding radiance, Mollie Mae reached out. She felt the lump hidden beneath the covers of Jeffey's bed. Observing a slight movement, she hesitated.

Mollie Mae pulled the blanket back in one fell swoop. She became startled. Lying curled up in a ball, all six feet plus, was Jeffey shivering. Reaching out to her frightened grandson, Mollie Mae wrapped her arms around his torso.

"Good Lord, child, what happened?"

Not a word was spoken by Jeffey.

Stroking his head with one hand, Mollie Mae clung tight to his body with the other. Softly she hummed in a soothing manner, the melody of a hymn Jeffey so loved. Jesus loves the Children so. Over and over she hummed the tune. Slowly, he stopped rocking and opened his eyes.

"Are you ready to tell me what happened, child?"

He sat up, abruptly. Jeffey stared into her pleading eyes. Tears formed. Jeffey gazed straight ahead.

Continuing to hold him Mollie Mae simply asked, "what did you see, Jeffey?"

"Gehenna." Speaking a little louder, he added, "I was with Jesus. We saw Gehenna! It was Gehenna!"

Startled by his response, Mollie Mae remained silent.

"He was with me there, M&M."

123

"You mean Jesus? Child, I'm confused, where'd He take you?"

"M&M, you don't understand," Jeffey implored. "I had to go. I had to see it."

"What?" Mollie Mae stammered. "Why do you say this?" Scooting back a few inches, she took his right hand into hers. "Where did Jesus take you?"

Closing his eyes, he tried to visualize it. Jeffey repeated, "Gehenna, M&M."

Mollie Mae placed both her hands on his face. "What is Gehenna, child?"

Quickly opening his eyes, Jeffey shouted. "Hell!"

"Oh good Lord, child, what kind of nightmare did you have?"

Pulling his hand away from hers, Jeffey cried out. "I was there, I was there." Pausing for a moment, he continued. "Tall man's there. Evil, evil tall man."

More startled than ever, Mollie Mae sat silently and listened. Frightened by what he was saying, she knew she had to allow him to tell his story. She knew the best thing she could do was simply listen.

"There were creatures, dark evil creatures everywhere. But tall man was in charge." Jeffey stopped for a second. "Beelzebub," he shouted.

"Beelzebub? What's Beelzebub? And who's this tall man, Jeffey?"

"They all listened to him. Beelzebub, he told them what to do."

"Do you know the tall man, Jeffey? What'd he look like?"

Shaking his head no, Jeffey didn't respond immediately.

Reaching for his hand once again, Mollie Mae asked, "Who is tall man? Is he the same as this Beelzebub?"

Jeffey closed his eyes once again. "Dark skin, dark clothes, dark beard. He was tall."

"What was he doing, Jeffey? Do you remember anything else?"

"Yes." Rocking back and forth, he stared at the ceiling. "Yes, I remember."

"Go on, child. Tell me what else you saw."

Still rocking, Jeffey stopped. Cocking his head to one side, he glanced directly into her eyes. "He's evil, M&M. He wants to destroy the church."

Shocked, Mollie Mae asked. "Another church, where?"

Reaching up, Jeffey ran his hands all over his head. Back and forth the hands probed. Straining in frustration, he tried his best to remember what he saw. Then bobbing his head up and down, he continually blurted out two words. "McDonalds, Jacob. Jacob, McDonalds."

Mollie Mae placed both her hands on his shoulders. She tried to calm him down, but Jeffey kept repeating, "McDonalds, Jacob, Jacob, McDonalds."

Jeffey, Jeffey, calm down, child," she implored. "What about McDonalds? I thought you said a church?"

"It's the arches, M&M. He's gonna destroy them." Closing his eyes, Jeffey laid back down.

Cinching her eyes as if trying to piece it all together, Mollie Mae sighed in frustration. "I don't get it, child. It's too late; I'm too tired to try. First you tell me Jesus was with you. Then you saw some tall man, or Beelzebub. And you were in Hell?"

Exhausted, she stared at Jeffey. Pulling his covers up, she bent down to kiss him. He seemed to be fast asleep. No motion from him, only the sound of rhythmic breathing. "No more bad dreams, sweet child. I'll leave the light on in the hall." Mollie Mae turned to leave his room.

Jeffey mumbled in a voice only he could hear. "It's not McDonalds, M&M. Poor Jacob, poor Pastor Jacob. Tall man's gonna get him."

THIRTY THREE

St. Louis, MO / First Christian Church

Jacob entered the foyer of the church after returning from a luncheon meeting. The meeting had been with several pastors from the St. Louis region. Although the get-together was productive, one of his friends indicated that for a revival to be successful, the ground work still had to be laid. There was so much on his plate. Jacob wasn't sure where to start.

"Give me strength, Lord," Jacob softly prayed as he approached Getta's desk.

Getta was furiously typing away at her computer as he called out in passing. "Hey, Get, have a good lunch?"

"I really didn't have time, pastor." She continued to pound away on the keys without looking up.

Jacob paused for a second before proceeding into his office. He hesitated before deciding whether he wanted to close his door. Somehow he felt he shouldn't, but then again there were plenty of calls he needed to make that were sensitive in nature.

Feeling his right hand slip from the knob, Jacob quickly reached out with his left and caught the door before it shut. Something came over him that prompted him to stop in his tracks. Peering through the narrow opening between the door and its frame, Jacob caught sight of Getta.

She seemed frustrated. Guided by the Holy Spirit, Jacob stood poised in the doorway.

Sensing his presence, Getta glanced up and asked. "Something you need, Pastor?"

Twice now she addressed him as pastor. Jacob knew Getta was troubled. In as warm a voice as he could muster, he invited her into his office.

Motioning for Getta to take a seat on the sofa, Jacob sat directly in front of her in one of the matching chairs. From where she was seated, Getta knew that this would be a heart to heart conversation.

Jacob leaned forward, taking the initiative. "Getta, I know you well enough that something is wrong. So, if you want to talk, I'm available."

With a half-smile, she responded. "No, no I'm fine, Pastor. Just a little tired, that's all."

Sitting back, Jacob decided on a different approach. "In that case, would you mind if I prayed with you?"

Although it was not an unusual request, Getta was a little surprised by the offer. "Well, sure. Sure, that would be nice."

Bowing his head, Jacob began. "Heavenly Father, I ask for your presence to lift up my dear sister, Getta. Give her a sense of peace only you can provide. Show her how much we love her here at First Christian. She is so vital to this ministry and to the work that you call her to do. Please, Lord, wrap your loving arms around this dear person so that nothing can take the joy from her heart. Let her know that we will always be here for her as you are always faithful to us. We love you, Father, in Jesus name. Amen"

Jacob lifted his head and peered over at Getta. He could see her head was still bowed, but slowly it bobbed. She was clearly sobbing.

Standing to his feet he grabbed a couple of tissues and reached out to her. "I think you could use these."

She glanced up. Reaching out at the same time, Getta mouthed. "Thank you."

Jacob took a seat on the same couch as Getta. Angling himself a few feet away, he allowed her some personal space.

"Now," he asked. "You sure there's nothing I can do for you?"

Dabbing a tissue at her eyes, Getta responded. "I'm sorry, Pastor Jacob. Lately I've felt a heavy burden on myself…it's kinda like a funk that has taken me over. Honestly, I don't know why I'm crying. I guess I'm wearing my emotions on my sleeve."

"Are you feeling overwhelmed by what I've asked you to do, lately?"

"No, I welcome the challenge. Although, I am a little confused by what's going on."

"How so?"

"Well, I realize it's not my place to ask. But why do you want to contact so many different pastors across the country?" Staring directly into Jacob's eyes, Getta added. "Pastor Jacob, is there something wrong? I'm getting kinda worried."

Taking a deep breath, Jacob paused to think how he wanted to answer her question. His first instinct was to protect her from the battle yet to take place. He also knew he needed as much help as he could get, both spiritually and physically.

"You're right, Getta. It's time I fill you in on exactly what we're planning."

Smiling, she asked. "By saying we do you mean, Jim Calhoun and Dr. Palmer?"

Chuckling slightly, Jacob replied. "I guess I have been speaking to them quite a bit over the past months."

"You might say that."

"All right, then." Jacob nodded. "How much time ya got?"

"As much time as you need to take," she grinned. "You're the boss."

Jacob told her about what had happened over the past few months. Getta barely said a word. She sat astonished as she listened.

Taking the initiative to allow Getta to speak, Jacob asked. "You seem perplexed by what you've heard. Am I correct?"

Swallowing hard, Getta asked, Pastor, how do you do it? You've experienced such incredible things. I guess I don't understand how you can be so in touch with the Holy Spirit."

Jacob asked. "Getta, are you familiar with Jesus' parable of the mustard seed?"

"Well, sure."

"In Mark, chapter 4, He talked about the wonder of the mustard seed. That it's the smallest seed, yet it still grows into a huge tree."

"I remember that, yes."

"But do you know what His parable means?"

Again, Getta shied away from answering and Jacob immediately sensed it. "The meaning can be a hard one to translate." Smiling, Jacob continued. "Basically what it means is that spiritual growth, much like the mustard seed, is a continual, gradual process. It takes time to grow with the Holy Spirit. Time to reach spiritual maturity."

"I understand that part. I mean we're always growing in our faith, but how do you really grow with the Holy Spirit?" Shifting in her seat Getta was clearly engaged. "You have such a presence about you, Pastor. I guess I'm wondering how I can get it too."

Smiling broadly, Jacob paused. "Oh Getta, if only everyone had the same desire you have. Walking with Jesus is listening to your spirit man. Listening to the Holy Spirit inside you. By not listening to your flesh, or doing what the world says you should do, you then draw closer to Christ."

Sensing she was close but not quite there, Jacob added. "When you asked Jesus into your heart, your world changed, correct?"

"Immensely."

"The next step is growing with the Holy Spirit."

Getta nodded, so Jacob continued.

"When you sense something is wrong, that's the Holy Spirit prompting you. Unfortunately, so many ignore Him. They do what their flesh wants any way."

"Well, I realize I have to listen to my "spirit man" when he talks. I'm still not quite clear how to grow. How to become closer to Him."

"Do you know what it means to commune with the Holy Spirit?" Watching her expression, Jacob continued. "In II Corinthians 13:14 Paul says, 'and the communion of the Holy Spirit be with you all.' Communion basically means having fellowship, a friendship with another."

"So, are you saying I need to talk to the Holy Spirit?"

Jacob's eyes grew with excitement at Getta's response. "Exactly. He longs for you to talk to him, share with him. Getta, the Holy Spirit longs to be your closest friend."

Leaning back, Getta cocked her head to one side and replied. "I guess I never looked at it that way. If He longs to be my friend, then I guess the Holy Spirit is my connection to the Father?"

Clasping his hands together, Jacob replied with joy. "Bingo, Getta. One of the best examples I ever heard of how the trinity works together is this. Let's say God gives the command, let there be light. Jesus, the son, is the one who performs the command. But, the Holy Spirit is the power. He's the one who produces the light. In essence, when you pray in Christ's name, the Holy Spirit brings your request to the Father."

"Pastor Jacob, why do think some people have spiritual experiences such as you've had and others don't? What I'd give to be able to hear from Jesus the way you do!"

"All I can say is that the Lord uses each of His followers in different ways. It's really up to us whether we choose to use the gifts He has given us." Pausing, Jacob leaned forward and stared past Getta, like he was looking out at the world. "I think the real question is why do so many people choose not to follow Christ?"

"Something tells me that's why you're contacting so many ministries across the nation," Getta replied.

"Exactly. What Christian leaders and I are trying to stress is that we, as a nation, are being judged." Staring at Getta, Jacob waited to see if she understood. "Getta, it's up to the Christians to stand up and take the nation back."

Nodding in agreement, she commented. "So this is God's wake up call."

"Believe it or not an incredible spiritual battle is about to take place. Right now we're simply gathering our troops."

Standing to her feet, Getta glanced at her spiritual leader. "Then count me in too. I've got a lot of work to do."

Slapping the top of the couch to emphasize his point, Jacob added. "As do I, Getta. As do I."

THIRTY FOUR

The Church Parking Lot

Stepping into his Explorer, Jacob paused and glanced at the passenger seat. Various papers, folders, cds, and of course an old McDonald's bag covered practically every square inch of the seat. Sighing heavily, Jacob muttered. "How can I lead, Lord, when I can't even keep my own vehicle clean?"

He knew at that moment he wasn't leaving just yet. At least not until he cleaned up the mess in his car. Stuffing what he deemed to be garbage into the crinkled bag, Jacob started to make some headway. The papers he couldn't part with were soon neatly stacked upon the folders.

Scooting to the side, he lifted the lid of the center arm console. He tossed three writing pens inside, while scrutinizing a fourth. Where in the world did this one come from? Slowly rotating the instrument, Jacob smiled. Written across the length of the pen were the words, "Stand firm the battle has just begun."

Without hesitation, Jacob rummaged through the center bin until a shiny object caught his eye. Pushing everything else aside, he grasped the object with his right hand. Specks of sunlight bounced off its surface. Its silvery sheen commanded his complete attention.

Displayed on a tiny dial was the number 786. Mouthing the words, "so close," he palmed the object with his right hand. He stared straight ahead. Jacob thought back to when he first acquired this special gift. He remembered how it literally changed his spiritual life.

It was eight years ago, no, nine. Nine years past when Jacob was handed this item. He had been attending a prophetic conference in another city, at the invitation of a pastor friend. The three day event had been an incredible experience. Three speakers gifted with prophetic abilities ministered to hopeful individuals.

Jacob had been content with just hearing the teachings over the first two days. On the third day he had been blessed by a word spoken over him personally. It was the last session of the conference. The sanctuary was packed. Sitting among two thousand people, Jacob and his friend were seated three rows from the front. They were in a section reserved for ministers.

The service was about to start when Jacob had just finished talking to a pastor seated in front of him. He looked to his left and noticed a man staring his way. It was the featured speaker for the night. Their eyes locked. Jacob felt a movement from the spirit within. Any feelings of unease soon dissipated, for he sensed something big was about to happen.

Without hesitating the prophet approached Jacob. The man's eyes focused squarely on him. Standing two feet apart, the gentleman offered his hand and introduced himself. It was an introduction Jacob would never forget.

"I'm Ian Veater," he said. "God just instructed me to talk to you."

Slightly taken back, Jacob responded with the most logical thing that came to mind. "He did? What did he say?"

Ian smiled.

Jacob offered his hand. "I'm Pastor Jacob Conley…and I have to say I've enjoyed your preaching immensely."

Placing both hands on Jacob's shoulders, Ian gazed into his eyes.

Jacob returned his stare.

"Yes, God definitely has a word for you, Jacob. Sometime soon, He will call upon you. I can't tell if it will be this year or in years to come, but He will definitely call upon you."

Shifting his weight and cocking his head to one side, Ian continued. "When God speaks to you, you will know. It will be a calling to lead. To lead a great uprising." Ian's eyes widened, and he paused. "There will be a revival, a revival for my people."

Ian stared into Jacob's eyes. His voice inflected a different tone. He spoke like a father talking to his son. "But you must first grow, Jacob. Grow with the Holy Spirit, and learn to cry out to me." With intensity, Ian added. "And you must shed yourself of pride, Jacob." Stepping back, Ian broke off his gaze.

Tears formed in Jacob's eyes. They were tears of sadness, because he knew the last part was true. His ministry had been stifled. Humility was the key. Ian's words were prophetic and they hit a cord. To become the leader God wanted him to be, he needed to take the next step.

Ian took Jacob's right hand into both of his. A sense of peace instantly fell upon Jacob. Both men nodded. Then, without saying another word, Ian returned to his seat.

Speechless, Jacob stared straight ahead. He meditated on what he had just heard. All about him, people were singing and praising. The music grew louder. But to Jacob it felt like he was the only person in the room.

He closed his eyes and shut out all other sounds. In his mind, it was just he and Jesus. He instantly fell to his knees and sobbed, crying tears of repentance. Years of guilt bottled up inside soon washed away from his soul. He experienced a cleansing like never before. Jacob sensed a presence standing nearby. Instantly the sounds of the sanctuary filled his ears. Glancing up he saw his friend leaning over him, smiling as if he understood.

Standing to his feet, Jacob beamed at his friend and simply said, "Wow."

Nodding in agreement, his friend returned to worshiping. Jacob did the same.

One hour later Ian was wrapping up his sermon when he reached into his pocket. Pacing from one side of the stage to the other, Ian held up an object for all to see.

"For those of you toward the back you may not be able to tell what exactly this is. If we could get the camera to get a tight shot that might help." Pausing to hold his hand steady, Ian continued.

"One day God told me that my prayer life was lacking and as it so often happens, He told me in a place where I couldn't fully concentrate. It was while I was driving. So, I did what I felt was best and I pulled over in a parking lot."

Stopping for a moment, Ian faced the congregation. "How many of you know that's not where He wanted me to stop? God told me, not here, Ian, over there. The only over there was an office supply store. I quickly realized I better go, over there."

Pointing off in the distance, Ian continued. "I got out of the car and proceeded to enter the store. As soon as I entered the store, the Lord said, stop. There in a bin next to me was a display of these." Holding up the shiny object for the camera to zoom in on, Ian added. "I reached down, picked one up and asked, this Lord?"

"And you know what He told me?" Smiling, Ian added. "God said, just buy it. So I did." Pacing the stage again, he continued the story. "I went to my car, and removed the wrapping. Then I thought to myself, what am I going to do with a clicker?"

Ian started clicking the device as he kept count of each step he took. Then he stopped when he got to the center of the stage, and said. "I noticed the package read that this clicker would count up to 999. I could then reset it, and it would start from zero again.

"God then told me why he wanted me to use it. He said, each time you praise me, I want you to click the device."

Smiling at the audience again, Ian added. "And then God said when you get to one thousand...start all over."

Descending the steps in the middle of the stage, Ian stood a few feet from the front row. Pacing directly in front of the congregation, he held the clicker at shoulder height so everyone could see.

Softly, he spoke into his wireless mic, clicking the device after every word. "Jesus," click. "Savior," click. "Glorious," click.

With each praise his voice got louder. The words kept coming faster and faster. "Holy," click. "Almighty," click. "Abba," click. "Worthy," click.

With the clicker at his side, Ian continued praising and clicking for several minutes. He continued to pace in front of everyone. Abruptly he stopped and glanced down at the clicker. "156," he said. Then he started up again.

"After several weeks and several thousand clicks, something interesting happened to me," Ian announced. "I discovered I no longer needed the clicker to praise God. Automatically, I would praise Him throughout the day. My prayer and praise life had changed dramatically."

Ian then started walking toward Jacob's section, where most of the visiting ministers sat. Without hesitation, he stopped next to Jacob and held out the clicker.

"Here," he said, handing the device to him. "I now pass this on to you."

THIRTY FIVE

Church parking lot

Opening the door to his Explorer, Jacob stepped out into the warm summer air. The joy of rediscovering his prized clicker made him feel like a little child.

With arms raised up to Heaven, Jacob immediately started clicking the device, praising God. He paced around his vehicle, then moved on to the next. Jacob skipped about the parking lot like a little boy on summer vacation.

The warmth of the sun energized his core and the beauty of his praises filled the air. An image of King David urged him on. He thought about the joy David had when the ark of the Lord was brought into the city. Within moments Jacob was nowhere near his car. Somehow he ended up in the back of the parking lot.

Jacob glanced about. Looking at the church sanctuary a good three hundred feet away, it hit him. As he stood alone amongst the empty parking spaces he envisioned a crowd. It was a gathering so massive that it overflowed with people.

Closing his eyes Jacob could clearly see a revival…the resurgence that was needed to bring God's saints together as one. In his heart he knew that a spiritual renewal was imminent. Now, Jacob realized where and why.

Holding the clicker, Jacob smiled and praised God. Looking up he asked. "It's here, Lord, isn't it? The revival will take place here in St. Louis."

Realizing he no longer needed the clicker, he dropped it in his pocket. In his mind a new vision rose. Jacob saw a sea of people all gathered in one spot. Thousands upon thousands were huddled along a mighty river's edge. On the other side of the gathering were tall buildings. They barely contained a mass of humanity. Directly in the center of the crowd was a towering object. Beams of sunlight reflected from it in all directions. It acted like a beacon.

The vision brought him amongst the people. Swarms of worshippers cried out in unison as Jacob looked upon their anguished faces. "How long, Lord? How long must we endure?" The saints cried out continually.

Turning about Jacob faced a massive stage. It was framed within the towering object. It sat beneath the Arch. The glare from the arch brought a warmth to the crowd. Scanning the people once again, Jacob could see joy replace their sorrow. This time they cried out as one saying, "now Lord, now we will make a stand."

As quickly as it appeared, Jacob's vision suddenly ended. Alone in the church parking lot, he noticed someone approaching. Feeling a bit awkward, he tried to compose himself. Jacob recognized the individual and half chuckled.

"You know if you're gonna dance around out here, maybe next time we can put it on YouTube."

Shaking his head in embarrassment, Jacob replied. "What can I say? Sometimes the Lord moves me in strange ways."

"Well, if it happens again," Dave, the head of maintenance replied. "Keep me in mind. I make a great dance partner."

Jacob placed his hand on Dave's shoulder. "You think anyone else saw?"

"Naw, but don't worry. I'll keep it between us."

Laughing, both men headed back toward the sanctuary. Jacob stopped abruptly. Reaching into his pocket he retrieved the clicker and held it out.

"You know what, Dave?" Handing the device to his friend, Jacob continued. "I no longer need this. I want to pass this clicker on to you."

THIRTY SIX

White House Conference Room

Senate majority leader Hank Dugan sat pensively, tapping the fingers on his left hand. It was bad enough that he had to wait for the other party to arrive. The power that he, Senator Dugan wielded, almost always had him in control. Not today though.

The finger drumming grew louder. The smile Senator Dugan usually displayed was replaced by a frown. Even his sparkling blue eyes, still vibrant for a man in his seventies, seemed dull on this day.

No matter how much he tried, the Senator couldn't control his nerves. Never in his illustrious career of forty plus years had Senator Hank Dugan been so apprehensive about meeting with one man. And he despised every moment of it.

Startled by the swiftness of the door opening, Senator Dugan leapt to his feet. Cursing himself for acting like a school boy in the principal's office, he remained rigid in place. The President strode across the room toward the conference table where the Senator stood. Dugan couldn't help but see the manila folder in the President's hand.

"Ah, Senator Dugan. I appreciate your patience."

Glancing at his watch to emphasize how long he had waited, the Senator met the President's eyes. He automatically offered his hand. "Good to see you, Mr. President."

As the two shook hands, the Senator could sense something different about the President. It was as if a certain energy flowed from him. Yet, his hand was cool to the touch.

Motioning for the Senator to sit, the President waited before doing the same. Seated side by side, the Senator glanced about the room wondering why the President chose this immense conference room and not his own office.

"Something wrong, Senator?" The President quickly got his attention.

"Why no, not at all." Senator Dugan paused. "Mr. President, why here? Why now, for this meeting?" Feeling his blood pressure rise slightly, he continued. "I must admit, I'm surprised by this clandestine meeting and its urgency."

The President waited for him to finish. He sat back and remained silent. Smiling, the President quickly leaned forward. "I can appreciate your concerns, Senator Dugan." Gesturing with his hand, he continued. "This room, of all places, why here? And just what is my urgency?" He asked in a patronizing tone.

Swallowing hard, Senator Dugan felt a chill in the air. "I didn't mean to question you, Mr. President. I mean, we're both busy men..."

"Indeed we are, Senator." The President interrupted. "What say we get right to the point?" Cocking an eyebrow for emphasis, he continued. "In less than four months, you along with a handful of our party's key leaders are up for reelection. An election you no doubt know will be very tight across the board."

Taken back by the President's frankness, Senator Dugan was poised to answer.

The President slapped his hand upon the folder in front of him. "Well, Senator, I'm here to tell you. With your unwavering support of this agenda, I'm prepared to go all out to make sure you and the others retain your positions."

Dugan wondered what exactly that meant.

Opening the folder, the President retrieved a document and placed it in front of Senator Dugan. "Since we last spoke I told you how important this Anti Inflammatory Defense Bill is to me, correct?"

Glancing down at the paper in front of him, the Senator replied. "And?"

"The gist of the bill states that it would be a defamatory offense to speak out against Islam, which in theory is politically correct. But the beauty of this bill is twofold."

Holding the document in his hands, Senator Dugan asked. "How so?"

Sitting back, the President answered smugly. "One, Christianity would take a big blow because the whole basis of their existence is to spread the gospel. But by doing so they would essentially be speaking out against Islam." President Pollard gestured with both hands. "After all, they do claim Jesus is the only way."

"And how does this benefit me?" Senator Dugan squinted. "I don't care one iota about what it does to Christianity."

The President nodded in agreement. "Here's the beauty of the bill, Senator. We would levy very stiff penalties against those who get caught, if you will." Pointing at the document the President continued. "Those penalties would go to a secret fund that, how should we put it, would benefit those loyal to its success."

Rising from his seat, Senator Dugan waited for the President to join him. Quickly offering his hand, the Senator's engaging smile returned. "I would say you have me and my colleagues' support, Mr. President."

President Pollard grasped the Senator's hand. "Glad to hear it, Senator." Squeezing a tad forcefully, the President added. "Just don't let me down, understood?"

Sensing a change in the atmosphere once again, Senator Dugan retrieved his hand as quickly as he could. Eyeing the President cautiously, he answered. "Yes, Mr. President. I understand."

THIRTY SEVEN

St. Louis, MO

Jacob sat at his desk reflecting on what was in store. He had fully accepted his new role. He needed to assemble as many people of faith as possible to bring about revival in the nation. Still, something was troubling him. There was another piece to the puzzle that involved him. Why exactly was God bringing forth the plagues of Exodus? And how did it involve him?

He stared at his desk calendar. A single item stood out. As bold as day, circled in red, was the number nineteen. Even though this was the start of a new month, he knew that July 19th was significant for some reason.

With eyes closed Jacob started to meditate. He prayed for the Holy Spirit to bring revelation. Within moments his mind drifted off. He saw himself on top of a hill. Jacob looked out over a valley. Before him was a terrain like one he had never seen before. The basin was almost desert in appearance. It had hot, dry air circling about.

Off in the distance he saw a battalion of men. They were dressed in ancient uniforms. The more he stared at these soldiers it became clear they were from another time. They spoke a dialect he was not familiar with. And in their hands they carried swords and spears. The soldiers were oblivious to his presence.

Crying out, Jacob asked. "What is it, Lord? What do you wish for me to know?"

Startling Jacob, a familiar seraph appeared before him. It was Briathos, the angel.

"Don't be alarmed, Jacob," Briathos stood before him. "You are here to witness an important event from ancient times. One that will answer your questions."

"Who are these people, Briathos? Who are they going to battle?"

The soldiers passed by and continued off in the distance. Jacob now felt more confused than ever.

"Those men are Philistine warriors and they are searching for David."

Awestruck, Jacob asked. "King David?"

"Yes, Jacob." Pointing to his right, Briathos added. "Look, there is David, camped with his men."

Staring in admiration at Israel's greatest king, Jacob was unable to reply. He watched as David remained motionless, like a cat preparing to pounce.

"Why are you silent, Jacob?" Briathos asked. "Surely it is clear by now that no one can see or hear you."

Still amazed by the sight, Jacob motioned with his hand. "If that is David, and he is going to battle the Philistines, then is this the Valley of Rephaim?"

"That is correct."

Moving closer to David and his men, Briathos and Jacob waited for something to happen.

Turning to address Briathos, Jacob asked. "Since this is the Valley of Rephaim, then that means David hasn't cried out to God yet."

"Now you see, Jacob. It's not the battle you are to witness...

"It's the plea from David," Jacob interrupted. "This is incredible. Am I really going to witness King David calling out to God?"

Smiling, Briathos turned and motioned toward David.

Kneeling on the ground, King David was heavy in prayer. His face was one of anguish, uncertain of what to expect. Yet, the more he prayed the more confident he appeared, until he boldly asked of God. "Shall I go and attack the Philistines? Will you hand them over to me?"

With his mouth agape, Jacob hung on David's every word. He silently urged him on.

"I know what history says," Jacob said to Briathos. "But how exactly did God help an army so vastly outnumbered?"

"You must realize that the spiritual world always controls the physical."

"You mean something must first happen in the spiritual realm before we can see the results?"

Briathos nodded.

Jacob dared to ask for one request. "Show me the spirit world, Briathos. Can you show me who stood in front of King David?"

Briathos waved his hand across the valley.

Falling back in awe, Jacob glanced at the sight before him. Score after score of warrior angels stood ready to do battle against the demon army of the Philistines. They far outnumbered the enemy.

Grinning at the remarkable sight he was granted to see, Jacob fell prostate. He worshipped the Lord for this privilege. Then, in an instant, David and his men were gone, leaving Jacob alone.

High above Jacob was Briathos, looking inquisitively at him.

Jacob called out to him. "I think I know what God means."

Reaching out, Briathos grasped Jacobs's hands. "You asked earlier, 'Lord, what is it you want me to know'?"

Nodding his head, Jacob urged Briathos to continue.

"Before going to battle, like David, you must first ask God for his presence and guidance. Then you will receive help."

Confused, Jacob asked. "Have I not prayed to God diligently? Have I not been patient wondering what else He wants me to do? And now, you mention a battle."

"You have done all these things, Jacob, and the Father is pleased. Now I must ask you. Through this entire experience what have you learned about David's opponent?"

"The Philistines?"

"Yes, they are the ones."

Scanning the valley's floor as if looking for them once more, Jacob drew a great breath. "Well, the Philistines were Israel's constant enemy. They did everything in their power to torment the Hebrews."

"Correct, Jacob," Briathos glowed. "And now, who would you say is the enemy of Christians today?"

Taken aback by the question, Jacob remained silent. He was lost in thought. Suddenly he frowned. "The enemy is the one who is in charge…more precisely, the President."

"Now you know your other role, Jacob." Releasing Jacob's hands, he continued. "Be the spokesperson God has asked you to be. Stand before the enemy who is persecuting His saints."

Jacob fell to his knees and sobbed. He cried out for forgiveness for being so blind.

Reaching down to place a hand on Jacob's shoulder, Briathos said. "He is not angry with you, Jacob. You would not have seen everything thus far if you were not carefully chosen." Guiding Jacob back to his feet, Briathos added. "Now go and do what is in your heart and know that the Holy Spirit is always with you."

Totally humbled, Jacob had one more question to ask. "What about you? Do you have another role, other than messenger?"

For the first time since he had been in Jacob's presence, Briathos did not return a smile. "There is a great spiritual battle yet to be fought. You can be assured I will always be at your side, only hidden from your sight."

Instantly Jacob awoke from his vision. Glancing about his office he quickly acclimated to his surroundings. Staring at his calendar brought a quickening chill. Jacob knew he had exactly twelve days before the nineteenth to determine what would happen next. Even more daunting, he had less time to gain an audience with the President of the United States.

THIRTY EIGHT

Driving home

Without hesitating, Jacob dialed the number for his friend, Colonel Carlin Hather. It had been months since they last spoke. Jacob hoped that Ben Palmer had kept the Colonel updated.

Colonel Hather recognized the caller ID, and answered in a booming voice. "Pastor Jacob, to what do I owe this call?"

"It's good to hear your voice, Colonel. I apologize for not being in touch more often."

"Contact goes both ways, Jacob, and we seem to be very busy men."

Feeling a little relieved from the Colonel's response, Jacob settled back into his chair. "Colonel, do you have a moment? I may have a very big favor to ask."

"I do indeed…and I must admit I've been anticipating this call."

Jacob wondered what the Colonel meant. Shifting in his seat, he asked. "What exactly have you been anticipating?"

Chuckling, the Colonel replied. "Don't worry Jacob, I haven't had any visions like you. But, Dr. Palmer has kept me up on everything that has happened."

Now laughing himself, Jacob interrupted. "Well Colonel, I have a new one Ben hasn't even heard about. Although, you've got me intrigued by what you've been anticipating."

"That's a simple answer, Pastor. I knew there would come a time that you might need my help in contacting the White House administration. Has that time come?"

"Let me first tell you about my latest experience? It literally happened merely ten minutes ago."

Enthusiastically, Colonel Hather replied. "I'm all ears, Pastor."

"Colonel, for weeks now I have had a number going through my mind, and up until this morning I hadn't been able to figure out what it meant."

"You mind if I ask what the number is."

Glancing at his desk calendar, Jacob answered. "No, of course not. It's number nineteen. Does this mean anything to you, Colonel?"

"Possibly, but tell me more, Jacob."

Jacob spent the next twenty minutes recounting his vision with Briathos and how they saw King David in the Valley of Rephaim. He described everything in detail as if he was still standing in King David's presence. Jacob then emphasized that his experience was not to see David in battle but to learn how important it was to pray to God before encountering the enemy. He needed to proceed just as the great king once did.

The last part of Jacob's vision was the most important to him, the final conversation he had with Briathos. Jacob wondered how he could tell this military man that he, Jacob, was chosen to confront the most powerful man on earth.

Sensing that Jacob was struggling for words, Colonel Hather interrupted. "Pastor, I've always been a man who can read people. Even though we're miles apart, I think I know what you're trying to tell me."

Jacob cocked his head to one side, visualizing his friend's image. "Then you probably know this isn't easy for me to say."

"I do Jacob. You are probably the most soft-spoken man I've ever met. But now that may have to change." Colonel Hather paused before continuing. "Two plus two tells me that not only do you need to become as fearless as King David, but now you must become as bold as Moses."

Speechless, Jacob thought about the analogy Colonel Hather used. He was right of course. In order to stand before the President of the United States and tell him to back off, he would need to be fearless and bold.

Feeling a rush of adrenaline course through his body, Jacob replied. "The wonderful thing, Colonel, is I truly feel ready to do this. Maybe I just needed confirmation from my dear military friend."

"Hardly, Jacob." Believe it or not, I saw something in you when we first met on that plane. At the time, I wasn't sure what, but I do now."

Trying to divert the subject, Jacob changed his tone and asked. "So Colonel, what do you make of the nineteenth?"

"I'm glad you asked," Colonel Hather answered in a more serious tone. "In regards to the President, I know for a fact he plans on vacationing at Camp David during that time frame."

"Camp David?" Jacob asked surprised. "This keeps getting better and better."

"Great parallel to your vision, isn't it?"

"God is amazing, Colonel," Jacob glanced at the ceiling. "How do you propose I get in touch with President Pollard, before July nineteenth?"

"It won't be easy, but I'm hoping my contact will at the very least relay a message to him."

Leaning forward, Jacob quickly replied. "That's not gonna be enough, Colonel. I really think I need to see him face to face."

"And what exactly is it you need to tell him?"

Closing his eyes, Jacob visualized ancient Egypt and saw Pharaoh being swarmed upon by the third plague from God. Continuing the conversation, he replied. "That by the will of God, the third plague from the Book of Exodus is going to take place at Camp David. It will, unless…"

"Unless what, Jacob?"

"Please do what you can to get me an audience, Colonel. When you do, the Holy Spirit will surely guide me in exactly what to tell President Pollard."

THIRTY NINE

Suffolk, VA

The forecast called for another day of sunshine in this region of Virginia. Temperatures could be expected to hover in the high nineties. Not unusual for mid-July. In fact, the summer weather thus far was ordinary to say the least. With the humidity sticking its nose into the mix, the overall heat index could reach an unbearable 105 degrees on this bright sunny day. Most folks made way for the beach. One could generally find some relief from slightly cooler coastal breezes, if you had a means of getting there.

For the non-human inhabitants of this neck of the woods, weather was never really a factor. The creatures of the swamp lived and died through a cyclical pattern that never allowed them to leave. That is unless they were forced to.

Dusk came quickly to the southern border of Virginia. As the sun slowly faded away casting shadows upon the darkening foliage, an evening gloom hung in the air. This was to be no ordinary night and all living things quickly sensed it. Scattering about, with primal instincts heightened and on alert, the only thing that mattered most was seeking refuge. From the largest to the smallest creature that God created, they all recognized something in the air.

Darkness blanketed the area as stars faded from view. The cloud cover was swift, virtually appearing from nowhere. Then again, everything happened for a purpose. Tonight was no exception, for the Great Dismal Swamp was about to be lit up.

FORTY

Jacob Conley's Home

Having cleared the table, Jacob finished placing the last dish into the washer. Another sumptuous meal prepared by Linda was always the perfect ending to a hectic day. Conversation had been light while the two enjoyed their meal together. Still, Linda sensed something was on Jacob's mind.

Jacob retreated into the den where he found his beloved bride flipping through the pages of a magazine. After twenty six years of marriage one thing was certain to him. His wife knew something was up, but it was her non-intrusive demeanor that always caught his attention. Linda never poked, she never pried. She was a Godly woman of few words.

Linda possessed the gift of discernment. With the Holy Spirit as her guide, seeing the truth came natural. Two minutes with any person and Linda had their number. No one knew this better than Jacob, though it hadn't always been that way.

When they first married Jacob vehemently sought the Lord with all his heart. Linda worshipped in silence. Jacob's single minded passion to serve seemed to carry both of them. His goal was her goal. His ministry grew, while Linda kept something hidden within her heart.

With her secret tucked away, the façade continued for the early part of their marriage. Slowly a wedge grew between them. The ugly truth about what happened in her youth was trying to surface. His desire for success kept him from noticing. But by the end of five years Jacob sensed something wasn't right.

Finally one day it took a television program to reveal the truth. During a quiet evening at home, Jacob turned to a news type program. Sitting side by side, the Conley's had no idea what to expect. The show consisted of three segments on three different topics. The first story instantly grabbed Linda's attention, while Jacob watched with a passing interest.

After ten minutes Jacob glanced over at his beloved bride. Tears streamed down her cheeks. Alarmed, Jacob grabbed Linda's hand. "What is it, hon? What's wrong?"

Staring straight ahead, Linda refused to make eye contact. The tears turned into sobs. Linda hung her head in shame.

The voice from the show rang true to Jacob's ears. Briefly glancing at the screen, Jacob saw a woman dabbing tissues at her own eyes. The television interviewer looked on sympathetically. Immediately Jacob knew. Some time in her past, Linda had been molested.

Instinct propelled Jacob to wrap his arms around his wife. She tensed and Jacob quickly drew back. "I'm so sorry, Linda. I didn't know...I didn't know." Scooting slightly away, Jacob gave Linda her space. Silence was all he could offer at the moment.

Jacob turned the television off. Reaching for a nearby lamp he clicked to the brightest setting. Then he hurried into the bathroom to grab some tissues. Everything seemed to move in slow motion. All he could think about was comforting his bride.

Handing the tissues to Linda, Jacob kneeled in front of her. "Please forgive me, Linda. Please forgive me." Tears formed in Jacob's eyes as well. "I should have known."

Leaning forward, Linda ran her hand through Jacob's hair. "How could you have?" Dabbing at her eyes, Linda added. "I'm the one who's sorry for keeping this secret. It's not what God had intended."

Breathing deeply Jacob gazed into the reddened eyes of the woman he loved. Climbing back onto the sofa next to her, he gently grasped both of her hands. "When you're ready," was all he said.

Taking a deep breath as well, Linda stared straight ahead. She remained silent for many moments. Finally she turned to face Jacob. "I was fourteen, he was a close friend of my father's. It seemed like he was always around. The two of them drinking till late into the night."

Jacob remained silent, allowing Linda the opportunity to continue.

Dipping her head slightly, Linda continued. "Then one night, sometime during the summer, I had been over at a friend's house. I came home late, and my Dad was passed out." Shaking her head with eyes closed, Linda paused. His friend was there. Drunk."

As Linda gathered herself, Jacob prayed silently to the Holy Spirit. He asked for peace to fall upon her and the courage to continue.

"He followed me into my room." Sobbing, Linda looked straight into Jacob's eyes. "I couldn't close the door fast enough. He forced it open."

Jacob placed his hand on Linda's shoulder. "You don't have to say any more." Offering her another tissue, he sat in silence. Thoughts of revenge tried to flow through his mind. He quickly cast them out.

Jacob repeated the words our precious Savior spoke, when He silenced the enemy in the desert. "It is written. It is written." Composing himself, he then asked Linda one question. "What is the man's name?"

Surprised by Jacob's request, Linda hesitated. "What does it matter, Jake? I don't even know if he's still alive!"

"Please, what is his name, Lin?"

"Rueben, its Reuben! Rueben." Linda buried her head into Jacob's chest reliving, crying, and trying to forget all at the same time. "Why does it matter," she moaned.

Gently lifting her chin, Jacob peered into Linda's eyes. "Because in order for you to heal, you have to forgive Reuben."

Startled, Linda asked. "Forgive him, how?"

"There's a great work that's going to be done in you. I just know it." Pleading with her, Jacob continued. "If you forgive this man, then all the pent up hurt will disappear, Lin. Ask the Holy Spirit to help you forgive."

The silence was pervasive as Jacob waited for Linda's response. Slowly, she slipped off the couch and fell to her knees. Facing away from Jacob, Linda lifted her hands toward Heaven, and in a broken voice cried out. "Dear God, I trust Jacob in what he's asked me to do. Please Lord, help me. Help me to forgive this man. Help me to forgive, Reuben."

Instantly Linda began to shake. Speaking in the spirit, she cried out to the Lord. Within seconds she coughed violently, releasing the hurt, the shame, the bitterness she had carried for so many years. The catharsis was completed. The secret had been revealed. Linda had forgiven the man who had haunted her so many years.

Over the next twenty years, Linda grew close to her beloved Holy Spirit. Every now and then she struggled with forgiveness, but a few moments on her knees put everything into perspective. He gifted her in so many ways, but none more so than the discernment of wisdom. Linda had become the perfect complement to Jacob, and he to her. Their love for each other grew as well.

Jacob's thoughts drifted to present time. Sitting just to the left of Linda in his favorite chair, he stole a glance in her direction. The nonchalant manner in which she turned the pages was all the confirmation he needed. It was time to share this latest vision with his soul-mate and confidant.

Clearing his throat, Jacob caught Linda's attention. "Hon, there's something I need to pass by you, that happened today."

Linda slowly met his gaze as she glanced up. "What is it, Jake?"

Closing his eyes reflective in thought, Jacob opened them and glanced up at the ceiling. "I guess I kept this bottled up because I'm not really sure what to make of it."

162

Linda silently urged him to continue.

Shaking his head as if he were disagreeing with someone, Jacob announced. "No, no, scratch that. I know what to make of this. I'm just not sure if I'm ready."

"Jake, what are you talking about?" Linda's smile faded away.

Jacob realized he was talking more to himself than her. "I'm sorry. Can I start over?"

Slightly amused, Linda wondered what he was going to say next. "Okay, in a nutshell?"

"Sure," she answered, soothingly.

"I had another vision, and it centered on King David."

"Really."

"Interesting, huh? Anyway, I called Colonel Hather afterwards because it became clear to me that I needed to get in touch with the President...

"The President?" Linda interrupted. "Wait a minute; what does King David have to do with President Pollard?"

"So much for my nutshell," Jacob grinned. "Okay, what I learned from this revelation is that God is telling me to be His spokesman and go before the President."

"To do what, Jacob?"

Standing to his feet, Jacob approached Linda and sat next to her. Taking her hands into his, he continued. "It's time for someone from the Christian community to take a stand against the White House policies. Linda, God has had enough of His people being persecuted. He wants me to engage the President."

"Wow, Jake." Linda interlaced her fingers with his. "For the longest time I've prayed for a revival. I've prayed for someone to stand like Moses.

Peering into her eyes, Jacob replied. "Do you think I can be that person?"

Nodding her head, Linda said. "I do, Jake." She hugged his neck. "But I'm curious. How does Colonel Hather fit into the equation?"

"Hopefully, he can get me in to speak to the President."

Drawing a deep breath, Linda asked. "Do you have any idea what you'd say?" Registering the look on Jacob's face, Linda added. "You'll know when the time comes."

The silence between them, suggested one thing. Both Linda and Jacob were engaged in prayer. Moments passed before a familiar sound interrupted them. Glancing to his left Jacob spied the object of distraction.

"Think I should get it?" Linda asked.

"At least see who it is."

Grasping the phone in her left hand, Linda quickly handed it to Jacob. "I think it might be someone from the White House."

FORTY ONE

Suffolk, VA

The lightning strike hit with such force that the ground shook hundreds of feet in all directions. The brilliance from a single bolt lit up the night sky before vanishing in a flash. Creatures scurried to and fro panicking from the aftermath.

A lone red maple stood out like a beacon, soon engulfed by raging flames. Incinerated within a matter of minutes, the inferno was temporarily halted, until it found a new path. Like a fuse in a firecracker the flame burned downward hunting for something to ignite.

Then it happened. Embedded within the roots and deep beneath the surface, a spark found its target. Peat. Often used as fuel in many countries, this decomposing plant matter was all it took for the fire to gain new life.

Throughout the history of this wildlife refuge there had been many a wildfire. With 111,000 potential acres to burn, the Great Dismal Swamp was no exception on this night. But this blaze didn't occur by accident, nor did man have anything to do with it. Everything happens for a reason, even a single lightning strike.

Within a matter of days the inferno would spread underground, fueled by the abundance of peat. Upward it would burn until the fire reached the surface. The aftermath would be smoke, and plenty of it. Hundreds of acres would smolder, with containment barely an option. Short of hopeful rains, controlling the blaze could take months.

FORTY TWO

Conley Home

Jacob grasped the phone. Quickly eyeing the caller ID he then hit the answer button. Mouthing to Linda, Jacob whispered. "Who's Anne Givens?"

Replying quickly, Linda said in a hushed voice, "she's the President's press secretary."

"Hello," Jacob answered.

"Is this Pastor Jacob Conley?" The party asked.

"Speaking."

"Good. My name's Anne Givens, Pastor Conley."

Covering the mouth piece, Jacob gazed at Linda. "Wonder if she's calling from the White House?"

"I hope I didn't catch you at a bad time, Pastor."

Returning his attention back to the call, Jacob responded. "No, no, Miss Givens. How can I help you?"

"Well, I realize this call is a little unorthodox," Anne replied. A mutual friend asked me to get in touch with you."

"And who would that be, Miss Givens?" Jacob continued to stare at Linda.

"Colonel Carlin Hather, Pastor…and please, call me Anne."

"Fair enough, Anne. How can I help you?"

Pausing, Anne responded. "I think it's I who may be able to help you Pastor."

Sitting back against the couch, Jacob sighed before responding.

"Pastor Conley," Anne interrupted. "By this time I'm sure you know who I am and who I work for."

"Yeah, I think I do."

"Well rest assured, I'm not at the office, and this is my private cell that I'm calling you on."

"That's very prudent of you, Anne." Jacob grinned. "So what exactly did Colonel Hather tell you?"

"Without going into any details, he made it very clear that you would like to get in touch with my boss."

Chuckling, Jacob replied. "What a country we live in when we need to speak in generalities for fear of retribution. Don't you agree, Anne?"

Laughing as well, Anne responded. "I wouldn't worry about that, Pastor. I get requests all the time."

Feeling slightly embarrassed by his last remark, Jacob answered. "I'm sorry, Anne. But as you can imagine, the Christian community is a little sore from all the new policies the President has enacted."

"Point taken, Pastor. I'm sure you can imagine I wouldn't be having this conversation with you if I didn't agree with you on some level."

Nodding his head in agreement, Jacob replied. "Good to hear, Anne. Now, how do you propose we proceed?"

"Pastor Conley, I wouldn't count on a face to face," Anne answered, somewhat sarcastically. "But I can certainly get a message to him if you feel it's that important."

Leaning forward and staring straight ahead, Jacob replied. "Then I'll take what I can get, Miss Givens. Now, here's what I want you to say."

FORTY THREE

July 15th / U.S. Fish & Wildlife Service-Suffolk, VA

Carter Hayes, Director of the Wildlife Refuge Center paced through his office with a phone to one ear. Stopping abruptly he glanced through a wall of windows at the control center. Monitors displayed every condition imaginable pertaining to the Great Dismal Swamp. Employees worked feverishly gathering information. Something caught Carter's eye.

Focusing his attention on a single television screen, Carter shook his head in exasperation. News reports kept coming in on the status of the wildfire that started two days ago. The reporter on the line was insistent on knowing what Carter thought.

Carter knew that it was too early to give an accurate assessment, especially since he didn't want to cause any undue angst. Due to the dry conditions that prevailed throughout the region people were naturally alarmed. But it wasn't the temperature or lack of moisture that concerned Carter. It was the winds.

The National Weather Service called for gusts up to 25mph on and off for the next few days. To Carter, that spelled trouble. If the fire kept burning at the pace it was on then the smoldering flames would be a problem.

Reporter Kim Posh, from UPI, wanted to know one thing and one thing only. Could this fire be a repeat of 2008? Back in June, 2008, the Great Dismal Swamp had a wildfire that burned over 2,700 acres. It affected the human population for several hundred miles around. It wasn't so much the actual fire that concerned the populists, since it really had nowhere to go. It was the smoke.

"I'm sure you can understand the public's concern, Mr. Hayes. I ask you again, what's the potential for another wildfire like 2008?"

"Miss Posh, for one thing it's too early to tell. But I can assure you fire crews are working diligently to contain this wildfire." Carter felt somewhat conflicted as he watched the screen on the television. The cameraman panned out over the vast refuge from a helicopter high above. From the chopper's viewpoint the fire looked nowhere near contained. Heavy plumes of smoke drifted NE, at the mercy of the wind.

"I'm sure you recall that fire was nothing short of alarming," Kim retorted. "The beach communities were not only threatened with the smoke but the insects were out of control."

Closing his eyes briefly, Carter nodded his head in agreement. He could only hope for a non-repeat of 2008, but he also knew they were doing all they could. "That was unfortunate, Miss Posh. As you probably know when a wildfire hits the refuge and burns underneath the ground, we're at the mercy of the fuel source."

"So are you saying because there's so much peat prevalent throughout the swamp that this thing could burn uncontrollably for weeks? Even months?"

"No, I'm not saying that." Carter grimaced at the tag line on the TV screen. 'Wildfire out of Control!' "Miss Posh, all I can say is we're doing everything in our power to contain this fire."

"Well, the weather service says there's no rain in the immediate forecast, how does that affect your plans?"

Pausing, Carter motioned for his assistant to join him. Holding his hand over the phone, Carter asked. "What's the latest, Jill?"

"Not good, sir. Maybe ten percent contained."

Nodding, Carter tried to concentrate on the question from the reporter. Sighing heavily, Carter answered Kim Posh's question. "Bottom line, only time will tell. We're doing all we can. Miss Posh, thank you for your call."

Ending the call, Carter focused his attention on the television for a brief moment. He pointed the remote and clicked it. He only wished he could turn off his current problem as easy as turning off the TV.

FORTY FOUR

The White House

Anne Givens had two days before the President was to leave on a weeklong retreat to Camp David, in Catoctin Mountain Park. Finding the opportune time to inform the President of her conversation with Pastor Jacob Conley was somewhat dicey. With the window of opportunity slowly closing she needed to act quickly.

The only problem was catching the President when he would be most receptive. His volatile nature was unpredictable. It often led to staff members walking on pins and needles. Knowing what mood Stuart Pollard was going to be in was like predicting the weather. There was always a slight chance of a storm when the temperature was high.

Having had a few days to digest her conversation with the pastor, Anne knew exactly how she wanted to approach the situation. The more she alluded to the source as someone who wanted to pass on information, the more the President would view her as a third party. As long as she came across as the messenger, she felt she would be safe. For now, that's how she would proceed.

Anne rounded a corner and spied the President's executive assistant, Jenny. No better person to ask about the President's mood than his assistant. Standing before her desk, Anne waited for Jenny to end her phone conversation.

Smiling, Anne spoke first. "Hi Jenny," Anne greeted her in the warmest tone she could muster. "Hey, I need to speak with the President for a few moments. How's his schedule?"

Returning a smile, Jenny glanced down at the President's schedule. "Well, whatta you know, you're in luck." Jenny looked back up at Anne. "There's nothing on the books for another twenty minutes." Glancing at the phone, Jenny added. "And currently, he's not on any call."

"Well, I guess I am in luck," Anne drew a breath.

"Shall I buzz him and ask if he's available?"

"Just one other question," Anne asked coyly. "What kind of mood is he in?"

Jenny smiled, then replied. "Between you and me, Anne, pretty good. I think he's already in vacation mode."

Nodding in confirmation Anne thought, not for long.

Anne closed her eyes and said a quick prayer.

"Anne, you may go in now," Jenny motioned toward the door.

Taking a step, then stopping abruptly, Anne turned back toward Jenny. "I got about fifteen minutes, right?"

"Thereabouts."

"Thanks." Anne reached for the handle and passed through the door.

As she stepped into the oval office Anne felt an instant chill. Her first thought was that the President had asked that the gauge be turned down. In the past she had always known that he liked it warm where-ever he went. To set the air on cool was out of character for him.

Anne paused and remained silent. She watched as the President finished writing a few notes. Keeping someone waiting was definitely part of his demeanor. President Stuart Pollard did everything in his own time. Fourteen minutes and counting, Anne thought to herself.

"That should do it," the President set his pen down. Popping his head up to meet Anne's gaze, he remarked. "I didn't know you were on my schedule, Anne."

Being a little taken back, considering Jenny had just cleared her to meet him, Anne simply smiled. "I'm not, Mr. President. But I wonder if I can have a few moments with you?"

Rising from behind his desk, the President gestured to the sofa at the center of the room. "Of course, Anne. Have a seat."

This is a little more promising Anne thought. She sat on the sofa, to the right of the President's wing back chair. He sat where she expected. Then, the President propped his right arm while slowly stroking his chin. Anne knew him all too well. He was trying to measure her motives.

Anne leaned forward. "Mr. President, I recently spoke with a gentleman who asked me to convey a message to you." She watched as the President's eyebrows peaked upward. "I talked to a certain pastor, via the phone, who had some startling things to say."

"Who was this man?" The President continued to rub his chin. "And does he pose any kind of threat?"

"Oh no, Mr. President, he's no threat. I didn't mean to come across that way."

Appearing more relaxed, the President replied. "In that case, Anne, tell me all about this conversation you had."

175

Sensing a slightly condescending tone from the President, Anne wasn't sure how to proceed. As she drew a breath, she noticed a smirk appear on his face, almost as if he knew what to expect.

"The man's name is Pastor Jacob Conley. He's from St. Louis." Anne paused, as she noticed a slight nod from the President. "Do you know him, Mr. President?"

"No, not really, Anne." Gesturing with his right hand, the President added. "Please, go on."

"Well, Pastor Conley claims to have visions from God." Anne tried to gauge the President's reaction before continuing. "Through these visions, he feels God is trying to tell him something."

"And what would that be?" He quickly interrupted.

Clearing her voice, Anne responded. "Well sir, Pastor Conley feels that if the administration continues to set forth policies that are detrimental to Christians…" Clearing her throat again, Anne waited for the President to jump in, but he didn't. "He feels God is going to bring more plagues that will affect you and those around you."

Still seated calmly, the President responded. "You say more plagues, Anne? I wasn't aware any had occurred."

Chuckling slightly, to ease her tension, Anne replied. "Pastor Conley claims there have been two so far…and he says there will be more soon."

Now leaning forward in his chair, the President asked. "Just for the sake of argument, what were the first two plagues?"

Feeling like a student being browbeaten by her teacher, Anne said. "From what he says, the first was blood in the water that happened in Montana. The second was, ah, frogs that appeared out of nowhere in Nevada, sir."

176

Cocking his head to one side, the President asked. "Now Anne, surely you don't think these occurrences are plagues from God?"

"Sir, I don't know what I believe," Anne answered sheepishly. "But Pastor Conley was emphatic about telling you what was going to happen next."

"Happen next. As in, if I don't change my policies?"

"Supposedly, sir."

Waving his hand in the air, the President replied. "Go on Anne, humor me. Tell me what Pastor Conley claims will happen and when."

Anne was clearly on the fence. On one hand Jacob Conley sounded very convincing and he had some very respectable people backing him up. On the other, the more she thought about what she needed to say to the President of the United States, the more she felt a little foolish.

Contemplating what to say next, she knew she was beyond backing out now. Anne realized that it was only a matter of time that the next prediction by Jacob Conley would either come to pass, or not. Any way she looked at it, she was now the messenger to the President. Knowing him, she wondered if her career would be in jeopardy.

Here goes, she thought. "Mr. President, on July nineteenth, a third plague will occur according to Pastor Conley. And as you and I well know, you will be at Camp David then."

"Believe it or not, Anne. I know that the Bible claims that the third plague that came upon Egypt was a plague of gnats." Laughing out loud, the President continued. "If your Pastor Conley is trying to tell me that a swarm of gnats will occupy the Camp David compound, high in the mountains no less, then he's as nuts as some of those TV evangelists." Glaring at Anne, he added. "I just hope you're not as well."

A sense of boldness came upon Anne, one that she had never felt before. As the words from Jacob Conley continued to fill her mind, sitting on the fence was no longer an issue. She now saw everything from a Biblical standpoint. Career or no career, God was about to act. The President's policies would soon be challenged.

Standing to her feet, Anne stared into the President's eyes. For the first time since she worked for him, she saw a man she no longer respected. She recognized an administration's guiding principles she could no longer stomach. Summoning all the courage she could muster, Anne responded.

"I guess in a few days the truth will come out. And for the record, Mr. President, I believe him."

Anne continued to lock eyes with her boss. The coldness he conveyed quickly confirmed what she needed to do next. With a determined look, she boldly announced. "I'll have my resignation on your desk by the end of the day, Mr. President."

Leaping to his feet, the President called out to her as she headed for the door. "Oh no, Anne. Draft that letter within the half hour."

Tears welled up as reality set in. Anne exited, wondering if she did the right thing.

FORTY FIVE

Camp David, MD

Nestled in the Catoctin Mountains of Maryland, located approximately 70 miles from the White House, is Camp David. President Pollard insisted on taking his short vacation there to escape the summer heat of Washington, D.C. Besides, it was often used as a summer retreat by past Presidents, so why not him?

The fact that Camp David derived its name from the grandson of President Eisenhower meant nothing to Stuart Pollard. Any history of the camp was irrelevant. All the President was interested in was how the Marines were going to provide security so that no one could bother him.

Security would be the least of the worries surrounding Camp David, though. Once all of the President's entourage arrived they would be faced with the supernatural. From that point on nothing could be done to help them.

At approximately 1:00 PM the President, along with his wife Collette, arrived at the retreat. Aside from the usual secret service assigned to the President, no one else was onboard Marine One when it landed. This escape from the White House was scheduled for five days with no visiting dignitaries and no key office personnel accompanying the President.

The lone guest yet to arrive was not expected till later in the afternoon. This would truly be a short vacation getaway for President Stuart Pollard and the First Lady. Of course any urgent matters would be brought to his attention, but for all intents and purposes the President was not to be disturbed.

The weather at Camp David on July 19th was a comfortable seventy three degrees. Having escaped the oppressive humidity of Washington, the President was anxious to relax outside and take in the gorgeous scenery of the Catoctin Mountains.

With Collette by his side, President Pollard strolled about the grounds. He felt more relaxed and confident than ever before. Pausing briefly to glance at an oblong shaped rock, the President's train of thought quickly reverted back to his conversation with Anne Givens. What was it she said, that this pastor fellow warned him about? Immediately the President remembered. He curled his lip in disgust.

"What is it, Stuart?" Collette asked. "You look like you swallowed a fly."

"A fly?" Stuart replied, putting the thought of gnats aside. "It's nothing. Just something I remembered I need to take care of when we get back."

Reaching for her husband's hand, Collette gave it a gentle squeeze. "Remember, we agreed no worries while we're up here." The First Lady gave him a knowing glance.

"Well, is there ever a time the most powerful man in the world doesn't have a worry?" The President chuckled as they continued their stroll.

"True, but let's keep them to a minimum." Snuggling up next to her husband, Collette Pollard sighed. "It just feels like no one or nothing can touch us up here."

Heading back toward Aspen Lodge, the Presidential cabin, the President commented. "At least no one better try."

FORTY SIX

St. Louis, MO / First Christian Church

While sitting at his desk, Jacob doodled on his calendar. Over and over again he circled the number nineteen. Not because today was the nineteenth, but because the number jumped out at him. This was the day the third plague was to occur. At least that was what his vision had told him. Jacob wondered if he did everything he could to get a message relayed to the President. He knew what happened next would change his status from this day forward. In his mind he couldn't help think of Moses prior to the Exodus.

"Jake, you there? You got silent on me." Jim Calhoun asked.

"Sorry, Jim." Jacob grasped the phone tighter with his left hand. "It's just that, within the next twenty four hours everything is going to change."

"Of course it is. Let's hope a certain individual comes around and things change for the better."

Sitting back in his chair, Jacob closed his eyes as he spoke. "I got to be honest, Jim. I don't see it happening. We're in for a long haul and we're in for a fight."

"Is that you speaking, or…"

"It's what I feel," Jacob interrupted. "It's what I know; it's what has to happen." Jacob paused as he felt his right hand ball into a fist. "And you know what, Jim…I feel like a warrior ready to do battle."

182

"Excellent," Jim replied. "We got the troops mounting and we're ready to follow you, Jacob."

A surge of adrenaline coursed through Jacob's body as he leapt to his feet. "This time tomorrow, I'll be waiting on an important call. A call that no doubt will set the war in motion."

"Praise God," Jim replied. "And I'll be praying for you through the night."

Jacob hung up the phone. Immediately a brilliant light appeared, startling him. Standing in Jacob's presence was Briathos. He approached Jacob.

"It is good to hear that you are readying yourself, Pastor Jacob."

Before responding, Jacob considered the salutation Briathos greeted him by. He had never referred to him as pastor in the past.

"Yes," Jacob answered. "I believe I am ready. Though, it sure would be great to know what I can expect."

"What you must know," Briathos gestured. "Everything changes from this point forward."

Standing to his feet, Jacob moved around his desk to face his guardian. "Well, sure, now that I have the attention of the leader of our nation." Jacob waited for Briathos to comment but he stared past him, not saying a word. "So are you telling me that my role with the President is going to change?"

For the first time since his arrival, Briathos changed his expression. An engaging smile appeared and his eyes softened. "That and much more, dear Jacob."

Gazing at Briathos, Jacob asked. "How so?"

"The enemy no longer has the power to remove that which the Father sends against them." Pausing, Briathos asked. "Do you understand?"

Jacob suddenly realized what to expect. "Starting now and in the future all plagues that occur cannot be stopped. Unless God chooses to do so." Nodding his head in agreement, Jacob added. "Now I know why everything changes."

FORTY SEVEN

US Fish and Wildlife Service / Suffolk, VA

"How could that be?" Carter Hayes asked, frustrated by the news from the other end of the phone. "Okay, all right, we'll keep an eye on it. Thanks."

Hanging up the call, Carter turned toward his assistant, Jill. By the look on his face she could tell he had bad news.

"That bad, huh?" Jill asked.

"I guess it shows. That was Ken from National Weather." Taking a seat at a desk piled with papers, Carter added. "There's a major shift in the wind patterns, not to mention we can expect an increase in gusts."

Leaning against Carter's desk, Jill inquired. "How major?"

"The westerlies have now turned northern." Drawing a breath, Carter continued. "And on top of that, gusts are projected to top 40 mph."

"That'll push the smoke up toward the Chesapeake."

Reaching for the phone, Carter replied. "With that kind of wind the smoke could possibly reach D.C., and who knows, maybe even Maryland."

"And along with it will come the gnats that have been plaguing coastal Virginia." Jill straightened up and wasted no time heading for the door.

"I can envision the phone ringing off the hook with every politician in Washington screaming for my head." Carter said defeated, as he immediately started dialing the phone.

Upon exiting Carter's office, Jill spoke under her breath. "Better you than me, boss. Better you than me."

FORTY EIGHT

Camp David

Secret Service agent J. Bullington heard the tiny receiver in his ear come to life. Standing some distance from the base helipad, he instinctively scanned the horizon. With nothing out of the ordinary to report, he lifted his left arm and spoke to his wrist.

"Bullington reporting, over" he responded.

"Bullington, this is Rosenburg. Marine One is on approach, touchdown in three minutes, over."

"Copy, I'm on alert." SS Agent Bullington scanned the horizon before asking. "Hey Burg, are we in for a storm tonight, over?"

"Not that I'm aware of, over," SS Agent Rosenburg answered.

"There's some dark clouds coming up from the south, and the winds have picked up, over."

"Do I need to bring you a blankie?" Agent Rosenburg joked.

Within seconds Agent Bullington could hear the distinctive sound of rotors whipping in the distance. Marine One was now in sight. "Bird in view, over."

Agent Bullington stiffened. The combination of the chill in the air and the guest he was to greet brought on a whole new persona. Being part of the Presidential detail was certainly an honor. But at times there was a definite downside. This was one of them.

Stepping out the side door of Marine One was the person Agent Bullington was required to escort back to President Pollard. Bullington gave up wondering how he was even able to ride on the chopper designated for the President only. Then again, Ra Farman was able to do a lot of things that broke protocol.

Bullington gestured toward the vehicle waiting to transport the two of them back to the main complex. From past experience he learned the President's advisor was not a person of many words. At least not to him.

Stowing Mr. Farman's bag, Bullington wasted no time climbing into the driver's seat. The sooner he delivered this man the sooner he could get back to his post guarding the main building.

"Rosenburg, this is Bullington. Do you copy?"

"This is Rosenburg. Do you have our passenger, over?"

"Affirmative, heading your way directly, over."

"Why such formality, Agent Bullington?"

J. Bullington was startled to actually hear Ra Farman address him.

"Feel free to refer to me as Mr. Farman, rather than the passenger." Ra added, sarcastically.

"Sorry sir, just following protocol."

"Very well, driver." Ra smiled smugly, as he turned to glance out the window.

Raising his eyebrows, Agent Bullington realized he was in for a long weekend.

It was a short distance between the landing pad and the Camp David complex, but to Agent Bullington it couldn't be short enough. Past experience with the President's unofficial advisor meant one thing. If it wasn't the President demanding something, it was Ra Farman demanding even more. Much to the chagrin of the secret service, he got what he wanted.

As he drove he couldn't help but notice the darkening sky coming up from the south. If this was some kind of storm it looked like it was gonna be nasty.

Pulling up to the main complex, Ra wasted no time exiting the vehicle. Agent Bullington proceeded to grab his suitcase when Agent Rosenburg joined him.

"Frosty ride?" Rosenburg joked.

"Nothing but." Bullington faced his fellow agent, with suitcase in hand. "What cabin is he in?"

"The Dogwood," Rosenburg gestured to their right. "Come on, I'll walk over with you."

The two agents remained silent until they were a safe distance. "Hey Burg," Agent Bullington said. "Something in my spirit has got me on high alert."

"You know what? When you mentioned the weather I didn't think much of it." Glancing off to the horizon, Agent Rosenburg continued, "I tend to agree. Something just isn't right."

Agents Rosenburg and Bullington had been two of the Agency's brightest and most dedicated members. Recently assigned to the President's detail, they came highly recommended by the assistant director, who happened to be a man of faith. Discreet by choice, Assistant Director Cummins instantly knew where to assign his Christian brothers.

Corruption aside, the leader of this great nation deserved complete protection. Of course it didn't hurt to have Godly men surround him as well. Agents Rosenburg and Bullington fully understood their obligation, yet they knew the price they could possibly have to pay. Persecution would show no bounds even in the line of duty.

Standing outside the cabin, Rosenburg waited for Bullington to place Mr. Farman's bag inside. He continued to squint at the darkness approaching. He wondered what kind of storm they were about to face. The sky not only changed but the winds picked up considerably.

"Bully, get out here," Rosenburg called.

"What is it?" Bullington raced out to join him.

Holding his right index finger up, Rosenburg spoke into the com. "Rosenburg to command, do you copy?"

"What is that?" Bullington asked, staring at a black mass heading their way.

"Command here, what's your status, over?"

Shaking his head, Rosenburg replied. "Command, I don't know if you've seen this, but there's an enormous swarm of insects about to overtake the camp." Rosenburg turned to face Bullington. "Command, do you copy, over?"

"Sweet Jesus," Bullington cried out. "What are they?"

FOURTY NINE

St. Louis, MO

Pulling into his driveway, Jacob was barely able to maneuver toward the garage. A sudden rush of adrenaline coursed through him as he parked the Explorer and stared through his windshield.

As anticipation followed, Jacob instantly knew what would happen next. Having a presence of mind to cut the engine, his mind rushed off into another realm.

There standing before him were two men dressed in dark suits staring up at the sky. Fear was set within their eyes as their images were quickly engulfed by a dark cloud. A mass moved about them.

Immediately, Jacob prayed for the men. Though, he didn't know who they were. Within seconds the men fell to their knees. A miracle began to unfold. The swarm surrounding them left them alone and quickly moved on. It engulfed the building beyond. The swarm claimed it, as if claiming it for its own.

Jacob was stirred by a pounding sound. At first it was muffled. Then it grew louder. Before long his mind went blank. He opened his eyes. The pounding grew louder yet. Startled, Jacob turned to his left and engaged the frantic eyes of Linda. She stood outside his car window.

As the pounding ceased, he heard her voice cry out.

"Jacob, Jacob. Are you all right?"

Gathering his wits, Jacob tried the door handle. It was locked. Flipping a button, the lock disengaged. Linda immediately swung the driver's door open.

"Dear God, Jacob. What happened?"

Stepping out of the vehicle, Jacob threw his arms around Linda. He held her tight.

Speaking softly into his ear, Linda asked. "What did you see?"

Pulling back so they were eye to eye, Jacob answered. "The third plague has started, Linda." Blinking his eyes as if conjuring up a clearer image, he added. "It's at Camp David."

FIFTY

Camp David

Shocked by what had just happened, Agent Rosenburg stared at the enormous mass of gnats. They engulfed the entire compound. Immediately he called into command headquarters. Rosenburg watched Agent Bullington approach the infested Dogwood cabin.

Amazingly, as Bullington moved closer the gnats scattered.

"Rosenburg, come in. Are you encountering these bugs, over?"

"Affirmative," Rosenburg responded. Everywhere he looked the gnats appeared. But not a single one was on his body. "They appear to be everywhere, over."

Moving deliberately, Bullington was amazed by the gnat's reluctance to be in the same space as himself. As he stood by Rosenburg's side, it was as if a bubble was surrounding them.

His receiver cackled grabbing Rosenburg's attention from the phenomenon. "Rosenburg, this is base. We need you and Bullington to report ASAP, over."

"Copy that, over" Rosenburg answered. "Let's go, Bully. You heard the man."

Shouts could be heard as the two men approached the main complex. Agents swatted at the pestering insects. Many stood outside securing the building. By this time, almost all the agents had scarves wrapped around their mouths and noses. They tried anything to keep the pests out of their airways.

Rosenburg and Bullington were still not bothered by the gnats as they entered the building.

"Shut the door!" An agent shouted. He hustled them inside.

It didn't matter. The inside of the building was as infested as the outside. Clouds of mist waffled throughout the air. Agents scurried to spray the bugs as quickly as possible. It was all for naught. The gnats kept coming.

The head of their detail, Agent Cooper, approached agents Rosenburg and Bullington. "We don't know where they came from, but the President wants them out of here as soon as possible."

Looking suspiciously at Rosenburg and his fellow agent, Cooper spoke through a cloth over his mouth. "What's the deal with you two? Why aren't the bugs swarming you?"

"No idea, sir." Bullington responded. He glanced at Rosenburg and grinned while tapping his chest. "Perhaps it's something inside."

"Whatever it is, I want you guys to escort the President and his party to Marine One. Pronto!" Cooper gestured toward three figures huddled together under a blanket. The number of gnats surrounding the trio was thicker than anywhere else.

Agent Cooper was still amazed as he watched Rosenburg and Bullington move as if there was a force field encapsulating them. They continued toward the President and the gnats flew away.

Rosenburg knelt by the three figures and said. "Mr. President, if you're ready we'll take you to the helicopter."

"Just get me out of here. Now!" Screamed the President.

Reaching his hand down, Bullington grasped the First Lady's hand and drew her toward him. As she stood near him, the gnats left her alone.

"Quickly, ma'am." Bullington said. "Let's head out to the vehicle and get you to Marine One."

The two moved off followed closely by the President and his guest, Ra Farman. The gnats continued to swarm the President and Ra. They hustled out to the vehicle. Diving into the Suburban, the four gained a respite from the pests outside.

A look of contempt appeared upon Ra's face as he watched Rosenburg approach the car. The swarm outside cleared out of his way, while he entered the driver's side.

"Did you see that?" President Pollard whispered to Ra.

"Of course I did," Ra sneered. He suspiciously eyed the two agents in the front seats.

"Agent?" The President asked.

"Agent Rosenburg, sir." Rosenburg turned from his seat and addressed the President.

"Yes, Agent Rosenburg, you say?" "How is it you two agents are not affected by these, these disgusting pests?"

Shrugging his shoulders, Rosenburg answered. "No idea, Mr. President." Turning back to the wheel, he drove the vehicle toward the helipad. Not a word was spoken within the confines of the car. All eyes peered out at the darkening mass.

Within a matter of minutes the Suburban arrived at its destination. Marine One's rotors whipped through the air. The sheer force of wind generated by the chopper kept the gnats at bay. It brought a cheerful shout from the First Lady.

"Thank God for small favors," she hollered over the deafening noise.

Not willing to acknowledge her glee, the President merely bolted for the awaiting chopper. Ra Farman closely followed. Agent Bullington dutifully escorted the First Lady from the vehicle to Marine One, as an assigned marine helped her ascend into the chopper.

The pilot wasted no time lifting off, leaving Agents Rosenburg and Bullington far below.

Once inside, the sound proof interior helped calm everyone's nerves. Except one. Trying his best to maintain composure, the President fumed on the inside. Glancing briefly at Ra, he was amazed by his friend's unruffled demeanor.

Sensing that the President was about to unleash, Ra quickly turned towards the President's ear. "Shall we discuss this when we arrive back at the White House, Mr. President?" The glare in his eyes conveyed more than his words.

Taking a deep breath, the President replied. "Yes, we'll talk then."

Relaxing his body, Ra stared blankly ahead. His mind worked at a feverish pace. Someone was going to pay for this. And they would be squashed like a tiny gnat.

On the ground, Agents Bullington and Rosenburg stared in disbelief. As quickly as the gnats converged on Camp David, they suddenly disappeared. The creatures were nowhere to be seen.

"You think they followed Marine One?" Bullington joked.

"You know as well as I," said Rosenburg. "Let's be honest. This was an act of God."

"Maybe so," Agent Bullington gestured with both hands. "But where'd they go?"

Rosenburg opened the driver's door to the Suburban. Staring over the hood at his fellow agent, he opened his mouth. Then he quickly closed it.

"What? No opinion on where they disappeared?"

Grinning, Rosenburg replied. "Who am I to question? Far as I'm concerned, I hope I never see those pests again."

Bullington took a few strides toward the passenger door. Looking around, he half mumbled. "Which ones?"

FIFTY ONE

San Diego, CA

A warm breeze flowed through the peaceful neighborhood of the Jeffers' residence. What had been a warmer than normal day for southern California was now the perfect front porch weather to socialize with neighbors.

Mollie Mae loved interacting with people in her neighborhood. A common bond was felt throughout the community. The warmth from Mollie Mae made her home the place to gather. The fact that she gave so much of herself was what made her so special. And what made her an incredible grandparent to Jeffey. But the one thing Mollie Mae craved, especially at the end of the day, was interaction with other adults. Her friends sensed this, and the porch gatherings fulfilled this need.

Polly from next door was Mollie Mae's best friend. Hardly a day went by that Polly and Mollie Mae didn't chat. As the wife of a preacher, with all their kids grown and gone, Polly went out of her way to look after the Jeffers.

Whether sitting on Mollie Mae's porch or sitting next to her during service the two friends had a strong bond. Tonight, they sat in comfortable chairs keeping watch over the busy neighborhood street.

It didn't take long before Jeffey burst through the open front door. In his haste he nearly ran pass the two ladies as he skidded to a halt near the porch steps.

"Child, what's gotten into you?" Mollie Mae called out.

Clearly agitated, Jeffey faced his grandmother. "I saw him, I saw him, M & M." Jeffey could hardly contain himself.

"Saw who?" Polly interrupted.

"Jeffey, you need to calm yourself," Mollie Mae said. "When you've calmed down you can tell me."

Jeffey started bouncing. His head nearly hit the porch ceiling.

"Good gracious, Jeffey. Yer gonna put a hole in that roof," Polly added.

Standing to her feet, Mollie Mae did the only thing she could. Grabbing Jeffey's right hand with both of hers, she held on till he slowly stopped jumping. Finally Jeffey focused on her face. His eyes lit up with excitement.

"Child, I'm getting too old to keep doing this." Releasing his hand, she took a step back.

"Tall man, it was Tall Man, M & M. He's mighty mad."

"Who in the dickens is Tall Man?" Polly asked.

Mollie Mae took a seat next to her friend and motioned for Jeffey to sit. He promptly plopped down on the floor. His gangly legs crossed as best he could.

Focusing on Jeffey, Mollie Mae met his eyes. "Jeffey, who did you see and where?"

"It was Tall Man," Jeffey said. He turned his attention away from Mollie Mae.

Nudging Mollie Mae, Polly asked in a whisper. Mae, who's this tall fella he keeps talking bout?"

"Last time he mentioned him, Jeffey said something about the arches. To be honest, I really don't know."

Immediately Jeffey became more agitated. Rocking back and forth, eyes shut, Jeffey mumbled something.

Leaning forward, Mollie Mae was inches from Jeffey's face. "What did you see, child? Who's Tall Man?"

"Evil, evil, Beelzebub," he blurted. Jeffey rocked more frantically than before.

Jumping to her feet, Polly reached out her right hand and laid it on Jeffey's shoulder. She stopped his motion in the process. Polly turned to face her friend and exclaimed. "Quickly, Mae. Lay hands on his body. We need to pray."

Both women held Jeffey as best they could. Tears streamed down his face.

"Lord Jesus," Polly cried out. "Remove these images of the evil one. Comfort this young man's soul. Satan has no authority over this boy, Lord. By your word, he must flee his presence."

Jeffey's rocking ceased, but the tears continued to flow. Mollie Mae held Jeffey and soothed him with words of comfort. Polly prayed silently in the spirit.

"It's okay now, M & M," Jeffey startled her. The tears had stopped. He was Jeffey once again. Standing to his feet he looked down at Mollie Mae. "I'm gonna play in my room." Off he went as if nothing ever happened.

Still on their knees, both ladies glanced in each other's direction.

"How did you know?" Mollie Mae asked.

"The word he used, Beelzebub. It's another name for Satan." Pausing, Polly added. "Jeffey just needed the power of the Holy Spirit to take control. That's all."

Reaching her arms out to embrace her dear friend, it was Mollie Mae's turn for tears to flow. Composing herself, Mollie Mae replied. "I should have figured it out the first time he said that name."

"The first time?" Polly asked.

"A while back, he said something about the Tall Man. He used that name."

Rising to her feet, Polly offered her hand to Mollie Mae. "Mae, we need to talk to Vernon about this." Taking a step toward the stairs, Polly paused. "There's a lot more to this than we know, Mae. I just feel it in my bones."

FIFTY TWO

The White House

Upon landing, the President immediately retreated to the situation room. Excusing himself from the First Lady, the President along with Ra closed the doors behind them. They left two agents to stand guard outside.

Reaching for the first thing to come into focus, President Pollard grasped an empty carafe. He hurled it across the room. The object bounced off a wall landing near Ra's feet.

Immediately the doors flew open. The two agents rushed into the room. They scanned the surroundings. Within seconds they stood before the President poised to ask the obvious question.

"Everything fine, Mr. President?" Agent Lex Parker towered over Stuart Pollard.

"Yes, yes agent," the President answered. His face reddened from embarrassment.

Stepping before agent Parker, Ra Farman gazed directly into the agents eyes. "A carafe was simply knocked from its place, Agent Parker." Placing his hand on Agent Parker's shoulder, Ra attempted to guide the agent toward the door.

Standing his ground, Agent Parker addressed the President. "Is there anything else, Mr. President?" Agent Parker glanced between the two men.

Still trying to compose himself, President Pollard meekly replied. "That'll be all."

As the two agents exited the room, the President took a seat at the massive table before him. Retrieving the carafe from the floor, Ra approached the President from the opposite side. He leaned against the table with his left hand. Ra slammed the carafe down directly in front of the President.

Startled by Ra's actions, the President quickly sat upright.

Glaring down at the President, Ra leaned on both hands. "Now that I have your attention, Stuart...maybe we can concentrate on what needs to be done next."

The President opened his mouth ready to reply. Then he quickly glanced downward, away from the man's gaze.

Ra took his time settling into a chair across from the President. Folding his hands upon the table, he sat in silence. Looking up, the President saw a look of determination upon his friend's face. Instantly Stuart Pollard knew something was about to happen.

"Tell me again about the conversation you had with your former press secretary." Ra's eyes burned with intensity.

Leaning into the table, the President replied. "It was a few days before we left for Camp David. She tried to warn me that a certain pastor had been in touch with her."

Gesturing with his hand, Ra asked. "This pastor she spoke of, his name was Conley?"

"Jacob Conley. Out of St. Louis."

Ra nodded. "This man, he sounds familiar."

"He's been on our radar," the President replied.

"What exactly did he say?" Tilting his head slightly, Ra added. "And why did he go through her?"

Shifting in his seat, the President answered. "I suspect he felt she was the best way to get a message to me."

Ra remained silent.

"Here's the interesting part," the President met Ra's gaze. "He knew what was going to happen. What happened today, up in the mountains."

"You're saying this pastor knew that the camp would be deluged with parasites?"

Taking a deep breath, the President answered. "This Pastor Conley told Anne that Camp David would be overrun by gnats. He also added that this would be the third plague to occur."

Ra burned with rage as he leaped to his feet. With his back turned to the President, he glanced up at the ceiling. "If He thinks a few plagues are going to make us change our direction. Then He is sorely mistaken."

Turning about, Ra faced the President.

"But it's not just this pastor who thinks this," the President commented.

"Do you take me for a fool?" Ra glared.

"Well, no. Not at all," the President stammered.

Leaning in toward the President, Ra added. "I know it is God, who is speaking. Just like you know it's not me!"

Hesitating, the President asked. "So what exactly should we do?"

"I don't anticipate a few plagues affecting our direction, Stuart. I have plans to meet with the association. When I return, we'll turn up the heat.

The President stood and reached out his hand. For the first time since they arrived, President Pollard smiled. "What would you like me to do?"

"Set a meeting with Pastor Conley, here at the White House." Retracting his hand, Ra strolled toward the exit. "Only, don't let him know I'll be in attendance."

FIFTY THREE

St. Louis, MO / First Christian Church

Reaching for the phone, Getta noticed that there was no caller ID displayed on the readout. That's odd she thought. She answered after the third ring.

"Pastor Conley's office. How may I help you?"

There was a brief pause before Getta heard a voice on the other end.

"Yes, this is Martin Ayers. Chief of staff for President Pollard. Is Pastor Conley available?"

A multitude of thoughts raced through Getta's mind. Is this a prank or is it legit? It's amazing how quickly one can react when motivated properly. The simple fact that no ID was displayed and the caller identified himself from the White House was all she needed.

Responding cautiously, Getta answered. "I'm sorry, Mr. Ayers, Pastor Conley is not in." Deciding to wait for a reply Getta offered no additional information.

"I see," Mr. Ayers replied. "Whom am I speaking with?"

Slightly taken back, Getta answered. "This is Getta Carter, Pastor Conley's executive assistant."

"Very well, Ms. Carter. May I leave a message for Pastor Conley?"

Getta reached for a pen. "You sure can."

"I have been instructed by the President that he would like to schedule a meeting with Pastor Conley at his earliest convenience."

"Really," Getta interrupted him.

"Yes, Ms. Carter. As soon as possible."

Getta was about to speak again, when Martin Ayers continued. "Please have him call me directly and we will make arrangements for his travel to DC, as well as lodging."

Still startled by this sudden request, Getta blurted out. "May I ask why? You know, just so Pastor has an idea of what to expect."

"I'll give you my direct number, Ms. Carter. Please have him call me...if that is acceptable."

The condescending tone was all it took for Getta to get the information and end the call. She wondered what was in store for Pastor Jacob.

Getta immediately dialed Jacob's cell.

"Hey, I'm pulling into the church parking lot right now. What's up?"

Taking a deep breath, Getta replied. "Pastor Jacob, I just hung up with the White House." Getta paused to hear his response.

"No kidding, the White House?" Jacob exited his vehicle and headed for the church doors.

"I'm serious, Pastor," Getta urged.

"Hold your thought, Getta. I'll see you in a minute." Jacob hit the disconnect on his cell. He glanced up and saw one of the leaders at First Christian, Mike Brothers.

As he approached Jacob, Mike threw his arms around Jacob's shoulders. "Hey pastor," Mike smiled. "You look troubled."

"Just a thousand things going on at once," Jacob smiled as best he could.

Taking a step back, Mike continued to search Jacob's face. Sensing that this was not the time to probe, Mike merely commented. "You've seemed preoccupied lately."

Jacob glanced at the floor, then back up at his friend.

Placing his hand on Jacob's shoulder, Mike asked. "Is everything all right? Better still, is there anything I can do for you?"

Jacob suddenly realized how daunting his role was becoming. Sure he had Linda, Jim Calhoun, and Ben Palmer's support. But, would that be enough? The fact that only a few minutes ago Getta informed him that the White House had called, verified the battle was about to begin.

Jacob realized that God had put Mike Brothers in front of him for a reason. That reason suddenly became very clear.

"You know what, Mike," Jacob spoke softly. "There is something you can do for me."

Grinning at Jacob, Mike already knew.

"Gather the intercessors, Mike. The war is about to begin and I need all my troops praying."

"I will handle it." Nodding once, Mike walked away.

A tear formed in Jacob's eye. He mouthed the words, "thank you, Lord. Now I know I'll be ready."

The clarity that Jacob felt faded quickly as he entered Getta's office. Seeing Jacob, Getta sprang from her seat.

"I didn't think you'd ever get here." Getta followed him into his office. Sitting in a chair across from his desk, Getta urged. "Sit, sit, I'll give you all the details."

Jacob never tired of her enthusiasm. Getta's exuberance was like the puppy he never had. Placing his elbows on his desk, Jacob waited patiently. Getta looked over her memo pad.

Glancing up, Getta said, "okay. It was actually the President's Chief of Staff that called. A, Mr. Ayers." She looked down at the memo. "The President would like you to come to the White House and meet with him, according to his Chief of Staff." Getta paused. "Oh, and they will make flight and hotel arrangements for you as well."

Jacob grinned. "You mean I don't get to stay in the Lincoln room?"

Sighing, Getta replied. "So Pastor, what do you think this is all about?"

Sitting back, Jacob started tapping his pencil on the edge of his desk. "It means God finally got their attention." Jacob set the pencil down and held out his hand. "It also means I need to get prepared."

Tilting her head slightly, Getta asked. "Pastor, if you don't mind me asking what exactly are you going to do?"

"I'm gonna obey God and take on the enemy...sometimes we need the help of others in order to achieve what He lays on our heart." Blinking rapidly, Jacob added. "I cannot have any crack in my spirit that Satan might take advantage of."

Frowning, Getta responded. "This is much bigger than anyone can imagine, isn't it?"

Nodding his head in agreement, Jacob asked. "You ever heard the expression, different levels, different devils?"

Getta simply shrugged her shoulders.

"It may have been something Smith Wigglesworth once wrote. Anyway, the saying means the greater the challenges we face, the more powerful the enemy will be."

Squirming in her seat, Getta said. "Well, that's a scary thought."

"If you think about it, Washington is the most powerful city in the world. So it stands to reason that the powers of darkness will be enormous in that area."

Noticing Getta's eyebrows peak, Jacob added. "Consequently, if I'm going up against something I've never encountered before. I'd better be ready."

Getta's demeanor shifted as she sensed the seriousness in Jacob's tone. "Pastor, is there anything I can do for you?"

Realizing this was the second time this morning that someone asked that question, Jacob closed his eyes. He remained silent meditating for a few seconds. Empowered by the Holy Spirit, he slowly opened his eyes and met Getta's. Jacob then simply replied.

"Just pray, Getta. Just pray."

FIFTY FOUR

Washington DC / Senator Hank Dugan's office

"What!" Senator Dugan exclaimed into his phone. Rolling his eyes, he glanced at his aide, Steffi Waters. She was seated across from his desk. "You gotta tell the President, that's not doable."

Shaking his head, the Senator frowned. He continued to listen. "All right, I'll see what I can do," he added, before hanging up.

"What's up?" Steffi asked.

"I know I have to toe the party line, but this administration is on a collision course."

"Let me guess," Steffi grinned. "Chief of Staff Ayers wants the senate to initiate a new piece of legislation. And you get to be the bearer."

"Yeah, something like that."

Leaning forward, Steffi inquired. "Anything I can do?"

"Not unless you have a great rapport with the Christian Coalition…and they'll listen to your every word."

Resting her elbows on the Senator's desk, Steffi asked. "What is it with the President and his vindictiveness toward that group?"

The Senator wondered about the question, but didn't respond.

"I mean, I don't really care about their problems. But the President seems intent on destroying all their influence. Isn't he?"

"That's just it, Steffi," Senator Dugan shrugged. "You and I both know it's not him pulling the strings."

Sensing that the Senator wasn't about to disclose the topic of his phone conversation, Steffi stood from her seat. "I gotta admit, Senator. That Farman guy gives me the creeps."

"That may be so, but he definitely has the President's ear." Senator Dugan reached for his phone. Mumbling, he added. "And I don't dare cross him."

FIFTY FIVE

The White House

Martin Ayers was feverishly red lining a document when his phone rang. Glancing at the caller ID, he set his pen down and answered.

"This is Martin Ayers."

"Hello Mr. Ayers, this is Pastor Jacob Conley. I received a message that you wanted to speak with me?"

"Pastor Conley, how nice of you to call me back. As you well know, I am President Pollard's Chief of Staff."

Jacob was barely able to reply, "uh ha."

"And the President has asked me to set up a meeting with you at your earliest convenience."

"That's what I understand," Jacob replied. He was about to ask why when Mr. Ayers continued.

"Would you be available next Monday? We have a driver ready to pick you up. We'll fly you out of Scott Air Force base first thing in the morning."

Finally Martin Ayers allowed Jacob time to respond to this one-sided conversation.

"Mr. Ayers, I can appreciate the President's schedule. I don't even know why he wants to see me, let alone if I'm even available." Jacob paused, before adding. "After all, I do believe you said at my convenience?"

With a slight air of condensation, Martin Ayers replied. "I can assure you, Pastor Conley, that the President has good cause to schedule a meeting with you."

Jacob thought for a second before responding. "So what you're telling me is that you don't really know why President Pollard requested this meeting. Would that be correct?"

"I don't question the President, sir." Mr. Ayers paused to let his statement sink in. "Now, according to your schedule will you or will you not be available next Monday?"

Jacob glanced at his calendar and realized there was nothing too urgent that he couldn't reschedule. Plus, if God wanted this meeting to take place, who was he to stand in the way of the timing.

Taking a deep breath, Jacob replied. "I apologize, Mr. Ayers. I most certainly will be available this Monday."

"Very good, Pastor Conley," Martin Ayers responded as dignified as he could. "I'll fax over the complete itinerary. If you have any pressing questions feel free to call me back."

"Thank you." Jacob waited till he heard the President's chief of staff hang up. He shook his head in amazement. "Lord God, what am I getting myself into?"

Jacob stood. He opened his door and popped his head in Getta's office. "Getta, you should receive a fax shortly from Martin Ayers, from the White House."

Eyes widening, Getta replied. "A fax from the white house?"

Holding his finger up to his lips, Jacob responded. "For now, let's keep this as quiet as possible." Grinning, he added. "Oh and Getta, I need to clear my schedule for Monday." Jacob retreated back to his office. He knew he had to do some major strategizing over the weekend.

FIFTY SIX

The White House

Martin Ayers strolled toward the Oval Office knowing that the President wanted verbal confirmation on Monday's meeting. He still wasn't sure why this meeting was going to take place. He had every intention of finding out. After all, he was the President's Chief of Staff.

As Martin entered the room, he saw the President wave him over to one of the couches. Stopping briefly, Martin saw a familiar face. Setting some papers on the coffee table, he smiled briefly.

"Mr. Ayers, how pleasant to see you again," Ra Farman grinned.

Offering his hand over the table, Martin waited patiently for Ra to stand and properly greet him. Just as the moment hit the peak of awkward, President Pollard joined them.

"Sit, sit, Martin," the President pointed. He sat in the wing back between the two facing couches. "You bring me good news, I hope?"

"Yes, Mr. President," Martin focused completely on the President. Reaching for the papers he set on the table, Martin glanced down. "Pastor Conley will arrive here at approximately 1:00 PM, and he is scheduled to fly back..."

"Good, very good," Ra Farman interrupted. "That's exactly what we needed to know." Ra waited for a response from the President.

"And I'll inform my staff, no interruptions Monday afternoon." The President nodded. Turning his head to the left, the President addressed his Chief of Staff. "Martin, will you see to it that this request is known by all?"

"Well, certainly, Mr. President," he stammered. "But may I ask what this meeting is all about?"

Martin could feel a cold stare from Ra bearing down on him. Not backing down, he sat back waiting for a reply.

"As my Chief of Staff, you may certainly ask," the President answered. Glancing first at Ra, then back at Martin, the President continued. "Martin, we've had some concerns about this Pastor Conley."

"Oh? What kind of concerns, Mr. President?"

Leaning forward in his seat, Ra spoke before President Pollard had a chance to answer. "It seems Pastor Conley may be part of a coalition trying to stir up trouble against this administration."

Searching for confirmation, Martin glanced at the President. Nodding in agreement, the President focused his attention back to Ra.

"So, you see, Martin," Ra added. "We feel it's necessary to meet with Pastor Conley, before his group gets out of control."

Sensing that he wasn't getting the full story, Martin took the opportunity to end this one-sided conversation. He'd do some digging on his own. Rising to leave, Martin simply replied. "Very well, sir." Addressing the President directly, he added. "Let me know if there is anything else I can do."

The President stood and reached out his hand. "Thank you, Martin. I always know I can count on you."

Ra remained seated. He waited for Martin to leave and for the President to sit down.

"We must keep an eye on him," Ra spoke.

Staring at the door and then back at Ra, President Pollard simply nodded in agreement.

Ra placed his hand on the President's right knee. "Now, let us prepare ourselves for Monday's meeting."

FIFTY SEVEN

St. Louis, MO / First Christian Church-Sunday morning

Approaching the stage, Jacob felt an incredible presence of the Holy Spirit. As the last song was winding down, he leaned toward his worship leader, Carson. Jacob whispered into his ear.

Carson nodded at his worship team. Then he played his keyboard in a subdued tone. With the music at a gentle lull, Jacob stood silently in prayer. The congregation of almost two thousand people waited upon his every word.

Grinning with arms raised heavenward, Jacob laughed out loud. "Yes, yes, precious Holy Spirit, fill this sanctuary with your presence."

Feeding off Jacob's energy, scores of people cried out in the spirit. Before long the building rocked with excitement.

Jacob motioned with his hands, gathering everyone to silence. "Good morning, precious saints." Pumping his fist into the air, Jacob continued. "Oh, don't you feel it? Can you sense His Holy presence?"

Jacob waited for the whistles and hand claps to die down before he continued. "The Lord has told me to tell you something very special today. Something incredible has happened to me over the course of a few months."

Gesturing for everyone to take a seat, Jacob leaned against a stool. "Some time ago, I guess it was actually several years' back, I was awakened from a dream. Well, it was more like a nightmare, if you will, than a dream. At the time it was very troubling.

Stepping away from the stool, Jacob paused. "In this dream I was bound by some unknown force. I couldn't move…I couldn't even cry out. Then as I glanced down at my rigid body, I saw what it was that had me in its grasp."

Jacob descended to the next level of the stage. He stopped abruptly. "Coiled around me from my feet up to my neck was a giant snake. It's ugly head, bigger than my own, was poised in front of my face. The more I tried to break free, the tighter the snake wrapped about me."

Shaking his head, Jacob paused. "I felt helpless in its grasp." Jacob held up his right hand. "How many know that snake was Satan? His intention was to keep me in place?" Scanning the audience, Jacob then continued. "As I prayed to God, I suddenly woke from this horrible dream. Then I rolled out of bed. I fell to my knees and cried out in prayer."

Up until now, I shared this dream with only a few others. Now, let me tell you why I share it with you." Jumping in anticipation, Jacob glanced about. People were riveted to their seats waiting on his next word. "Saints, for the past few years I have felt like something was holding me back. For every step we took forward, corporately, we seemed to be halted in our growth. Halted in our vision."

"I only say that because the church can't move forward if the leadership doesn't lead the way. As the head of this church, I just couldn't seem to get going."

Jumping in excitement, and grinning like it was Christmas day, Jacob screamed out. "But Hallelujah!" He pumped his fist in the air. "The snake is gone!"

Rising to their feet, multitudes of the congregation shouted in praise. Jacob did his best trying to settle the roar. Finally, after several moments, the noise from the crowd lessened. A single voice cried out. "Preach on, Pastor."

Turning to acknowledge him, Jacob responded. "I think I will. Here's the beautiful part. Over the past several weeks I have sensed a new direction…a new shift in the atmosphere here at First Christian." Pumping both arms over head, Jacob added. "And I have never felt freer, more in tune with the Holy Spirit, than I do now."

Jacob ascended the steps. He took a seat on the stool. "Here's the confirmation that brought it all together. About a week ago, I got a call from Jim Calhoun. How many of you know that Jim truly has a prophetic gift?"

Scores of hands were raised as Jacob scanned the audience. "Anyway, Jim called and said, 'Jake, I had a vision I must share with you.' So I said, okay. What did you see? He says. 'In this vision, I saw you preaching at First Christian and really speaking the word, when something flashed by me.'"

Shifting his weight on the stool, Jacob paused. "What was it?' I asked. Well, at this point, Jim's voice got real animated as he said. 'It was a snake, a giant serpent.'"

Leaping from the top tier to the lower tier of the stage, Jacob stood motionless. "He then said. 'Its tail was at the bottom of your feet, Jacob. Its head flew by me. The snake headed down the aisle and out through the doors.'"

Once again, people jumped to their feet and sang out. Shouting above the crowd, Jacob added. "But I knew it was gone! Jim confirmed it was gone! Now we all know it's gone. Brother, let me tell you, nothing's gonna hold us back now!"

Jacob waited for the frenzy to die down. Then he closed his eyes, and silently prayed. Jacob realized he needed to address a serious matter. Standing quietly, he waited upon the Lord to fill him with the right words.

Jacob knew how much he loved the people seated before him. This was his family. He had leaders he could truly count on. He had people who would pray alongside him. It had been a long process gaining the trust of the congregation. Now it was time to share with them the Lord's new vision for the church.

"I told you the story of how I was set free, only to share with you another dream that God has set before my eyes. You see, this new vision also involves you." Sweeping his hand across the audience, Jacob zeroed in on the eyes of the people.

"How many know that this nation is changing right before our eyes? Laws have been enacted and rights have been taken away that affect Christianity like never before. Now, I have never been one to preach about politics." Chuckling, Jacob continued, "at least from the pulpit. But the rules have changed."

Pacing in front of the congregation, Jacob added. "We have an administration that is determined to bring Christianity to its knees and to govern from a socialist standpoint."

Stopping suddenly, Jacob faced the audience. "I know there are bound to be some who disagree with me. There will inevitably be some who choose to leave this church. But I tell you God has called us to make a stand. He will provide signs and wonders for those who choose to see. Because of all that, I know that I know that I know, there's no way I'm gonna back down."

Jacob spoke even louder. He could sense the people starting to stir. "For that matter, I'm moving forward, for God has called me to help start a revival of faith. We're going to start an awakening right here in St. Louis. One that will surely send a message that this is God's country. And Christianity is here to stay. Romans 1:16 says. 'For I am not ashamed of the gospel of Christ: for it is the power of God unto salvation to everyone that believeth.'"

Shouts of encouragement rang throughout the sanctuary. A thunderous applause reverberated. Raising his hands to quell the response, Jacob waited. In a hushed tone he whispered. "Thank you, Jesus. Thank you." Jacob's praises started to grow louder and louder until the only sound heard was Jacob glorifying the Lord.

"Precious saints, here is what I ask you to do. At the request of the White House, I am meeting with President Pollard tomorrow afternoon. Believe me; I was quite surprised at the invitation. Honestly, I don't really know what is on his agenda. I can assure you, he's going to know mine."

"So from now until tomorrow afternoon-no, strike that. Make it starting now, please pray that God gives me wisdom and favor. May the Lord allow us to create a revival in this nation like none before. May He supernaturally impart the power of the Holy Spirit to engage the enemy, whenever and wherever so that victory is ours. So that thy will be done. Those opposing us will know that we will not stand down."

Jacob signaled for the worship team to start playing again. People leapt to their feet shouting their approval. Jacob felt a rush of relief flow from him knowing that he now had a multitude of saints praying for this cause.

Hushing both the music and the many voices, Jacob added one more thing. "I leave you with this quote by the great John G. Lake. 'Men have said that the cross of Christ was not a heroic thing, but I want to tell you that the cross of Jesus Christ has put more heroism into the souls of men than any other event in human history.' I say, let us be heroes too."

By the power of the Holy Spirit, Jacob knew he had God's blessing. By the support of his congregation, he knew the awakening had begun.

FIFTY EIGHT

Washington DC / the Executive Office

Jacob was about as prayed up as he could possibly be. By the power of the Holy Spirit he was no longer nervous. He glanced at his watch. It was twenty minutes and counting waiting to see the President. Jacob grinned at Jenny Davis, the President's administrative assistant. Not once did she try to disrupt Jacob while he was deep in prayer. Her eyes suggested that she wanted to.

Jacob decided one thing. If he was going to be kept waiting, then the best way to pass time was to be in communication with his best friend. Once again, he called upon the Lord.

"Pastor Conley," Jenny abruptly announced. "Excuse me, sir!"

Glancing up Jacob saw Jenny standing before him. He stood as well. "I guess I'm up?"

Taking the lead, Jenny moved toward the northeast door to the Oval Office. Reaching with her left hand, she opened the door inward and gestured to Jacob to enter.

Jacob paused before entering, "thank you, Ms. Davis." He then entered into a sanctuary he had only read about and seen in movies. Taking in everything, Jacob spoke under his breath. "So this is the Oval Office."

Sensing Jacob's awe and replying to a comment not meant to be heard; Ra Farman stepped past President Pollard. Putting a clear emphasis on his statement, Ra spoke out. "Yes Pastor Conley, this is the office of the most powerful man on earth."

Surprised by the forwardness of this stranger, Jacob's eyes darted between the President and his guest. Within seconds Ra stood directly in front of Jacob. He blocked his view of President Pollard.

"Allow me to introduce myself," Ra offered. "I am Ra Farman, the President's closest advisor."

"My pleasure," Jacob retrieved his hand. Turning to engage the President, Jacob felt a hand guide him toward the sitting area. Sensing a slight chill from the encounter, Jacob stood his ground and waited for President Pollard to greet him.

"Pastor Conley," President Pollard reached out. "How good of you to join us."

Forcing a grin, Jacob replied. "I appreciate the invitation. Although I must admit, I'm not quite sure why you called me."

"Surely you do," Ra interrupted. This time he left both men behind and took a seat on a sofa facing them.

"Please, Pastor Conley," President Pollard gestured toward the sofa opposite Ra. Clearing his throat, the President sat in a wing back between the two men.

Barely moving his lips, Jacob prayed silently, waiting for this mysterious meeting to start. He hoped to escape the chill he sensed in the air. Jacob focused his attention on the President.

Expecting President Pollard to at least acknowledge him, Jacob could tell that something was not right. It was as if time was frozen and everyone but him was moving in slow motion. Yet, that was the least of Jacob's concerns. Grinning at him across the way was Ra Farman. And he was not alone.

FIFTY NINE

San Diego, CA

By the time the phone rang for the ninth time, Mollie Mae was startled from her nap. She hadn't meant to fall asleep but watching Wheel of Fortune sometimes had that effect on her.

Groggily she glanced at the cuckoo on the wall and noticed it read 10:32. She reached for the phone, wondering who was so persistent in trying to call her. She didn't believe in answering machines and figured anyone who hadn't given up by now must really be desperate to reach her.

"Hello," she positioned the phone as tightly against her left ear as possible.

"Ms. Jeffers!" The voice called out frantically. "It's Gail Masters, from Lincoln High."

Mollie quickly straightened up in her chair. She realized something must be wrong with Jeffey.

"Jeffey had an incident, Ms. Jeffers. But we were able to get him to calm down."

Hearing the urgency in her voice, Mollie Mae immediately asked. "Well, what happened to him?"

"We just don't know, ma'am. His teacher, Mr. Patrick, said Jeffey suddenly lost control and started screaming at the top of his lungs."

"What, how?"

"This happened about five minutes ago. It took four teachers to restrain him, Ms. Jeffers."

"Dear God, how is he now?"

"That's just it, Ms. Jeffers. He won't communicate with or acknowledge any one in the room." Gail's voice paused for a moment before continuing. "It's just not like Jeffey, Ms. Jeffers. He's, definitely not himself."

Mollie Mae gripped the phone tighter.

"Ma'am, is there any way you could come down here? I know it's not easy for you to get around, but I could come get you."

The fact that the school urged her to come brought Mollie Mae back to her senses. "Yes, of course I'll come. But are you sure he's alright for now?"

Mollie Mae could hear Gail speaking with someone at the school. She couldn't make out what was being said, but she thought she recognized the voice.

"Ms. Jeffers, this is Mr. Patrick."

"Oh Mr. Patrick, how is my Jeffey doing?"

Mr. Patrick asked Mollie Mae a question in response. "Ms. Jeffers, Gail Masters is on her way to your home to bring you here. Is that okay?"

"Yes of course," Mollie answered.

"Good, Ms. Jeffers. Right now I think the best thing we can do for Jeffey is have you come here. Try to talk with him directly."

"I just want to help my Jeffey."

"Of course ma'am. In the meantime can I ask you a question?"

Dabbing at the tears which had started down her cheeks, Mollie Mae said. "Why yes, anything."

"Before this all happened with Jeffey he was perfectly fine. But out of nowhere he lurched forward across a table and started flailing his arms."

"Why, Mr. Patrick?"

"Well, Ms. Jeffers, I was hoping you could tell us."

"I'm so sorry, Mr. Patrick. I really have no idea...but then again he's acted a little odd the last few months."

"How so, ma'am?"

"Well, Jeffey has had some disturbing dreams and visions."

"What kind of dreams?"

Mollie Mae suddenly realized this was not a topic she was comfortable talking about. Her hesitation was noted by Mr. Patrick.

"Ms. Jeffers, if there is anything you can tell me about Jeffey? It might be helpful."

Again, Mollie Mae paused. How does one talk about the enemy to someone from the secular world? These visions could be understood by a person with faith, but...

"Ms. Jeffers, perhaps it would be helpful if I tell you exactly what Jeffey was saying."

Beating him to the punch, Mollie Mae asked. "Did Jeffey shout out the word 'Beelzebub'?"

This time it was Mr. Patrick's turn to take pause. Only his answer was not what Mollie Mae expected.

SIXTY

The Oval Office

Blinking rapidly, as if trying to clear his vision, Jacob was stunned by the sight before him. Gathered on each side of Ra Farman were several of the most hideous creatures he had ever seen. Clearly they were meant to intimidate him. Or at least try.

In the spiritual realm Jacob understood the Holy Spirit was allowing him to see these demons, but in the natural world it was still disturbing. He tried his best to remain calm.

Jacob quickly diverted his eyes from the gathering over to President Pollard. It was obvious the President was not seeing the same thing as Jacob. At least at this point, everything was back to real time.

As the President gestured to Ra for him to speak, some of the demons inched their way closer to Jacob.

"Pastor Conley," Ra's voice boomed across the room. "We have become concerned by the movement afoot."

Jacob focused his attention back on the President. He became alarmed when he saw President Pollard nod his head in agreement. Tiny demons whispered into his ear. The more they danced about upon his shoulders, the more the President's head shifted back and forth.

All the while, Ra grinned with delight. He waited for a reply from Jacob.

Jacob quickly rose to his feet. Pointing his finger directly at Ra, Jacob spoke out with authority. "Don't you realize that the weapons we fight with are not the weapons of this world?"

Not expecting an immediate response from either man, Jacob continued. "On the contrary they have divine power to demolish strongholds, II Corinthians 10:4-5."

The demonic presence intensified around the President. Ra continued his sinister grin.

"This is absurd!" Jacob lifted his hands toward Heaven. "By the power of Jesus Christ, I command all evil spirits to flee this instant."

A screeching sound that only he seemed to be able to hear emanated throughout the room. Jacob then witnessed the power of the Holy Spirit as the creatures in front of him instantly vanished.

"Do you think that's going to change anything, Pastor?" Ra countered in a condescending tone.

Rising to his feet, President Pollard glanced directly at Jacob. "Pastor Conley, there's no need to be insulting." The President stared at Jacob as if he was looking at a mad man. "I can assure you, Mr. Farman and I have good intentions for this meeting. Certainly not evil."

"Exactly," Ra interjected. His eyes glowed momentarily.

Jacob realized he was being played by both people present. He sensed the President had no idea he was being manipulated. Jacob took his seat. He briefly closed his eyes and began to pray. At this point he didn't really care whether anyone else approved or not.

"Now, if you are ready Pastor Conley, perhaps we can continue this meeting." President Pollard spoke again.

Glancing about the room, making sure all evil spirits were kept in check, Jacob grinned and nodded his head. Looking directly at Ra, he replied. "You may masquerade as an angel of light, but I know better."

"There's no masquerade here, Pastor." Ra countered. "I certainly have nothing to hide."

"Gentlemen," President Pollard interrupted. "Why don't we cut to the chase?" Focusing on Jacob, he continued. "It has come to our attention that a potential uprising, if you will, from certain religious factions are under way."

Jacob tilted his head, as if he was surprised.

"Surely you are aware that the Christian Coalition is upset with recent administration policies, Pastor Conley?"

"Oh, I'm aware of the actions against Christians, Mr. Farman. But, I have no idea what this has to do with me."

Ra pointed directly at Jacob. "Have you not become a leader of sorts for this group of fanatics?"

"Fanatics!" Jacob sat forward. "Do you suggest Christians take a back seat to White House politics, just because this administration chooses to discriminate against them?"

"Not all people," Ra smirked.

"Then who are you referring to?"

"Gentlemen, this doesn't need to get ugly," the President interrupted.

"With all due respect, Mr. President, from where I'm sitting this has been nothing but ugly." Jacob continued to stare at Ra, waiting for him to answer.

"Pastor, there's no need to be uncivil." Ra answered in a condescending tone. "What would your father think of this?"

Jacob felt like a knife had been pierced through his heart. How, and why, were the thoughts running through his mind.

Clearly Ra knew he had struck a chord. "Surely Gideon Conley would be disappointed with his son addressing the President of the United States in such a manner?" Ra stated.

Memories of his dad cascaded through his mind. Jacob stared blankly straight ahead. Thoughts of Gideon Conley chastising his son for not trying hard enough at a little league game. Biting words from his father that he wasn't tough enough to play high school football. Abject disappointment when he had told him he was going to become a pastor.

Now it was Jacob's turn to sit mindlessly, while evil spirits moved closer. All the while, Ra Farman spoke louder and louder trying his best to beat Jacob's defenses.

Half way across the country, Jim Calhoun suddenly fell to his knees. He startled his assistant pastor in the process.

"Quickly, quickly," he cried out. "Start praying for Jacob Conley. Now!"

Prayers from Jim's office cried out. Staff members joined in. All they knew was that a beloved brother was in trouble. They knew they had to pray.

###

Jacob's body jerked forward in such a way that President Pollard shouted. "Pastor Conley, are you all right?"

Jacob locked eyes with pure evil. Collecting himself, he ignored all that was around him. Gathering a deep breath, softly he prayed to the Holy Spirit.

Appearing completely composed as if nothing happened, Jacob addressed Ra directly. "It doesn't matter what you say, or how you try to manipulate. The spirit of offense between me and my father is gone!"

Staring intently back at Jacob, Ra offered no words.

"I still believe there is one question yet to be answered?" Jacob looked from one man to the other, eventually focusing on Ra. "Exactly what religious group are you targeting, Mr. Farman?"

Perhaps he had underestimated Jacob Conley. Or perhaps the game was now in full swing. Either way, Ra remained unfazed.

"Why Pastor Conley," Ra smirked. "You knew the answer to that before you even got here."

Jacob paused before responding. Of course he knew the answer. He knew this entire meeting was but a ruse for intimidation. He also knew neither side was about to back down. The sole purpose for this meeting was to make it official. The battle line between light and dark had been drawn. Only one question remained.

"You're right, Mr. Farman." Jacob rose from his seat, suggesting it was time for him to leave. "Now, it's just a matter of who is going to back down first."

"Ah, but history has shown that Christianity doesn't have the backbone to stand for very long." Ra stood. He glared at Jacob.

236

Jacob returned his stare. "When we are weak, He is strong." Jacob paused, before addressing the President. He hoped he still had a chance of getting through to him. "Mr. President, this persecution can be stopped. It must be stopped."

Briefly the President had a faraway look in his eyes. It was as if he was contemplating what Jacob had said.

Jacob then noticed that Ra was staring intently at the President. A new spiritual battle was about to unfold, and Jacob knew he had to act. Within seconds, new demons appeared. They focused directly on President Pollard. His eyes started to glaze over.

"What are you called?" Jacob spoke promptly to the largest of the creatures. It stood no more than three feet tall, thin and gangly in shape. Its protruding dark leathery snout dripped with saliva. Its eyes were void of any life.

Turning its attention away from the President, the power spoke. "We are emptiers."

The demon took a step toward Jacob and snarled. "There is nothing you can do for this human. Nothing!"

Without pause, Jacob confronted the entity before him. "You have no power over me, darkness. I speak with the authority of Jesus Christ."

Backing off slightly, the emptier's raspy voice added. "For now, Jacob Conley. But, all it takes is a single crack." Gesturing toward its accomplices, the demon continued. "It is then we empty those of all hope, and joy. Things that are worthless in our world."

It was Jacob's turn to step forward. He was not there to debate with Satan. He knew it was time for this interaction to end. Approaching the President he stopped short and addressed the emptier one last time. "That's where you're wrong! By the power of prayer and the power of Christ all things can change." Pointing his right index finger, Jacob cried out. "By the blood of Jesus I command you to flee this man's presence. Now!"

Instantly, every demon vanished. Glancing back at Ra, Jacob stared defiantly. Ra simply grinned in return. Turning his attention to the President, Jacob paused before speaking. He watched as the President's demeanor changed from transfixed to focused.

Gesturing with his hands, Jacob asked. "Mr. President, are you familiar with God's judgment on Pharaoh's sin…when he refused to let the Israelites go?"

Standing rigid as a board, the President answered without any emotion at all. "Do not compare me to a Bible character from thousands of years ago."

Jacob shook his head in disappointment. "God has mercy on whom He wants to have mercy. But He hardens the heart of whom He wants to harden." Holding his hand out, Jacob added. "I pray you do the right thing."

Firmly grasping Jacob's hand, President Pollard ended the meeting. "You do what you have to, Pastor Conley…for I assure you, I'll do what I must."

SIXTY ONE

San Diego, CA

The office that Mollie Mae sat in was not at all what she expected. There were very few books on the shelves, and the ones she could make out seemed out of place. The cramped confines of the room were no more than ten by ten.

In front of the two mostly empty shelves stood a cluttered desk with a single wooden chair tucked beneath it. The hard plastic seat she patiently sat upon was brought in from another room. If the door had not been left open, Mollie thought for sure she would have passed out from the lack of air circulation.

"So this is what our tax dollars have amounted to," Mollie Mae mumbled.

"Afraid so, Ms. Jeffers." Mollie was startled by a male voice.

"Oh, Mr. Patrick," Mollie Mae blushed. "I hadn't expected anyone to hear."

Oliver Patrick squeezed in behind his desk and fought to pull his seat out from underneath. After briefly struggling to get situated, he grinned sheepishly at his guest.

Fortunately, Oliver stood no taller than five nine, and weighed less than one forty. But what Oliver Patrick lacked in physical stature he made up for in kindness. Mollie Mae was glad she was meeting with him.

Immediately recalling his manners Oliver extended his hand across the desk. He tried his best to half stand in doing so.

"Please, that's not necessary, Mr. Patrick." Mollie Mae briefly shook his hand.

Mr. Patrick quickly spoke up. "Let's talk about Jeffey."

"They said it was best if I didn't immediately see him." Mollie Mae's eyes conveyed sadness. "I guess I understand, since he's now calm, but..."

"Truthfully," Mr. Patrick interrupted. "I wanted to be able to speak to you before you saw him. Believe me, he is doing fine."

Sighing deeply, Mollie Mae waited for Mr. Patrick to continue.

Interlocking his fingers and leaning forward, Mr. Patrick commented. "Ms. Jeffers, I can tell that what we spoke of on the phone has you worried. I understand why."

"You'll have to forgive me," Mollie Mae frowned. "I don't exactly remember what was said."

Oliver Patrick realized how fragile the situation was. On one hand he felt obligated to protect her from something she really had no control over. On the other hand, she had a right to do whatever she could to help him, through both conventional and unconventional means. And it was the unconventional he wanted to focus on.

"Ms. Jeffers, I know you and Jeffey have a strong faith."

Mollie Mae's eyes perked up from that statement.

"This may surprise you, but I do too."

"I didn't know, Mr. Patrick. I mean, Jeffey certainly never mentioned that."

Mr. Patrick squirmed in his seat. "I try to keep my views to myself, given the state of the public school system and all."

Mollie Mae nodded in response.

"Anyway, when you asked me on the phone if Jeffey called out a certain name."

"Yes, Beelzebub." Mollie Mae grew excited. "Now I remember."

"To be honest, I've never heard that word before." Pausing, Mr. Patrick seemed lost in thought. "But then I put two and two together, and figured you meant something else."

"What do you mean?" She asked.

"Because of what Jeffey was screaming."

This time it was Mollie Mae's turn to squirm. "I'm confused, Mr. Patrick. What did he say?"

"He started by yelling a person's name at one of the other students. Then he pointed his finger at him. Jeffey kept repeating the name, Jacob Conley."

"Jacob Conley, who's he?"

Mr. Patrick stared at Mollie Mae. He suddenly realized she didn't know. "I isolated Jeffey from the other students. Then I asked him what he meant."

"So who is he?" Mollie Mae pleaded.

"He's a pastor, Ms. Jeffers. Jeffey eventually started calling him a pastor."

"We don't know any Pastor Conley. Where did he get that name?"

Mr. Patrick waited for a moment before replying. He could see that Mollie Mae was trying to process this information. "That's not all he told me, ma'am."

Cocking her head, Mollie Mae begged the question. Is there more?

"Jeffey also said, Pastor Conley warned the President." Waiting for Mollie Mae to grasp the seriousness, Mr. Patrick continued. "Jeffey added, it'll swarm before he eats."

"What?" Mollie Mae sat forward.

"I know this all sounds bizarre, Ms. Jeffers." Mr. Patrick waited before continuing. He could sense her frustration and concern. "I went ahead and did a search on whether there actually is a Pastor Jacob Conley."

Mollie Mae didn't respond.

"Well, I found one. He lives in St. Louis."

"St. Louis? Mr. Patrick, what's this all got to do with Jeffey?"

Throwing his hands up in the air, Oliver Patrick sighed. "I honestly don't know…but I'd be lying if I wasn't concerned for Jeffey's safety."

SIXTY TWO

New York City

The New York Marriot Marquis Hotel, situated at Broadway and 45th, had always been a hotel of stature and elegance. With its regal entrance and opulent lobby, it was no wonder the elitists from the Pollard administration chose to have a benefit dinner at this location.

The hotel consisted of 49 floors of meeting space, restaurants and an abundance of guest rooms. Besides its obvious amenities and its Broadway Ballroom, the hotels Manhattan location made it a great choice for a Presidential event.

The dinner had been planned for months and the invitations were long sent out. No one had declined to attend. How could anyone resist being part of this festivity? Who would dare not?

The dinner regalia was set for a Friday evening which meant security for the President's entourage would be tight. Aside from the President there would be a total of fifteen staff members accompanying him.

The official purpose of the dinner was to thank those who had been so loyal throughout the past tumultuous year. The unofficial purpose was to gather support for his recent initiatives. Bottom line, it was a dinner party at $1000.00 a plate with invitations to some of the nation's wealthiest progressives.

Only the best of everything was going to be served for the event, so the Marriot had its work cut out for them. President Pollard insisted on steak as the main dish in this five course meal. And not just any steak; it would be Kobe beef flown directly from a premier Japanese meat processing farm.

Often considered by many to be the most succulent beef available in the world, true Kobe beef is almost impossible to acquire. Depending on the person of course. With its origins in Japan, pure Kobe comes from a single strain of cattle called Wagyu, and is prized for its flavor, tenderness and marbling. Unfortunately for almost everyone, Kobe beef cannot be legally exported from Japan. But when you have the pull and power of the President of the United States, it's not an issue.

The logistics of the food preparation were left up to White House head chef, Arthur Gordon. At the insistence of President Pollard, Chef Arthur would be flown in with the Presidential staff to supervise the preparation of this dinner. Thus, the Marriot kitchen staff would have to relinquish control.

To assure the freshness of the Kobe meat, Chef Arthur required that the steaks be flown in on the day of the event. Fearing the worst, the Marriot staff set forth a plan B in case there were any delays. Little did they know that they would be scrambling at the last hour.

SIXTY THREE

St. Louis, MO

Pleased that he was home and safe in a familiar setting, Jacob sat at his desk lost in thought. As always, he had taken everything to prayer. He was still concerned about what had happened in Washington the previous week. The Holy Spirit had so far revealed nothing to him that was significant, but it didn't mean He wouldn't.

Having conferred with his own staff along with Jim Calhoun and Ben Palmer, they had all come to the same conclusion. God was going to move in a big way. The question was when and how?

Something was definitely stirring within Jacob and he could sense something was about to unfold. Closing his eyes, he sat in meditation, knowing it was times like this that the Lord revealed His plans.

The utter stillness brought Jacob further into prayer. As his mind drifted to thoughts of Jesus, every other distraction sifted away. His vision became clearer than ever before. Standing before him were the throngs of people he had seen in past dreams, openly worshipping the Lord.

A sea of humanity crying out for redemption, crying out for healing, amassing for a battle yet to come. "When Lord?" His lips pursed the question. "What do I need to do?"

The scene changed abruptly from one of hope to one of chaos. Stirring in his seat, Jacob squinted as if trying to get a clearer picture. Gone were the people worshipping in unison. Darkness started to unfold. He now saw a mass of different people screaming in panic, looks of anguish upon their faces.

"What is this, Lord? What am I seeing?" He begged. Two sentences flashed before his eyes. 'They will squirm. They will swarm.' Startled by the words, as the scene faded away, Jacob sat back in his chair and opened his eyes.

A knock came from his door, bringing Jacob back to reality. "Yes, come in."

"Pastor, I'm sorry to bother you." Getta poked her head around the door. "I know you're busy.

"No, no, come in." Jacob insisted. Staring intently into Getta's eyes, he added. "There's something important you need to tell me, isn't there?"

Taken slightly back, Getta replied. "Actually there is." Stepping closer to his desk, Getta shifted her weight to one side. "There's this woman who has called twice now. She insists she needs to speak with you."

Cocking one eyebrow, Jacob remained silent.

"Anyway, she's calling from San Diego. Her name's Mollie Mae Jeffers." Shrugging her shoulders, Getta asked. "Does this name seem familiar to you?"

Jacob grinned. Although he didn't know her, he knew Mollie Mae Jeffers had to somehow be part of the puzzle. Reaching across his desk, he waited for Getta to hand him a piece of paper.

"I hope she makes sense," Getta offered the paper. "Cause, she seemed a little odd to me."

"Thank you Getta," Jacob stared at the number.

As she turned to walk out, Getta paused at the door. "Pastor, are things about to get weird?"

Jacob chuckled slightly, thinking about the question she had asked. In his mind he thought, how does one define weird? Then it dawned on him that In God's infinite wisdom, weird was just another word for revelation.

Looking back at Getta with the most compassion he could muster, Jacob answered. "In the natural, yes. But in the spiritual, it all makes sense."

"Okay," she said, as she continued out through the door.

Jacob picked up the phone and glanced one more time at the slip of paper. Dialing, he softly prayed. "May this person give revelation, Lord."

SIXTY FOUR

San Diego, CA

"Hello," a female voice answered. It was neither an irritated nor overly friendly voice. But it was definitely one that suggested, get to the point.

Deciding that he didn't want to waste time, Jacob stopped analyzing and asked. "Is this Mollie Mae Jeffers?"

"It is," she replied. "Who's calling?"

Jacob hadn't given any clear thought to just what he wanted to ask her. So determined to place the call, he almost forgot the circumstances. "Ma'am, my name is Pastor Jacob Conley."

"Pastor Conley," Mollie Mae interrupted. "I sure hope you know what's going on, cause my Jeffey has been calling out all kinds of weird names, including yours."

That's the second time someone has used the word weird, Jacob thought. There's got to be some kind of connection. "How about we start from the beginning, Ms. Jeffers? Maybe you can tell me why you called me?"

Mollie Mae was poised to pick right up from where she left off, when she felt an urging from within. She knew instantly what was prompting her, and she knew immediately that the Holy Spirit was nudging her to slow down. Taking a deep breath, Mollie Mae paused.

"Pastor, we're gonna be talking about things of a spiritual nature, and I sense you already know that. You have to call me Mollie Mae, and stop with the ma'am, and miz stuff."

"Absolutely, Mollie Mae," Jacob couldn't help but grin. "And I'm comfortable with you calling me Jake, if you like."

"Oh no sir, that won't do. I've never been disrespectful to a man of God in all my seventy years. I'm sure not gonna start now."

This time Jacob took a deep breath, as he settled into his chair. "That's fine. So, Mollie Mae, how can I help you?"

Back to pulling no punches, Mollie Mae simply asked. "Pastor Jacob, what exactly did you warn the President about at your meeting?"

Stunned, Jacob took a moment to think about the question. How did a woman half way across the country know that he had met with the President of the United States? For that matter, how did she know he basically gave warning to him before he left?

Jacob wondered if he should be somewhat coy with this person. He didn't know her after all, but then again, he felt an overwhelming ease with her. It was as if he felt he needed to comfort her, somehow. Sensing this, Jacob decided to take a chance.

"Mollie Mae, have you, or your Jeffey had some kind of dream or vision about me and the President?"

"Jeffey has, I haven't. Of course, he's always been able to talk to God."

"You mean he prays?" Jacob asked.

"He does more than pray, Pastor. My Jeffey carries on conversations with the Almighty. Always has, and I believe him. Everyone believes him, including Pastor Vernon."

249

"Is he your pastor, Mollie Mae, Pastor Vernon?"

"Has been for the past thirty years. Oh, he knows all about my Jeffey. Sometimes during service when Jeffey gets all excited you can really sense the presence of the Holy Spirit. My oh my, we sure get to shaking."

Smiling to himself, Jacob listened intently to this dear woman. After about twenty minutes of hearing about Jeffey, including everything he had said at school, Jacob had but one question to ask.

"Mollie Mae, when can I meet the two of you? I think I need to spend time with you both."

"Well, you're welcome to stop by any time you like Pastor Jacob," she graciously offered. "Just give me a little notice so I can prepare a room, and prepare Jeffey."

Shaking his head, Jacob stared upward before responding. Whispering, he said. "This is beautiful, thank you, Lord."

"He is beautiful, isn't he, Pastor?" Mollie Mae spoke softly in response to a comment not meant to be heard.

Jacob had given up being surprised; he was just in awe with the connection he perceived between two of God's faithful children and himself.

"Would there be room for one more, Mollie Mae?" Jacob asked.

"Mrs. Conley is welcome as well, but like I said before, let me know in advance. Jeffey needs to be prepared for visitors."

"I understand, Mollie Mae." Glancing at his calendar, Jacob saw no openings any time soon. He didn't want to leave her on the line without making a commitment, but he would have to shuffle some things around. That would take time.

Sensing the urgency from both Pastor Conley and The Holy Spirit, Mollie Mae spoke up. "You know, Pastor Jake, I've always wanted to see St. Louis. Believe I might even have some relatives from that area."

Jacob waited to respond.

"Can't say for sure but the Jeffers line is spread out all across this country." Mollie Mae paused to take a breath. "Anyhow, I just know my Jeffey would love seeing that arch."

"Then it's settled," Jacob squeezed in. "You pick a weekend, so Jeffey doesn't miss too much school, and we'll fly you two out here. You'll be our guests, Mollie Mae."

Chuckling and humming at the same time, Mollie Mae answered. "Pastor Jake, we'll take you up on the flight getting there, but I'm afraid it would be difficult convincing Jeffey to stay at your home."

Somewhat disappointed, Jacob still understood. Autistic children craved familiarity and since the flight alone would be new grounds, perhaps their own space was best.

"Mollie Mae, we'll take care of everything. In fact, there's a wonderful hotel near my home and my church. I think Jeffey would be very comfortable staying there."

"That's very hospitable of you. We'd love to come," Mollie Mae hummed.

As Jacob thought about the best weekend for them to visit, he again glanced at his agenda. There didn't seem to be any time that was better than another. Still, he sensed the urgency of them meeting soon. As his eyes scanned from one week to the next, Mollie Mae announced.

"Pastor, if it works for you I believe we can come the weekend of October 24th. Jeffey only has half a day of school that Friday."

Problem solved. Jacob would have liked to have prayed about the best timing, but if it worked for them then it would work for him.

"Perfect," Jacob replied. "I'll have Getta make flight arrangements and book a room for the two of you. How's that sound, Mollie Mae?"

"Oh, Jeffey's gonna be so excited, Pastor Jake." There was a pause before she continued. "Time can't come soon enough for my Jeffey."

Jacob wasn't quite sure what that statement meant. But he knew to trust in the Lord, that He did.

SIXTY FIVE

New York City

The Presidential Suite on the 45th floor of the Marriot Marquis was silent for the moment. The hotel lobby was a different story. It was the morning of President Pollard's appreciation dinner for his key supporters. The advance buzz surrounding the event was so great in expectation that throngs of uninvited admirers were clamoring for tickets.

Key White House staff were peppered with requests, but to no avail. The event was sold out. The President couldn't have been happier. With public approval hovering in the low forties, everything the President did seemed to go against the consensus. But there was only one faction President Pollard directly focused on.

With a well-crafted speech in hand, the President decided to spend the morning familiarizing himself with the content. The rest of the day would entail sightseeing and pressing the flesh with elite officials and the media.

Continuing to memorize key points of his speech, President Pollard's cell suddenly came to life. Glancing down at the number, his first reaction was to ignore it. Taking a second look, the President thought better of that.

"Ra," the President answered. "How nice of you to call me."

"Have you committed my speech to memory yet?" Ra asked.

253

Standing to his feet, Stuart Pollard responded. "I'm looking it over right now, Ra. It's a marvelous play on words."

"It's more than that, Stuart," Ra responded. "This speech is designed to not only grab the attention of those we oppose. It will bring them to their knees."

Swallowing hard, President Pollard felt a tinge of guilt. His passion was not the same as his mentor. He was interested in one thing, the limelight. Not some obligatory lecture.

"Focus, Stuart. You need to focus tonight," Ra said.

"Of course, of course, my friend." The President thought, for once I'm glad Ra's not going to be here. Then he quickly got a check in his spirit. "I'm just sorry you can't be in attendance. You'll be missed."

"I'll be there in spirit," Ra snarled. "Make sure you call me when the dinner has adjourned."

President Pollard ended the call. He glanced out his window taking in the sea of high-rises from the New York skyline. Still holding the papers in his hand, he moseyed across the suite. Picking up the room's phone, the President dialed his chief of staff. From this point forward all morning activities would be cancelled. He had a speech to memorize after all.

Unbeknownst to the President, a ripple in the menu for tonight's dinner had taken effect. The jet from Tokyo to New York transporting the special Kobe steaks was not going to make it in time. In fact, the plane never even took off.

Accusations flew with abandon. No one was willing to accept responsibility. The mere fact that the menu might have to be changed was all that mattered. Refusing to focus on this change was Chef Gorden, the White House head chef.

Instead of searching for other options he continued to throw his considerable weight around. In a last ditch effort he made numerous calls overseas. He did whatever he could to receive the prized steaks. "The President wants the meat from one place and one place only," he continued to rant.

The only thing the staff from the Marriot could do was wait for him to calm down. Finally, Chef Gorden, dejected and exhausted allowed Damon Ruiz, the Marriott's head chef to approach him.

"If you're finished with your tirade, we have an alternative solution," Chef Ruiz said defensively.

With a flip of the hand, Chef Gorden turned his head away and replied. "I leave it up to you."

"Thank you!" Chef Ruiz answered brusquely. "I'll contact our own source here in the city. I know we can purchase enough Kobe steaks for tonight."

Standing abruptly, Chef Gorden met his co-chef's eyes. "You are certain we can get enough meat for tonight?" With a smirk, he added. "And this source will provide the best the city has to offer?"

Chef Ruiz returned the smile. "It will cost you, but consider it done."

In the most condescending tone he could muster, Chef Gorden replied. "Just tell them to bill the White House." Turning to leave the kitchen, he added. "Just get it done, Ruiz. I'll be back at four."

After Chef Gorden and his assistants left, the remaining Marriot staff stood dumbfounded.

"I just saved his butt," Damon Ruiz exclaimed. "What nerve." Turning to his assistant, Damon motioned. "Call Revelation Packing, Sid. Tell em to bring the steaks over pronto."

Damon made one more request, before his assistant left the kitchen. "Oh, and Sid, make sure they charge the White House. I don't wanna get stuck with this bill."

SIXTY SIX

St. Louis, MO / the Conley Home

Three images came up on the screen as Jacob and Linda watched their laptop. One by one each person offered a greeting until all four parties were officially welcomed.

The Conley's screen was divided equally between Dr. Ben Palmer, and his wife Amy, Jim Calhoun, who was alone, and finally Colonel Carlin Hather. They had all agreed to this web meeting at the request of Jacob. Since it was Jacob's meeting he didn't waste any time getting the ball rolling. "Everyone, thank you for joining Linda and me in this impromptu meeting. I only wish we could all be together in the same place, but the good Lord is awesome in providing this type of technology."

"You couldn't afford to fly me in if you wanted to, Jake." Colonel Hather chimed in. "Even though I'm retired and single, my consulting fees are quite hefty," he laughed.

"Hey now, you can't be charging more than a doctor," Ben Palmer retorted.

Laughter abounded, as Amy added. "I ought to know, I take care of his invoices."

"Well, I'm glad somebody is making some money," Linda chuckled. "This economy has been brutal."

Smiling at his wife, Jacob decided to grab the reigns of the meeting. "Okay, let's get this show on the road, everyone. Something has come up recently that I really need your input on." Feeling Linda squeeze his hand, Jacob added in a more serious tone. "Not everyone knows this, but since we are all connected as brothers and sisters, and with Jim's permission, I want to divulge this."

"What is it, Jim?" Ben quickly asked.

Nodding his head, Jim didn't immediately reply, so Jacob spoke again.

"Lisa didn't join us today because she has recently become ill. Now the doctors have told Jim they think it's the H1N1 virus, but we know better."

"What are the symptoms, Jim?" Amy asked. The Palmers were clearly concerned.

Jim Calhoun answered with a hoarse voice. "You'll have to excuse my voice I may be coming down with the same virus. Anyway, she's been laid up for the past several days with chills, and a fever."

"Did they actually confirm it with testing?" Ben asked.

"Not yet," Jim coughed.

"That is why we're nipping this illness right now," Jacob broke in. "This is the work of the enemy, and we are not going to allow it."

"I agree," Colonel Hather spoke up. "Jacob please lead us in prayer binding this spirit."

As Jacob raised his hands toward Heaven, everyone followed suit. With eyes closed, Jacob spoke out against Lisa's illness. "Precious Holy Spirit, we ask that you cast out this spirit of infirmity. Bring instant healing upon our beloved sister, and allow your glorious peace to reign in the Calhoun household. We claim that the enemy has no authority over Lisa or Jim, and we claim by the authority of Jesus Christ that all sickness leaves their bodies. By the blood of Jesus, we shout out healing now!"

"Amen," everyone spoke in unison.

"Thank you," Jim whispered. Then, in his normal boisterous voice he added. "Now, let's get down to business."

"A few days ago," Jacob started. "I called a woman from San Diego, who had been persistent in trying to reach me. Instantly, I knew I had a connection with her."

"How so?" Ben asked.

Gesturing with his hands, Jacob replied. "Like everything that has happened recently, I was prompted by the Holy Spirit. Her name is Mollie Mae and she has a sixteen year-old autistic grandson named, Jeffey."

"He's autistic? That could be interesting," commented Amy.

"Why does that intrigue you, Amy?" Linda asked.

"I read one story where the parents of an autistic child claimed that the child could talk to God."

"Amazing," smiled Linda. "That gives me goose bumps."

"I believe that Jeffey can do the same thing," Jacob interrupted.

"Jake, what makes you think that?" Colonel Hather inquired.

"Because through Jeffey, Mollie Mae knew all about my meeting with President Pollard. Specifically, he knew about the indirect warning I gave the President before I left."

"Refresh our memories on exactly what you said," Ben asked.

"Well, bottom line, I basically told him to change his mind on his current policies." Shifting in his seat, Jacob continued. "To be honest guys, the evil I sensed in that room was overwhelming…by the sheer power of the Holy Spirit I was able to stay. To stand firm."

"Jacob," Jim Interrupted. "I just received a revelation that I need to share with you all."

Everyone was silent, waiting on Jim to continue.

"God said that something huge is about to happen tonight in New York." Jim paused as he strained to see clearly. The plagues, something about the next plague occurring there."

"New York!" Colonel Hather exclaimed. "President Pollard has some huge gala scheduled in the city."

"It's got to have something to do with that," interrupted Ben.

"Jacob, there's something else that the boy said. Isn't there?" Jim asked.

"That's the part I can't make sense of," Jacob frowned. Glancing at Linda, then back at the screen, he added. "Mollie Mae said her Jeffey mentioned two sentences over and over again."

"What did he say?" Asked Amy.

"It will squirm. It will swarm." Jacob shook his head in frustration.

Flipping through her Bible for confirmation, Amy turned to Exodus and read. "Exodus 8:20, then the Lord said to Moses. Get up early in the morning and confront Pharaoh as he goes to the water and say to him. This is what the Lord says: let my people go, so they may worship me. If you do not let my people go, I will send swarms of flies on you and your officials, on your people and into your houses."

Silently, everyone reflected on the scripture read.

Ben was the first to speak up. "I get the swarm part; it obviously is the flies about to happen. But what did this Jeffey mean by it will squirm?"

Contemplating the question Ben asked, no one commented immediately.

Jacob spoke with concern. "The fact that Jeffey knows, means the enemy knows. I'm afraid that he's probably in trouble."

"We got to do something, Jake." Linda grasped his hand.

"How did you end the conversation with Mollie Mae?" Colonel Hather asked.

"We agreed that she and Jeffey would come here to visit."

"When?" Ben interrupted.

"Two weeks from today."

The silence once again was overwhelming as each individual thought and prayed about what to do. Clearly if the enemy got hold of Jeffey his fate would be in their hands. Aside from the fact that he needed protection, Jeffey was now part of the bigger picture.

"Jake, you mentioned that they live in San Diego." Colonel Hather said. "Is that correct?"

"Yeah, not sure exactly where."

"Being the military town that it is," Colonel Hather responded. "I have some old Navy buddies that still live out there. Let me contact them and see what kind of surveillance we could provide for the family."

"Do you think they would do that?" Linda blurted.

"Well, seeing how one is actually a minister, I've no doubt he'd get involved somehow."

Ben Palmer broke into the conversation and asked a question. "Not to get off the topic, but I've been trying to line up some pastors on the west coast for our alliance, and if this minister you know would be willing to help our cause…"

"Let me see what I can do first, Ben," Colonel Hather interrupted. "I don't know about the rest of you, but I'm really worried about this kid."

SIXTY SEVEN

New York City

Not a penny was spared on the decorations of the Marriot's Broadway Ballroom. Minus the pre-function area which included twelve elevators and one escalator, the ballroom occupied over half of the sixth floor. With approximately 29,000 square feet of space, this ballroom was immense.

The east side of the room consisted of a spectacular state of the art stage with two widescreens flanking it. At its foot the guest of honor's table sat. It ran parallel to the entire stage. Interspaced throughout the remaining ballroom were the guest tables. Elegance was the theme, from the fine linens, and abstract floral arrangements to the numerous ice sculptures strategically placed.

The premise of the sculptures was the Greek gods of mythology. Each sculpture depicted power and strength. The focus piece was a carving of Zeus and Hades standing side by side. Beams of light danced around the sculpture. Eyes were instantly drawn to this grand statue. Icy flames of fire protruded from the head of Hades, allowing this character to dwarf that of Zeus.

The room was filled to capacity with some of the nations wealthiest and most elite. Champagne flowed in abundance. Small talk filled the air. The only person missing was the guest of honor, though he was due any moment.

As the emcee for the evening took hold of the microphone, the music in the background faded away.

"Ladies and gentlemen," he announced. "May I have your attention, please?"

Conversations slowly ended, as heads turned toward the dais.

"Could everyone please take your seats?" He said. "In a moment I would like to introduce our guest of honor."

The eruption of applause echoed throughout the room as those still milling about made way for their seats.

"Now, without further ado," he announced. "Please welcome the President of the United States, Stuart Pollard."

The applause became even greater as President Pollard strutted to the stage. Waving and gesturing, he fed upon the adoration from those standing in attendance.

Champagne glasses held high, a small but growing chant emerged. "We are in charge, we are in charge." The mantra grew louder with every passing moment. Finally, waving with both hands, the President was able to bring the chanting roar to an end.

"We are in charge!" The President shouted. "And the nation will hear us tonight!"

The response was deafening. Those who supported Stuart Pollard were clearly in attendance. As if on cue, the band in the background started playing again, the music feeding the fire.

With shouts of "We are in charge," and with the music blaring, President Pollard bounced back and forth pumping his fist in the air. It didn't take long for his eyes to defiantly peer upward and mouth the words, "I am in charge."

Returning to his seat and giving one final wave to the audience, the noise slowly abated. The guests took their seats, while the emcee approached the microphone.

"Ladies and gentlemen, if you please, we will begin to serve the meal." Pausing, he glanced over at the President. "Immediately following our dinner will be a speech by our esteemed leader, President Stuart Pollard."

Within seconds, scores of Marriot staff brought exquisitely decorated salads to every table. The sounds of Bach reverberated in the background, while muted conversations echoed across the hall.

Back in the kitchen, Chef Gordon barked instructions to any and all around regarding the preparation of the main course. Sniffing the air, the hotel's assistant chef, Sid, stepped back as he opened one of the chilled boxes of steaks. Something didn't seem right.

Motioning for Chef Gorden, Sid stood poised over the box. "Does this meat seem alright to you?"

Waving him to the side, Chef Gorden took Sid's place. Scanning the contents and breathing in heavily, Chef Gorden frowned.

"What's the problem?" He asked indignantly. "I would think you would know a good cut of meat when you see it."

The hotel's assistant chef, Sid's first duty was to make sure all food was edible. His second duty was to help prepare it. As far as he was concerned if the pompous white house chef was okay with the meat, then he was okay with preparing it.

"You're right, Chef Gorden, there is no problem." Sid took a step closer to the counter. "What would you like done next?"

"As soon as the fourth course is served, throw the steaks on."

"Fourth course, sir?" Sid asked.

265

"Where's Chef Ruiz?" Chef Gorden whirled around. "I want Ruiz now!" He barked.

Heads turned in unison as the kitchen staff focused on the irate White House chef.

"Don't just stand there you nimrods," Gorden's tirade went up a notch. "Find me Ruiz." Gorden left abruptly.

Standing in place like a little boy who dropped his sucker, Sid waited for the upheaval to calm down. Within moments Damon Ruiz joined his beleaguered assistant's side.

"What's going on, Sid?" Chef Ruiz asked. "I could hear yelling inside my office."

"Do me a favor, before that nut job from DC gets back," Sid motioned toward one of the boxes of steaks. "Tell me if ya think the meat smells a little odd?"

Just as Chef Ruiz was leaning over the carton, Chef Gorden reappeared.

"There you are. Is there some reason your assistant can't follow orders, Ruiz?" Chef Gorden stood before him with hands on his hips. "There are plenty of other cooks who'll do what I tell them."

Scrunching his nose slightly, Chef Ruiz turned to face Chef Gorden. "Sid seems to think the meat might be a bit tainted." Cocking one eyebrow, he continued. "I might tend to agree with him."

Snapping the box closed, Chef Gorden faced the two chefs. "You're not being paid to make assessments. You ordered it, now we're gonna use it." Throwing his hands up in the air, Chef Gorden turned around. "Just throw some extra sea salt on them."

Chef Ruiz scanned the other boxes. "How bout the rest of the cartons, Sid?"

"Haven't checked all of em, but so far this is the only one that's a little off."

"Well, you heard the man," waving his hand toward the grill. "Throw em on when it's time. But let's put this carton to the side."

Burrowed deep within some of the steaks foul creatures squirmed. Undetectable to the eye, larvae only 3 to 9 mm long and creamy white in color, wriggled in rotting flesh. The question was which steaks?

The growth of these maggots was about to be supernaturally transformed. Some would eventually crawl out and squirm on the plates. Others would remain embedded in the foul meat of the steaks. Once consumed, the larvae would hatch and burrow through a human body. The maggots would then cause damage to vulnerable organs, and even death.

SIXTY EIGHT

San Diego, CA

Thousands of miles away from the celebration in New York City, Jeffey and Mollie Mae finished praying over their own dinner.

Ravenous, and impatient, Jeffey dug into his plate. It was one of Jeffey's favorite, Arroz con Pollo. Mollie Mae always made extra, which meant enough food for five. Lately, it seemed that Jeffey couldn't get enough food to satisfy him. Of course she attributed this to the still growing young man he was.

With his plate overflowing with the steaming dish, Jeffey didn't bother looking at Mollie Mae.

"Jeffey, you need to slow down. Lord's sake, you're like a steam shovel."

Peering back at her from the corner of his eye, Jeffey paused a second. He then went back to scooping his food.

Glancing at the roaster in front of them, Mollie Mae chuckled. "Good thing I made a lot." Humming between small bites, Mollie Mae loved to see her Jeffey eat.

She noticed that his glass of milk was almost empty. Rising from her seat, Mollie Mae made her way over to the fridge. With her back to the table, she swung her arm to close the door.

A loud crash followed. Jeffey screamed. Turning about, Mollie Mae was appalled at the scene before her. Chicken and rice were strewn across the floor, bits of a plate at her feet.

Jeffey had scurried into a corner. He was curled up into a ball. Shocked and dismayed, Mollie Mae cried out. "Good Lord, Jeffey. What happened?" Stepping gingerly around the mess in front of her, Mollie Mae hurried to Jeffey's side. Now rocking back and forth, he seemed inconsolable.

"Child, child," she reached out. "What is it, Jeffey?"

Jeffey barely opened one eye. He peered at the mess. Quickly he shut his eye, and grimaced as if he had bit into something sour.

Scanning the wreckage, Mollie Mae looked for anything out of the ordinary. Satisfied that nothing stood out, she reasoned that Jeffey saw something she didn't.

Placing a comforting hand upon his shoulder, Mollie Mae spoke soothingly. "It's all right, child. It's all right. Whatever it was, it's gone."

Jeffey trusted her by gingerly opening his eyes. Darting to and fro, his eyes finally rested upon Mollie Mae. Meeting her stare, he responded. "They were wiggling." Scrunching his lids trying to escape the vision, Jeffey began rocking once again.

"Wiggling, Jeffey what was wiggling?" she calmly asked.

With his head buried, he mumbled. "The rice, it was alive, M & M."

"You mean you saw the rice moving?"

He raised his head slightly. Jeffey peered over his forearm. "Has it stopped?"

Scanning the floor, more to appease him than anything else, Mollie Mae answered. "There's nothing moving, child." Placing her hands on his forearm, she asked. "Was it the rice you saw moving, or something else?"

269

"It looked like the things that eat dead animals. They squirmed. The rice was squirming."

Mollie Mae gasped, then turned her head away. She suddenly realized what he was saying. Her conversation with Pastor Conley flashed back in waves. They will squirm, they will swarm, she had told him.

It was all making sense. Jeffey had just seen the squirming part while eating this meal. Looking back at her beloved grandson, tears began to form in Mollie Mae's eyes.

Suddenly she was brought back to reality as she felt a finger gently stroke her cheek. Meeting her eyes once again, Jeffey whispered. "It's okay, M & M, it's only God talking to me."

As the tears flowed freely, Mollie Mae wrapped her arms around Jeffey. "Dear child, you're so right," she said. "It is God, and He loves you."

Silently she prayed for peace, and that this would all end soon. But in her heart she knew that the battle was just beginning.

SIXTY NINE

New York City

The doors burst open and the waiters scurried in, carrying piping hot plates loaded with succulent Kobe steaks. Within a matter of minutes everyone in attendance was biting into the mouth-watering meat.

Peering discreetly through the kitchen door, Chef Gorden would have patted himself on the back if he could have. Satisfied that he had delivered the goods, he retreated into the kitchen. Off to the side, sat Sid and Damon.

"My work here is done. I'll leave you and your crew to the kitchen," he boldly announced.

"Yeah, nice working with ya," Sid snarled.

With a passing glance, Chef Gorden proceeded out the door and into the lobby. He stopped dead in his tracks. Screams were heard echoing from the main ballroom.

Aghast from the cries coming from the President's party, Chef Gorden bee lined straight for the gathering. Shrill voices shrieked out in disgust. Chef Gorden's heart palpitated ferociously. What in the world happened? Everything had been going so well.

Bursting into the ballroom he stopped abruptly, as a wave of humanity bowled him over. Arms raised in a defensive posture, Chef Gorden managed to keep most of them from running into him. But not all.

271

He crumpled to the floor, splayed out on his back. The chef looked up just in time to see the gaze of a terror filled guest. As she struggled to right herself, the guest vomited directly into Chef Gorden's face.

Shoving the girl aside, Gorden scrambled to his feet and slid across the floor. Landing in a pool of vomit, he stared at the scene. Scores of people were shouting. Many were pointing to various plates.

Righting himself, Chef Gorden stared at a table nearby. Writhing on top of a piece of meat, hundreds of festering maggots teemed on a plate. Instantly he joined the spewing crowd, adding to the puddle surrounding him.

Then something truly supernatural occurred. Gathering in the center of the cavernous room a darkened cloud appeared. The screams of many diminished to the shouts of a few as those still in attendance stared in shock.

In a deafening cacophony of sound the cloud spun like a whirlwind becoming immense in size. Millions of screw worm flies, the size of a thumb nail, descended on the unfortunate guests.

Batting madly at the insects in the only defense possible, people fought against the swarm. Scores of the pests feverishly infested any open orifice. Panic ensued among those attacked. The massive swarm of screw worm flies continued unabated.

###

Briskly whisked away, President Pollard bounced between several handlers. The shouts of his entourage overshadowed the screams from behind. Still trying to process what had just happened, the President remained silent.

Momentary confusion led the group to a standstill. One agent insisted they go one way, while a Presidential advisor urged the opposite. Within seconds the service elevator sprang to life and a decision had to be made. Per protocol, the senior secret service agent won out after shuffling the team aboard. Pressing the button for the garage, the decision was finalized. The President would be taken away.

"Let it be known I do not agree with this course of action!" Chief of Staff Ayers spoke vehemently. "We should be going back UP to the Presidential suite so we can all regroup!"

"Duly noted, Mr. Ayers," agent Cooper retorted.

The elevator reached its destination. Martin Ayers attempted one last plea. "Mr. President, surely you want to get cleaned up before we do anything else?"

Eying his own dinner jacket then Mr. Ayer's, the President spied a noticeable difference between the two men. The President's coat had been wiped down from unwanted projectile, while his chief of staff's was quite drenched.

"You'll survive, Martin," President Pollard responded, as the team proceeded toward awaiting limos. "Just make sure he's in another vehicle," his remark was directed to agent Cooper.

Sitting for the first time since the panic occurred, Stuart Pollard glanced out a blackened window. Scanning the faces gawking at his convoy, the President had one thought on his mind. It's not over yet.

His train of thought broken, the President turned to see a phone held before him.

"I'm sorry, Mr. President," agent Cooper held out the receiver. "I didn't mean to disturb you. But it's Mr. Farman."

Snatching the phone, Stuart Pollard took in a deep breath. "I gather you've heard the news?"

"Before you allow yourself to become undignified, listen to me," Ra answered curtly.

The President remained silent.

"Tonight's event is not a slap at you. It's a slap at us."

With no response from the President, Ra continued.

"Don't think for a second because I was not there, that the message will go unnoticed, Stuart. Things are already in motion to strike back."

"Strike back. Do you know what happened to me?" The President focused his eyes out his window. "What exactly do you mean by--

"How dare you question me?" The harshness of Ra's voice forced the President to retract the phone a few inches. "What the coalition decides is what you shall do. Period."

Shaken and somewhat embarrassed, the President responded in a hushed tone. "Please forgive me, my friend...I meant no disrespect."

An eerie stillness engulfed the vehicle. Static emanated from the phone. Shifting in his seat, the President did not speak a word. Out of the silence he heard agent Cooper remark.

"Do you all hear that?"

"Hear what?" another agent replied.

As the static continued to come from the phone, President Pollard glanced out the opposite window. He pointed. "There, over there."

Keeping pace with the vehicle was a massive black cloud. It moved as one, yet was comprised of many. The closer it moved alongside the car, the more thunderous it became.

All eyes strained to make out what this mass was. Finally after a few moments it disappeared. A solitary creature peered through the President's window. Shifting his head, he couldn't quite make out what was clinging to the outside glass.

"Excuse me, Mr. President," agent Cooper pointed a small flashlight toward the glass.

Turning away from the window, the President briefly acknowledged agent Cooper. They both stared ahead as a beam of light focused on the creature. A single fly clung to the glass.

A voice finally projected through the phone.

"Are you still there?" Ra shouted. "What is going on in that car?"

Realizing that Ra probably heard all the commotion, the President brought the receiver back to his mouth. "It's definitely not over, Ra." He spoke with bitterness. "You're right; we need to strike back quickly."

In a calmer tone, Ra remarked. "Soon as you get back to Washington, start laying the groundwork for the next piece of legislation. Understood, Mr. President?"

"What about the media? They're gonna be all over this."

"Never mind them. Retribution must come first."

SEVENTY

Atlantic City, NJ

In a darkened room showing just a glimmer of the surrounding city, a man sat engrossed in the screen before him. One after another, images popped up as his fingers danced across the keys. High speed and great desire were a wicked combination.

The hotel room itself was opulent and offered any amenity a person could want. Wide screen TV, fully stocked bar, a breathtaking view of the skyline that never faded…it was everything a man could want. Any ordinary man, that is.

The desires of this world were few for this individual, but then again everyone has his vice. Thoroughly taken in by the provocative poses before him, he barely noticed the palm-sized instrument vibrating to life. His eyes darted briefly from his enticement to the object. Reaching for the cell, the text simply read, call me.

Placing his laptop off to the side, Gaether rose from the comfortable sofa in search of another object. The lack of light was no detriment in his efforts. He in fact saw much better because of it. Grasping yet another phone, Gaether hit speed dial on the encrypted device.

"I have a job for you," a voice spoke on the other end.

"I'm listening."

"Friday, October 23rd, St. Louis airport. Two packages, one retrieval."

"Names?"

"Mollie Mae and Jeffey Jeffers."

"Which one?" asked Gaether.

The voice on the other end paused briefly, as Gaether waited for the final instruction.

"I want the boy!"

"Understood," Gaether replied, ending the call.

SEVENTY ONE

New Egypt, NJ

In a small town of roughly three thousand people, located somewhere in the middle of the state, notoriety would soon occur. There was no coincidence in the town's name, the event soon to unfold, or God's impeccable timing. But none of that mattered to twelve-year-old Aubrey Cousins and the place she called home.

Cousins' Cattle Ranch was not overly large in area. At just under two hundred square acres, walking from end to end was not an option. The main farmhouse fronted an old dirt road that eventually led to town. The white batten-board two-story had a wraparound porch offering views as far as the eye could see.

Off to the left was a matching barn that dwarfed the farmhouse. A lone, towering maple stood between the two structures, offering the only shade. The opposite end of the farm consisted of a pond and a forest, leaving the majority of the land for grazing. The field was divided into multiple sections by electrified fencing. The section Aubrey had occupied was a good distance from the house.

Sprinting across the field Aubrey suddenly felt like her lungs were on fire. Panic, fear, and sorrow urged her on. A single thought played over and over. They're dead.

As the comfort of her home came closer, Aubrey caught movement to the side. It was one of their four wheelers. Her dad was driving it. Veering slightly off course from the house, Aubrey frantically waved her arms.

"Dad, Dad," she shouted, knowing that there was no way he could actually hear her. Her only hope was to keep waving to get his attention.

Her heart sunk as he sped off in the opposite direction. Not wasting any time, Aubrey ran toward her original destination. She realized no one else was home. But she had to tell someone, and the phone was her only alternative. Stumbling through the back door, Aubrey reached for the nearest cordless. Frantically she dialed her mom's cell, hoping she had it with her.

In two rings Maureen Cousins answered. As a mother, wife, and co-owner of two hundred head of cattle, running errands never ended. Maureen frowned as she glanced at her cell. "If you're calling to have me pick something up, I've already left the store."

"Mom, you've got to get home," Aubrey struggled to catch her breath. "There's a bunch of em dead."

"Aubrey? Aubrey, honey, what's wrong?"

Straining to look out the window, hoping to see her dad, Aubrey cried out. "The cattle. I went out to check on the new calves…and there were so many of em dead." Now sobbing and still searching the horizon for her dad, she added. "Mom, what's happening?"

Maureen felt her foot press down on the accelerator, willing her Suburban to move even faster. "Sweetie, try to calm down. Are you sure the calves weren't just lying down?"

"I'm not joking, mom. It wasn't just the calves. There was so many of em just lying there, with huge flies all over them."

Not sure what to say next, Maureen asked the most logical question that came to mind. "Did it look like some animal attacked them?" Something had to cause this."

"I don't know," Aubrey gulped. "I just wish you and dad were here."

Gasping, Maureen asked, "Aubrey, where's your father?"

"I don't know, I don't know. I just know I can't go out to that field again."

Gripping the wheel tighter than before, Maureen tried to think ahead. "Listen, I'm almost home. I'm gonna hang up and try your dad's cell, okay?"

Still sobbing and staring out into the field, Aubrey murmured. "Just hurry."

SEVENTY TWO

Orlando, FL / the Palmer Household

Amy Palmer sat riveted to the television watching a breaking news segment on Fox News. Barely hearing the door to the garage close, she called out as if on autopilot.

"Hey Babe. Quick, come over here."

Dr. Ben Palmer threw his keys on the counter and followed his wife's voice. "What's up?"

Pointing to the screen on the wall, Amy spoke excitedly. "This just might have something to do with the incident from the President's dinner party in New York."

Joining her on the mocha colored couch, Ben settled in and stared at the television.

"Joining us on this breaking news story is noted entomologist Dr. Arthur Corby." The screen widened to show news correspondent Fran Schaeffer and Dr. Corby across from each other. "Dr. Corby, since your expertise is the study of insects, specifically the fly species, what can you tell us about this breakout at two livestock facilities that occurred today?"

"From what I've read thus far, there appears to be an unusual infestation." Pausing, Dr. Corby added. "What I mean by unusual is that this species of fly, the Chrysomya bezziana, or old world screwworm fly has not been seen in this part of the world for quite some time."

"Dr. Corby, what do you mean by not seen?"

"Well, for some time now, the United States has controlled the screw worm fly populations by successfully mating sterile males so that the eggs of the female do not hatch." Frowning, Dr. Corby continued. "To have an infestation of this proportion by a species thought to be wiped out, in the northeast no less, is unbelievable."

Cutting to live footage, hundreds of dead cattle were shown.

Fran's voice was heard in the background. "What we're seeing is live shots from the air of the devastation below at the Cousins' Cattle Ranch. For stated health reasons, officials are not allowing news crews to get close to the areas affected."

Cutting back to both individuals, the camera zoomed in on Fran as she asked. "Dr. Corby, just what is the health risk in this situation?"

"The risk is the possibility of an animal disease called myiasis, occurring in humans." Panning to Dr. Corby, the camera focused solely on him. "Myiasis is a disease caused by parasitic dipterous fly larva that feed on a host's dead or living tissue. In other words, maggots hatch in the flesh of cattle, in this instance. Then the maggots eat both dead and live tissue and can actually burrow into the host's body and attack various organs."

Not realizing that the camera had focused on her expression, Fran swallowed as if she was trying to keep something down. "So what are the signs that a person may be infected, Dr. Corby?"

Taking a deep breath, he responded. "The maggots can invade open wounds in a body or as I previously mentioned through unbroken skin. Some can actually enter through the ears or nose, but the symptoms that one should look for are non-healing wounds, itchiness, and even movement under the skin."

The camera man clearly was having fun with this interview as he immediately zoomed in on Fran for her reaction. "Did you say movement under the skin?"

"Oh yes," Dr. Corby's eyes lit up. These larvae are very invasive if given the opportunity." Waving his right hand near his head, he added. "With Aural Myiasis, which is the invasion of the middle ear, a person will experience crawling sensations and buzzing noises."

Shaking her head, Fran stated. "What you're saying is the host, or individual can actually hear the maggots inside their ear."

"Not only that, but the larvae can actually get to the brain, and in the process cause deafness."

Gesturing to the background shot of dead cattle, Fran implored. "So what needs to be done to prevent this outbreak from spreading, Dr. Corby?"

"To my knowledge authorities are presently applying what is called vector control. This is the spraying of the areas with insecticides such as organophosphorus or organochlorine. These chemicals will then eradicate the adult flies before they can repopulate."

"Truly amazing." Smiling for the first time, Fran addressed her guest one last time. "Dr. Arthur Corby, thank you for your time." Staring into the camera once again, she added. "I am sure our viewers are wondering about two things. Will this 'vector control' work?" Fran paused, as a new graphic appeared behind her. Looping footage revealed the aftermath from the President's dinner in New York City. "And is this outbreak of screw worm flies somehow tied into the huge disruption of President Pollard's gala from the other night? White House officials are not commenting."

Muting the sound from the television, Amy glanced wide-eyed at her husband. Sitting perfectly still, Ben was silent.

Breaking the silence, Amy asked. "Do you think Jacob knows?"

Briefly acknowledging her, Ben picked up the nearby phone. Glancing back in her direction, he simply replied. "He will soon."

SEVENTY THREE

First Christian Church / 3 days before Mollie Mae
and Jeffey's arrival

Searching various news sources, Jacob focused on the screen. The devastation from the fly larvae at five separate livestock facilities had become far worse than the Mad Cow scare of 2003. Even though no new outbreaks had appeared in several days, officials were still cautious. Both the beef and pork industries in the northeast part of the country were basically shut down. Consumers were up in arms as meat prices sky rocketed.

Jacob was still amazed by how little had been said by the President, concerning the livestock incidents. In fact, all statements had been issued directly through the White House press secretary. He began to wonder just how much the President may have been affected.

All because of the hardened heart of the White House, Jacob thought. If only the people really knew. With the fifth plague virtually over Jacob knew what he needed to do next. Much to his displeasure, he had to try and contact President Pollard. He needed to see if he was finally getting the picture. God would not be mocked any further.

He dialed the number to Martin Ayers, the President's Chief of Staff. After four rings the call went immediately into voice mail. Hesitating, Jacob almost hung up. Sensing the urge of the Holy Spirit, he knew it was right to leave the ball in their court.

"Mr. Ayers, this Pastor Jacob Conley." Jacob closed his eyes, and paused. "I wish to leave a message for President Pollard. Please have him call me regarding all that has transpired over the past several days." With a hint of mystery in his voice, Jacob finished the message. "The President will no doubt know exactly what I mean. Thank you."

Jacob pondered what the Lord had in store. If he was to believe that history was playing out in modern times, this contest between good and evil was only half-way done. There was still five more plagues that could occur.

The key to what might happen in the future seemed somehow connected to one young man. "Is Jeffey the answer to this nation's next great revival, Lord?" Jacob cried out in earnest. "Or is he simply just one piece of the massive puzzle that I count myself blessed to be part of?" No matter what happened next, Jacob felt intensely responsible for keeping the movement going. And the next order of business was meeting with the Jeffers in three days.

It didn't take long for Jacob's cell to ring. Glancing at the ID, Jacob thumbed reply. "Hi, this is Jacob Conley."

"Pastor Conley, I got your message," Martin Ayers paused. "Call it déjà vu, but just this morning President Pollard asked me to get in touch with you."

Grinning, Jacob replied, "I prefer to call it divine intervention, Mr. Ayers."

"Humph," was the response.

"Since the President had me in mind, what was it he needed?"

"It's imperative that he see you in person, as soon as possible, Pastor Conley." In a softer tone, Martin Ayers added. "How soon can you come?"

Seizing the moment, Jacob asked. "You're going to have to tell me what this is about, Mr. Ayers. If I'm going to drop everything--

"Now see here," Martin Ayers interrupted. "This is the President of the United States. If he wants to see you I would expect you to accommodate him!"

Taking a few seconds before responding, Jacob composed himself. "Mr. Ayers, why doesn't President Pollard simply call me if it's so urgent?"

Hesitating in his response, Martin Ayers thought carefully about what to say. "Pastor Conley if I speak bluntly with you, can I be assured this conversation stays between us?"

Recognizing the concern in his voice, Jacob responded in like manner. "Mr. Ayers, is everything okay? As a man of God, my first concern is the well-being of the President."

"I appreciate that. I really do." Pausing, Martin Ayers continued. "The President has some health issues that resulted from the dinner party several nights back. Suffice it to say, he really needs to see you in person."

Without hesitation, Jacob answered. "I can be ready first thing tomorrow. Will that work?"

"Thank you, Pastor Conley. If you like I'll set up the details with your secretary."

"Very good."

"Oh, and Pastor Conley, I appreciate your discreetness in this matter."

"I understand," Jacob confirmed, as he pressed the end button. Rubbing his chin, Jacob reflected on their conversation. Things were moving swiftly and the last thing he wanted was to be anxious. Fortunately he knew the cure for that and for all matters.

Bowing his head, Jacob did what came so naturally. He simply prayed.

SEVENTY FOUR

The White House

Standing outside a single door, Jacob had no idea what part of the White House he was in. As soon as he had arrived he was ushered through an entryway, down a winding corridor and finally to this location. Two stern marines stood guard. Jacob had no doubt the President was on the other side.

A few anxious moments passed. The door opened, and Martin Ayers appeared. His boyish face appeared withdrawn. No longer did he possess an arrogant smirk, nor did he use a condescending tone. Martin Ayers simply motioned for Jacob to enter.

"Please, Pastor Conley, come in."

Jacob entered the room as a heaviness fell upon him. Scanning his surroundings, he took in the relaxed, informal décor. A nearby hearth held a peaceful fire, crackling soothingly. With his back facing Jacob, a man sat staring intently at the licking flames.

"President Pollard?" Inquired Jacob, as he addressed Martin Ayers.

Breathing deeply, Mr. Ayers replied, "yes." He took a step in front of Jacob.

Sensing something wrong, Jacob waited for Martin Ayers.

Staring intently at Jacob, he added. "The President can't hear you. He lost his hearing after the incident in New York."

289

Initially taken back, Jacob then moved toward the President. A nearby agent quickly stepped in his way. The commotion alerted the President. The burly guard blocked Jacob's direct view, but in his peripheral vision he noticed the President stirring.

"It's okay, Agent Cooper," the President's voice sounded slightly altered. "Let him pass."

Standing face to face, Jacob eyed the President cautiously. No words were spoken as each man sized up the other. Assessing the gravity of the situation, Jacob took a step forward, within reach of the President.

President Pollard flinched slightly, as Jacob slowly raised his right hand toward him. Staring intently into the President's eyes, Jacob paused. Placing first his right hand over the President's left ear, Jacob continued to peer into his eyes.

Covering the President's right ear with his left hand, Jacob closed his eyes. Tilting his head up, Jacob prayed silently. The President gazed at him.

Grasping the President's head between his hands, Jacob shouted out loud. "Ephphatha! Ephphatha!"

Freeing himself from Jacob's grasp, the President stepped back. Violently, his body shook. He collapsed to his knees. Within seconds both Agent Cooper and Martin Ayers were at his side.

Raising the President to his feet, Agent Cooper looked on in amazement. Tears streamed down the President's face as he mumbled over and over. "I can hear, I can hear."

Agent Cooper guided the President out of the room. The agent paused to look back at Jacob. Returning the agent's steely gaze, Jacob stood motionless. Without saying a word, Agent Cooper continued toward the door, steering the President away.

Placing a hand on Jacob's elbow, Martin Ayers grasped Jacob's attention. "What was it you said?"

"Ephphatha," Jacob grinned. "Look up the passage from the book of Mark. Chapter 7, verses 34 and 35."

Cocking his head to one side, Martin Ayers asked. "But how, and why?"

"The power of God is limitless, Mr. Ayers. The question is, now that the President can hear again, will he listen?"

SEVENTY FIVE

St. Louis airport

Stepping from the plane into the galley-way, Mollie Mae and Jeffey moved along with the crowd. It had been quite a few years since she had last flown. Much like back then the experience had left a bad taste in her mouth.

Jeffey took everything in with his usual combination of curiosity and wonder. Now able to stretch his lanky frame, Jeffey was raring to go. Grabbing Mollie's hand he literally dragged her along, not having any idea where they were heading. He was excited to be somewhere new.

"Slow down, child," Mollie Mae yanked back. "We need to be looking for our greeter."

Stopping in his tracks, Jeffey spun around and cocked his head to one side. "Greeter, what kinda greeter, M&M?"

Half smiling and half glancing about, Mollie answered. "It's someone from Pastor Jacob's church, Jeffey. He's here to pick us up and bring us to a hotel."

"Hotel? I've never stayed in a hotel."

Mollie Mae sensed Jeffey's agitation. She grabbed both his hands. "Now Jeffey, we talked about this, remember?"

Jeffey glanced away.

"I thought it best that you not be around too many people, and have your own space."

"Yeah, space. I like my space," Jeffey smiled.

"Okay then, let's look for our greeter. I believe the man from the church's name is Pastor Will."

"How will we know Pastor Will?"

"Good question, Jeffey." Mollie looked around nervously wondering to herself. "I'm sure he'll have a sign."

"A sign," Jeffey blurted. "What kinda sign?"

Glancing back and forth among all the people in the greeting area, Mollie replied. "We'll know, child. We'll know.

Mollie knew if she got too worried or it seemed to be taking too long she could always call Pastor Jacob on her cell. For now, she was content moving along with the rest of the herd.

They had almost made it to the baggage claim area when something caught her eye. Off to the side stood a single man, dressed in black blazer, white shirt, and black pants. Held in his hands was a homemade sign that read, JEFFERS.

Instantly the man locked eyes with Mollie Mae as if he had known her forever. Smiling broadly, the man took a step toward Mollie Mae and Jeffey, while holding the sign.

"There, over there," Jeffey exclaimed, pointing at the man.

"Child, I believe we found our ride," Mollie answered.

The man now stood a few feet from Mollie and Jeffey, and grinned. "Would you be Mollie Mae Jeffers?" he asked.

"I sure am," Mollie motioned toward Jeffey. "This here is my grandson, Jeffey."

"Very good," he replied. "I'll be your driver, ma'am. Gesturing toward the luggage carousel, he added. "Shall we get your bags?"

As the man walked toward the baggage carousel, Jeffey stood still.

"Well, come on child. Don't want to keep the man waiting."

Jeffey refused to budge.

"Jeffey? Don't you want to help the man get our bag from the plane?"

"That's not our driver," Jeffey stammered. Glancing around something caught his attention.

"What are you looking at, child? We need to tell the man which bag is ours." Grabbing his hand, Mollie tried to lead him toward the man.

Still staring off in the opposite direction, Jeffey refused to move. "We need help M & M." He looked directly at Mollie Mae. "That man is evil, he's not Pastor Jacob's friend."

Now feeling uncomfortable, Mollie Mae watched as the man scanned the revolving carousel. He was oblivious to their absence.

"Jeffey, what makes you feel this way? Tell me, child?"

Bouncing up and down in a nervous state, Jeffey closed his eyes not saying a word. Again Mollie glanced at the baggage carousel looking for the man. He was gone.

Suddenly Jeffey stopped bouncing and looked over Mollie Mae's shoulder and screamed. "He's with Beelzebub."

Startled, she whirled around to see the man standing behind her with her suitcase in hand.

"All set to go, ma'am?"

"What?" She asked. "How, how did you know which bag?"

With a smug expression, he answered. "By the tag." Holding the tag out for her to see, it read, Jeffers.

"What did you say your name was?"

"I didn't ma'am. But you can call me, Gaether. Now if you're ready, the limo is parked right outside."

Confused by the man's directness but also uncomfortable in his presence, Mollie Mae wasn't sure what to do. She suddenly became startled by the ringing of her cell phone.

"Excuse me," she smiled nervously at the man. Turning her back towards him she answered the call. "Hello, this is Mollie Mae."

"Miss Jeffers, thank God I got you. This is Pastor Will, from First Christian. I am so sorry that I'm running late."

Mollie could feel her face flush as she listened, then she abruptly interrupted. "Pastor Will, if you're running late, then who's this Gaether guy?"

Will paused, before answering. "Gaether? I don't know any Gaether. What's he want?"

Jeffey grabbed Mollie's hand. He pulled her toward the object he was staring at earlier. It was the USO commissary room, filled with traveling military personnel. Jeffey sensed it would be safe.

Before they proceeded through the door, Mollie Mae glanced back at the man still holding her suitcase. He didn't budge an inch. He stared straight ahead at the glass wall they stood in front of.

Pulling Mollie Mae through the glass partition, Jeffey stopped abruptly in front of the check in desk. He glanced around at every type of military uniform imaginable. Hundreds of soldiers milled about, relaxing and enjoying the incredible opulence of this first rate facility.

Startled by a voice behind the desk, Mollie Mae turned to her right.

"Ma'am, can I help you? Is there someone here you need to see?"

"Oh no young lady, I have no one but me and my Jeffey."

Jeffey didn't wait for Mollie Mae to finish. He simply screamed. "Help, we need help!"

As if a bomb exploded, the entire commissary drew quiet. They waited to hear what this young man might say next.

"There's an evil man." Jeffey pointed through the glass partitions. "He's after M & M and me, he's gonna hurt us!"

Instantly chairs screeched backward and the commotion of bodies filled the room.

"What man?" Someone bellowed. He approached Mollie Mae and Jeffey. Air Force reserve Staff Sergeant Lance Brown, stood a menacing six foot two with mountains for shoulders.

"Right there, right there," Jeffey pointed.

Suddenly the wall of windows was full of prying eyes eager to see this evil presence. Gaether simply stood his ground. He stared back defiantly, still holding onto the suitcase.

"What exactly has he done, ma'am?" Sergeant Brown asked.

"My grandson, Jeffey and I flew here from San Diego to meet with a pastor friend. Our friend was supposed to send someone to pick us up and bring us to the church."

"Not the church, M & M. Hotel, not the church," Jeffey interrupted.

"Sorry, child. Anyway, that man out there said he was here to get us. Then one of the pastors called me and said he was running late to pick me up."

"So, who's this guy?" Asked the desk receptionist.

"We don't know, but Pastor Will said he never heard of him."

"He's got our luggage," Jeffey blurted. "He shouldn't have our luggage."

"That's another odd thing," Mollie added.

"What's that?" asked Sergeant Brown.

"Well, how'd he know which bag was ours?"

"I've heard enough," one young marine pushed his way through. "It's time to have a talk with this dude."

"Hold on private." Placing a hand on the private's shoulder, Sergeant Brown stopped him momentarily. "I'll go with you. But let me do the talking."

With Sergeant Brown in the lead, three men approached Gaether. He stood motionless.

Glancing down at his vibrating cell, Jacob recognized the caller. He then returned his attention to his guest.

"I'm sorry, Evelyn. You mind if I answer this?"

Pastor Evelyn Connors smiled, then rose from her chair. "No, go right ahead," she replied.

"I wouldn't bother but it's Will and he's supposed to pick up the two guests I was telling you about." Jacob answered before the call went into voicemail. "Will, everything going well?"

"Pastor Jacob, something strange just happened."

The concerned look on Jacob's face caused Evelyn to interrupt. "I'm gonna run, Jacob. Call me if there's anything else you need."

Holding his right hand over the cell, Jacob replied. "Thank you, Evelyn. I'll call you as soon as I know more."

Jacob returned the phone to his ear as Evelyn left his office. "Sorry Will. What exactly is going on?"

"I called Ms. Jeffers at the airport to tell her I'd be there shortly and she said some guy was waiting for her."

"Some guy? Who was he?"

"All she said was the guy's name was Gaether, and then the call ended. I've been trying to get her back but there's no answer."

Jacob paused before replying. "All right listen, Will. Get to the airport as fast as you can. How close are you?"

"Almost there."

"Good, head straight to the baggage area. And just park the car right out front. I'll keep trying to reach her."

"Got it."

"Oh, and Will? Call me as soon as you know something."

Ending the call, Jacob fumbled through some papers searching for Mollie Mae's number. A sick feeling sat in the pit of his stomach. "No Lord, no." He softly pleaded. "Let no harm overtake those two."

SEVENTY SIX

St. Louis Airport

Flanked by three burly men in military fatigues, Gaether maintained a steely gaze. Looking past the largest of the three, he kept his eyes on Mollie Mae and Jeffey still secured inside the commissary.

"I'm gonna ask you again, mister," Sergeant Brown glared directly at Gaether. "What's your business with the lady and her grandson?"

Ignoring the sergeant's question, Gaether took a step to his right in an effort to move closer to the USO.

"Well now, we're trying to talk to you buddy." The brass young marine cut Gaether off by stepping directly in front of him. "No need to dis us."

Instantly the other two soldiers joined their comrade forming a human wall.

"Mister," Sergeant Brown spoke up. "You can try to ignore us all you want, but I can assure you, you will not take a step inside that office without our consent."

Gaether sneered at the sergeant.

"Aw now, no need to pout," the marine chuckled.

The third soldier, also a young marine, held his hand up in front of Gaether's face. "This is as far as you go, Jack."

Stepping back two paces, Gaether pressed one button on his cell. He held the phone to his ear. Gaether's eyes scanned from one soldier to another as he waited for an answer.

"Oh oh," Jeffey cried out. He peered through the commissary window.

"What is it, Jeffey?" Mollie Mae grabbed his hand.

Throwing his hands up in the air, Jeffey answered. "Big trouble. Big, big trouble."

"Have you acquired the object yet?" The voice on the other end asked Gaether.

"The object is in sight," Gaether answered. "But I have a few obstacles." Gaether emphasized his reply to make sure the three soldiers heard him.

"Whatever it takes," came the reply. The call ended.

Placing his cell back in a pocket, Gaether proceeded to go around the shield before him.

Stepping quickly to head him off, the first marine held up both hands in a stop position. Shoving him aside with little effort, Gaether drew closer to the commissary.

Watching the scene from the commissary, four more soldiers poured out from the office. Stopping momentarily, Gaether stood completely encircled. Seven against one. Heated words were hurled toward him. The circle tightened.

Raising his hands above his head, Gaether spun round in a complete 360. Each soldier was flung backwards from a force unseen. The glass wall before him shattered into a million pieces. There was no longer a barrier between the Jeffers and Gaether.

Pandemonium ensued from the sound of crashing glass. Patrons screamed and ran amok trying to avoid the area. Gaether simply stood still. His glowing eyes fixated on Jeffey.

"Jeffey, Jeffey, someone help Jeffey." Mollie Mae cried out.

Scores of soldiers no longer stunned stepped in front of Mollie Mae and Jeffey. Seizing the opportunity, Sergeant Brown dove at Gaether trying to knock him off balance.

Falling to the ground Gaether laid pinned. Soldiers' dog piled on top of him.

"Don't let him up, keep him down," shouts rang out.

Scrambling to his feet, Sergeant Brown turned toward Mollie Mae. Motioning for her to join him, he shouted. "Quickly, while we have him subdued! Come on, come on." He waved at her frantically.

Stepping over the shards of glass Mollie Mae guided Jeffey toward Sergeant Brown. Grabbing his hand she pulled him along trying to get away from the evil presence.

In a deafening screech, Gaether propelled the mass of soldiers away from his squashed body. Rising to his feet he roared at his fleeing subjects. Bounding past fallen bodies, Gaether was soon upon them.

"Arrogant human," Gaether bellowed at Jeffey's lone protector. "Do you really think you're a match for me?"

"I don't know what you are," Sergeant Brown stood with feet and arms spread wide. "But I'll die before I let the likes of you take these people."

"So be it."

301

Advancing forward Gaether suddenly stopped. He turned toward a voice coming from behind.

"Wait! You have no authority over these people!" Pastor Will shouted. "Pray, Ms. Jeffers, pray out loud like never before!" Will stood at their side. "By the authority of Jesus, you have no power over us."

Raising her arms in the air, Mollie Mae joined him in prayer. Sergeant Brown looked back and forth between them.

High above in the atmosphere, and unseen by human eyes, a battle raged on. Scores of hideous demons engaged the spirits of light. The prayers from Will and Mollie Mae drifted toward Heaven. The darkness weakened. It started to diminish.

Standing motionless, Gaether seethed with rage. The two continued crying out for protection from his dwindling powers. Sensing a shift in the surroundings, Sergeant Brown summoned all his courage. He approached Gaether.

Situated mere feet from the most evil presence he ever encountered, Sergeant Brown swallowed hard. He somehow managed to say, "I think your time here is done." He paused to wait on Gaether's response. Chilling fear coursed through the sergeant's body.

Echoing in the background the prayers from Will and Mollie Mae continued. Finally, Gaether took a step back and glared at Sergeant Brown. The face of a hideous demon appeared. Its eyes focused on the soldier. "You," it whispered. "Soon, soon enough."

Instantly the creature turned back to its original form. He turned and walked away. Gaether vanished as if he never existed.

"Whoa," Sergeant Brown said. He turned to face Pastor Will. "I pray I don't ever see that thing again."

Placing his hand on the sergeant's shoulder, Will responded. "Then I suggest you indeed pray and pray often."

Cocking his head to one side, with his mouth slightly ajar, the sergeant stared intently at Will. "Who are you?"

Extending his hand, Will grinned. "Will Foxx, I'm a pastor at a church here in St. Louis."

"I don't know if you realize it, Pastor. But you just took down one of the most powerful guys I've ever encountered."

Glancing briefly at the ceiling, Will answered. "It's the power of the Holy Spirit. No demon can stand against His authority."

Joining the two men, Mollie Mae appeared disheveled from the encounter. Throughout the melee she was so busy in prayer that she didn't realize one important thing. Her beloved Jeffey was nowhere to be seen!

ABOUT THE AUTHOR

Tom Bazow

Tom is an accomplished Christian author with four published books to his credit and multiple manuscripts in the works. Previous works include "Gedden's Armor," a supernatural suspense thriller that has received several favorable critical reviews. Inspiration for this book developed while taking a group of his students on a field trip to the mysterious St. Louis City Museum. Tom also has written a faith based children's series called "Quest for God's Hidden Creatures." He and his wife, Warrine, live in St. Louis with their two daughters, Hannah and Molly.

Order all of Tom's books at:
www.amazon.com/author/tombazow

FUTURE TITLES:

Exit 57 – Fall 2014

Gary Thurston has a gift, a visionary gift he is struggling to understand. Besieged with his own demons and trying to make sense of these revelations, Gary is faced with one fateful day that could change his whole life and possibly prevent a national catastrophe of devastating destruction. In the tourist Mecca of the Midwest, Branson, Missouri, an incredible explosion is set to take place. Harvested by a fanatical terrorist group, plans are in the making for the worst destruction ever seen on American soil, during a Memorial Day celebration. Unbeknownst to him, Gary Thurston is the only hope to bring an end to this man made plan. An ensuing chase and battle between Gary and a lone terrorist results in a hold your breath climax with the clock literally ticking away.

The Joshua Generation – projected 2015

The action packed sequel to "Persecution of the Saints."

www.ingramcontent.com/pod-product-compliance
Lightning Source LLC
Chambersburg PA
CBHW071249170626
46809CB00001B/136

* 9 7 8 0 9 7 7 7 7 2 5 4 4 *